Beogall's Choice

HOW A BOY AND A BIRD RESCUE NATURE

by G.G. Neilson

Published by:

FriesenPress

Suite 300 – 852 Fort Street
Victoria, BC, Canada V8W 1H8

www.friesenpress.com

Distributed to the trade by The Ingram Book Company

Table of Contents

Part 4 – Westwind Bird Sanctuary

This book is dedicated to bird lovers everywhere

And for Gregory, Nicole, Martin, Linda,
Gemma and Oliver always

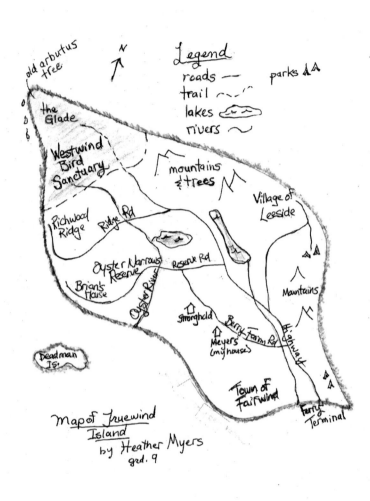

old arbutus tree

N

Legend
roads —
trail ~~~
lakes ⊂⊃
rivers ~

parks ⛺

the Glade

Westwind Bird Sanctuary

mountains & trees

Village of Leeside

Richwood Ridge

Ridge Rd

Oyster Narrows Reserve

Reserve Rd

Brian's House

Oyster River

Mountains

Stronghold

Berry Farm Rd

Meyers (my house)

Highway

Deadman Is.

Town of Fairwind

Ferry Terminal

Map of Truewind Island
by Heather Myers
grd. 9

Part 1 – Cypress Gardens

Hope is the thing with feathers
That perches in the soul
And sings the tune without the words
And never stops at all.
\- Emily Dickinson

Chapter 1

Last Day at St. Zallo's Private Boy's School

Toby was already awake when there was a short, sharp rap on his bedroom door.

He had dreamt about birds and awoke with a strange tingling running up his spine that made him shiver. *Weird,* he thought.

He squirmed as the tingling stopped right behind his ears. It was like, like... Then he heard the knock and opened his eyes. Just another overcast, west coast morning.

"Here are your clothes, Master Toby. It's time to get up for school," came the gruff voice of their butler, Duffin Wint, through the closed door.

Toby was reluctant to climb out of bed. It was so pleasant listening to the lilting songs of the robins, the familiar *yank-yank* of the nuthatches—the spring bird chorus was growing. At times he felt as if he could almost understand them. There was something more going on in their songs—that strange new sort-of register he had been hearing lately...

Probably just excitement—it was the last day of school before spring vacation. They were going to the Bahamas for the March break to a resort they had been to before. He and his father were flying from Vancouver airport early the next morning. But it would be the first time without his mother.

She always lined up an exciting itinerary for them. She knew all the best places.

His mother. The thought of her filled him with wracking grief. Where was she and why hadn't she called? Could things be that bad between her and his father? He sensed that his dad knew where she was, but wouldn't say. One night Toby had yelled and practically pulled a little kid tantrum to find out, but still his father remained silent on the matter.

He worried about his dad—always at work, too preoccupied to pay him any attention. Was it because he too missed her? Some of his school friends had parents who had split up, so he was not alone there. He had started talking to some of the boys he knew who lived with only a dad or a mom. Usually there was a step-parent though, and some were even pretty cool. But Toby was nowhere near ready for that.

Still, he wondered if maybe his dad had a girlfriend but wasn't telling, to save his feelings. His father had turned forty last year, but Toby thought he looked pretty good for an old guy—he kept himself in shape. He decided to bring up the subject some time on their vacation.

As the butler entered with his school clothes, Toby quickly wiped his eyes. On Fridays they got a break from the strict uniform in favour of a more casual outfit. Instead of a jacket and tie, there was a cashmere sweater with the school's insignia, worn with the standard pale blue shirt.

"Thank you, Duff. Leave them on the dressing chair. That will be all."

Duffin Wint, large, muscular and bald, looked more like a lineman than a butler, although he did his job impeccably. Dismissed, he walked stiffly from the room.

Toby leapt up and stretched at the room's largest window, like he did every morning. His bedroom overlooked a vast landscape of trees and gardens. Their forest included giant

G.G. Neilson

hemlock, fir and cedar trees. Two ancient yellow cedars grew at the very back of the mansion grounds.

There were birds in their legions—he had catalogued most of them and even sent his records to the local birding association. Absently watching the flitting nuthatches, he looked for a pair of swallows that should soon be eying a spot in the garden shed again this year.

Should he advise Walter to put up the hummingbird feeders? Lately, he had been helping their gardener, who welcomed his input as Lars became more withdrawn. "You decide, Walter," was his father's mantra.

His mother had never spent much time in the gardens, preferring instead to oversee the inside staff with her decorating ideas, gourmet meal planning and especially searching out works of art. Barbara Myers loved art and occasionally bought an expensive piece without consulting his father. But his dad said that she had an unerring eye for good art, and her choices invariably increased in value.

Toby looked in the mirror. It was weird watching himself stare back; medium height, medium build, and he figured, medium looks. He had his mother's blue eyes and his father's dark hair and dimples—in both cheeks. *Smile and show us your dimples*, she often said. He would dutifully smile and she'd say how cute he was. But did he really want to be cute?

On his way down the wide, curving staircase to breakfast, he regarded several spots on the walls where paintings had hung. His mother had not left empty-handed, a fact which upset Toby and his father, but for different reasons. Toby saw it as a sign that she might not be coming back. His only hope was all the beautiful art still left behind.

Duffin had prepared a fruit salad and hot cereal for Toby's breakfast. Freshly-squeezed orange juice and a steaming cup of hot cocoa were set at his place, just like every morning. His "This looks good, Duff," was reciprocated with a grunt.

Their butler spoke little, but went about his job efficiently. He was in charge of breakfast and a bag lunch for Toby and sometimes his father. The maid did not live in but arrived late morning to clean, do laundry and cook supper, which, more often than not, ended up having to be re-heated. Toby had after-school lessons and his father was staying at work later and later. His dad's little Porsche sports car was hardly ever there any more. He used to take Toby out in it and even told him he'd be able to drive it someday.

"Your lunch, Master Toby." Duffin held out the bag as if there was something rotting inside. He made it plain that he did not approve of Toby being a vegetarian, but what difference did it make? The man persisted in calling him *Master* with an undertone of sarcasm. When Toby's mother hired him a few years before, she insisted on it, but didn't seem to notice the butler's resentment. Toby was waiting for the best opportunity to tell him to drop it, especially now his mother had gone.

In silence Duffin drove him to the stately St. Zallo's Private Boys School. Although overcast, the day was mild, and Toby thought about getting his bike out soon to ride to school. He had done that a few times the previous year, over the objections of his father. It was a pleasant ride through their neighbourhood of mansions, lush trees and well-kept gardens. Better than Duffin's sullen silence.

Toby's first class of the day was English. He didn't go to his usual seat, but made his way to the back, next to Thompson Coyote. Thompson was there on a scholarship and called himself the school's "token native". No-one knew where he was from and he just replied "the sticks" if anyone asked.

Thompson leaned over and whispered, "What're you up to over the holidays?"

"Going to the Bahamas." As Toby told him, Thompson looked a little crestfallen. Could it be that he was looking for a place to spend the holidays? Quite the coup, since none of the boys had much success in drawing him out and Toby was not one of the popular boys. Maybe that was why Thompson had asked.

"Why don't you come over to my place sometime after spring break?" Toby whispered.

"Could do." Thompson looked somewhat cheered.

"What are you up to for the holiday?" Toby asked.

"Little of this, little of that." It sure sounded like Thompson was going to hang around the dorms. He was one of the students who boarded. Most of the others were taking off to go on family holidays. "Maybe hang with my auntie. She's over in the east end."

Their English teacher was giving them the beady eye, so they returned to their timed writing. It seemed like ages before the bell rang for break and then it was off to Socials.

The buzz of spring break excitement was almost palpable as the morning classes finished and they trooped off to lunch. The boys who boarded went straight to the dining room and the others went to the kitchen door to retrieve their lunches, which were kept chilled. The staff would heat them and even lay them out on plates if requested. Most of the boys who didn't board preferred to have their lunches packed by butlers or maids at home. Not that St. Zallo's didn't have decent food, but so many had their own particular tastes.

"What is it today, Myers? Peanut butter and jam?" sneered Milton Turf, who delighted in making fun of Toby for being vegetarian. Milton made meat-eating out to be a sign of superiority or even manhood.

"Lay off, Turf," Dalton Butter defended him. "Get with the times. Lots of people are vegetarian." Dalton was as close a friend as Toby had at St. Zallo's, and in spite of his slightly rotund build, was generally respected—mainly on account of his father and grandfather having gone there and being great donors and supporters of the school.

"Yeah, but we are different. We're better, Butter." Milton's comment drew some snickers. Dalton quelled the mirth with a withering look.

The friends finished their lunches in silence; Dalton had salmon rolls and a salad—Toby noticed that Dalton seldom ate meat and when he did, it seemed to be more for show. He never ate poultry but seemed to enjoy all kinds of seafood. They cleaned up quickly and left.

"I mean, should we really be eating animals?" Toby complained as they started to walk around the grounds. "I can't stand the thought. My mom told me that I gagged the first time she tried to feed me chicken," he confided, quelling the spike of emotion he felt mentioning his mother.

"Don't worry about that idiot. He has no clue about the outside world. He's insulated himself with all those violent video games and doesn't even follow the news. Did you hear some of his ignorant comments about current events in Socials today?"

They were now in the forested part of the school grounds, having ventured into a section with a grove of enormous trees—majestic red cedars with branches sweeping down like curtains, and the deeply grooved bark of Douglas firs reaching skyward with tall arms. The still air was lemon-fresh and pungent.

Suddenly the tranquility was broken as a great blue heron swooped down and settled onto the path in front of them. It stood there like a statue. The two boys halted, hardly daring to breathe as they stared at the stately bird. It gazed back. Toby had that strange, tingling sensation again. Was it there to see him?

He took a deep breath and said quietly, "Hi-ya fellow, do you want something?"

The heron began making peculiar noises. Toby, listening intently, wondered what it was trying to communicate. Then the bird repeated a sound several times.

"Beogall?" Toby finally queried. The heron made a nodding motion with its huge head and seemed satisfied. It flapped its giant wings a couple of times, got airborne and flew off as silently as it had arrived. A long, slim feather was left behind on the path.

"Whew! What was that all about?" asked Dalton. "It seemed to be speaking to you. What did you mean by 'Beogall'?"

"I… I think that's its name. It's weird I know, but I got the feeling it was trying to communicate with me." Toby bent over and picked up the gray-blue feather. His fingers tickled as he tucked it carefully into his pocket.

"Yeah, you've always had a thing for birds."

Toby looked at Dalton sharply. Was it that obvious? Then his friend added, "That bird was totally awesome! Can I see the feather?"

Toby was relieved that the afternoon bell rang then—he didn't want anyone else touching the feather. They hurried off to gym class. Before they got to the change-rooms, the secretary came to fetch him to speak to the counselor.

"Enjoy your little talk," grinned Dalton. Most students had already gone to discuss their course selections for the following year. Toby grinned back, glad to get out of Phys Ed.

After some small talk Mr. Forger, the balding counselor, got down to business. "Well Toby, have you and your parents discussed your courses for next year?"

Toby was pretty sure Mr. Forger knew his mother had left. There was that time the man had stopped him in the hall to ask how things were. But Toby was nowhere near ready to discuss it, even if he did like the counselor. He hadn't seen enough of his father lately to discuss his courses. He would just speak his own mind.

"Well sir, I'd like to go into Biology. Maybe ornithology."
As soon as he said it, he wondered if there would be ornithology in high school. But weren't there more choices in
senior science?

"Ornithology? Yes, well, Biology would be the one to take
then. Grade 10 Science is a general course, but it doesn't hurt
to be thinking ahead." Toby was relieved he didn't question
him further, although he felt tempted to bring up his odd connection with birds. Forger seemed okay, but...

"Physics and Chemistry are pretty math-based," the counselor continued. "You have to decide on taking higher math
or basic math."

Toby's performance in math had been less than stellar, and
his father wanted to get him a tutor. Toby had resisted—he
knew it was nothing but laziness on his part. "I'll start with
the higher math, if it's all the same. I could always switch
over if it didn't work out." Everyone knew that Basic Math
was as easy as pie.

Mr. Forger nodded then wrote in his file. "For elec-
tives, do you want to continue with Music? And what
about Technology?"

"Yes, Music for sure." Having endured two years of ridi-
cule, what was the point of giving up the flute now? He also
played the violin, but the school only had a band program.
Technology was a given and if he didn't take it, he'd probably
be the only one in the school. "And put me down for Tech. Is
there going to be an Outdoor Ed class next year?"

Toby didn't enjoy regular Phys Ed much, but you had to
take it until grade 10. Outdoor Ed was the alternate, if there
was enough interest.

"We have almost enough, but we won't know for sure for
a couple more weeks. There's always the community Phys
Ed option."

G.G. Neilson

Toby had heard about that—you got to go to your private gym for credit, which would be awesome. "What about my tennis lessons? Could they count too?" he asked eagerly.

"Sure they could. Well that's about it, Toby. Next year you'll have more choices to make. I assume you want to stay in French?"

Toby nodded. He liked languages and would have taken another one too, but being a small school, French was the only one St. Zallo's offered.

"You're all set for next year. You've got some good marks here so keep up the good work. Is there anything else you'd like to talk about?"

Toby shook his head.

Mr. Forger paused. "Are you happy here at St. Zallo's?"

"As happy as can be expected, sir."

"What would make you happier?"

It would be nice to have more friends. He and Dalton were buddies but they didn't hang out much outside of school. But, he wasn't about to ask Forger how to make friends. And he definitely wasn't going to talk about the kids that picked on him, or mention Milton Turf by name. Anyway, he was learning how to deal with them.

"Um, do better. Focus on my music—that helps me a lot."

Just then the bell sounded.

"You better be off to your next class. I know you don't want to miss Science. Toby, come see me if you ever want to talk, will you?"

Toby nodded but had a feeling it wouldn't happen.

He hurried to Science; his favourite class with his favourite teacher. Mr. Getty, a young teacher, had arrived at St. Zallo's two years earlier and he was passionate about science.

Toby looked immediately at the top far left of the board where a riddle was usually posted. Today's was, *Steals from the rich to give to the poor.*

Mr. Getty's riddles were often about birds and this one was no exception. Toby thought he knew the answer but would never say, knowing Milton always struggled over them. Sometimes their teacher made them hand in answers on a slip of paper before they got to leave the class. Milton purposely sat beside the smartest kid in order to copy the solution. He heard the boy whisper "robin" to Milton. *Why did he give it away?—make him sweat a bit.*

Mr. Getty came jogging in just as the bell rang. He was tall and thin, with unruly hair and always looked slightly disheveled. He wore his usual corduroy jacket with leather elbow patches, his plain, black tie askew.

"Since it's the last day before the break, I have a treat for you boys," he enthused. "After we hear about the status of your ecology projects, we'll be listening to some bird songs." Mr. Getty paused dramatically, "And then we'll go out to the grounds to see if we can hear any of them!" He waved a CD around with an almost boyish delight.

Some groaned—it didn't sound much like a treat to them—but most picked up Mr. Getty's enthusiasm. There were two other avid birders in the class besides Toby, and both Dalton and Thompson were usually interested in anything their teacher proposed.

By turns, they gave a two-minute summary of their independent projects. They had to study an ecosystem and focus on one organism and the interconnections between it and its surroundings. Their projects were due by the end of the month.

Dalton Butter went first. He explained how he was examining life in the pond on his parent's grounds. He was particularly interested in tree frogs. "They've really got a chorus going this time of year," he said.

"It sounds as if you have a good handle on your topic, Dalton. Excellent."

Next, Thompson talked about how wild salmon were in decline. Mr. Getty asked about why this was and Milton rolled his eyes when Thompson said, "I think it's because of salmon farms near where they migrate."

"I look forward to your report, Thompson," Mr. Getty commented.

Others projects included examining a compost pile and its slug inhabitants, studying loons at the cottage, and an intriguing one about the lifecycle of dragonflies.

When it came to Toby's turn, he spoke about studying the communication and nesting habits of the red-breasted nuthatch, to the snickers of some in the class. It had been hard to narrow it down to just one species, since there were so many birds he wanted to research.

"An excellent topic," Mr. Getty nodded. "Nuthatches have a unique voice and some think their communication patterns are quite complex."

"Yes," enthused Toby. "They are such funny little birds. They often walk sideways up and down tree trunks. And even upside down." Toby would have continued, but he saw some of the boys rolling their eyes and Milton Turf made a loud yawning noise, so he cut it short.

After three more students it was Milton's turn. It seemed as if he had just then pulled something out of the air as he mumbled that he wanted to see what happened after their gardener sprayed their lawns. "I want to learn all about the ingredients in herbicides," he added with a smirk.

A slight frown darkened Mr. Getty's face. "Yes, I know you're quite interested in chemistry, Milton. However, as this project is to be part of your ecology mark, you will need to choose some living creature. And remember the rule that no creature is to be harmed during your research. If the lawn is to be sprayed in any case, maybe a before and after study of the wildlife living there would be instructive. Do you know that birds and other wildlife can be quite affected by the sprays—an unintended consequence of the practice?"

Milton grimaced but raised no objection to this new direction. Toby had an image of him pulling the wings off any insects he found.

There was one more presentation and then Mr. Getty played several sections of the CD. "Now listen carefully. We should be able to hear some of these today." He paused first at the song of the robin, waggling his eyebrows towards them. Some people laughed since he made it so obvious that this was the answer to the riddle. He paused at a few other songs, including the red-breasted nuthatch and the varied thrush.

"Let's head out now and please don't disturb other classes."

Some took the assignment seriously while others chased each other around the woods. Mr. Getty and Toby ended up listening and watching for birds in a quiet section of the grounds. Suddenly the same great blue heron swept across their path. It stood before them and gazed at Mr. Getty, who said, "Have you met Beogall, Toby?"

Toby was stunned. "You know him?"

"Beogall followed me to this school from the previous one I taught at," he replied. "Do you still go there, Beogall?" There was a nod of the magnificent head. "However, his home is actually in Stanley Park."

Just then the bird made some earnest noises.

"Toby, I believe your life will be changing, but I would be happy if you kept in touch and let me know if there's anything I can do," said Mr. Getty. "Here's my card."

"What do you mean?" asked Toby, taking the card, which had a small varied thrush embossed on one corner.

"Well, Beogall gets around and has excellent hearing besides. I can't say any more than that."

The heron seemed to nod and then made some strange noises. Both Toby and Mr. Getty laughed. He had definitely communicated that birds are smarter than people think. Beogall got airborne, surprisingly graceful for such a large bird, and called back, "Take care of that feather."

Toby stood looking up, open-mouthed as the startling revelation hit him. He had understood the great blue heron perfectly. Mr. Getty realized too and nodded at Toby with a pleased expression. As they turned to go, there was Milton, peering from behind a tree with a smirk on his face. How much had he heard?

Just then, the last bell of the day sounded and Mr. Getty rushed off to round up the rest of the class and usher them back to the science room. Toby trailed behind, deep in thought. After packing up and wishing a happy vacation to Mr. Getty, he made his goodbyes to Dalton and Thompson.

Out in the hallway, Milton whispered loudly, "So Myers talks to the birds. You're as crazy as Getty. I think I should do some bird research too. I wonder what it takes to poison them."

"You do, and I'll poison you. Too bad you don't have enough brains to do proper research," Toby answered hotly as he hurried out to meet Duffin.

But the butler was nowhere to be seen. Standing there, waiting restlessly with a worried expression, was his father.

Chapter 2
A Pampered Life Disrupted

"Dad! Did you finish work early? We don't leave for the Bahamas until tomorrow, I thought."

"There's been a change of plans, Toby. I'll tell you in the car. Have you got everything?"

Toby nodded and climbed in. His father had brought the Prius, not his Porsche. As they drove away, Toby saw Thompson watching and they waved to each other.

"Something's come up," his dad said abruptly. "Things have not been going well at work. In fact, Toby, we've, well, we've lost everything. I'm sorry, but we have to move. Today."

Toby gasped as a giant weight landed on his chest—was this what Mr. Getty meant?

His father continued grimly, "I know who's behind it all. I should have realized earlier what was going on." Then he added in a voice that sounded artificially light, "But we're going to be okay."

Toby was too stunned to speak. He didn't know much about his father's work, other than that he was an investment banker. Finally he croaked out, "What do you mean we've lost everything! The mansion? The property?"

"The works." His father gripped the steering wheel. "We'll take just what we can carry. I've arranged for us to move into a condo in the east end. It's small but... cozy. There will be no house staff—we won't be needing help in that small place anyway."

"What about Walter? What if Mom comes back? How will she know where we are?" Toby's voice had risen to a howl. *This was too much!* Why hadn't his father given him any warning? It was totally unfair.

"I'm sure Walter can find other employment—maybe he'll be kept on. I will let your mother know where we are. It'll be okay, Toby. Collect yourself." His father's voice had become dead calm. He now sounded unworried, like he often did under stress—the worse the situation, the calmer he became.

Toby breathed deeply and visualized, just like the yoga instructor had taught them. He pictured their grounds. The lovely gardens, the birds now returning for the spring season. Helping Walter with the pruning and planting. The trees. The birds. He stifled a yowl of pain.

He was still in shock when they pulled up in front of their mansion. Is this what Beogall was trying to tell him (and how could a bird talk anyway)?

No, it was all a bad dream. He'd wake up soon.

Three vehicles were parked outside the mansion gates. One was a police car with two officers leaning against it. Another looked like some sort of official vehicle with a mousy-haired man waiting anxiously beside it, shuffling papers. The third vehicle was a long, black limousine with darkened windows, whose occupant had not yet emerged.

As they drove up, the mousy man scurried forward. "I'm the warrant officer," he said nervously and shoved a sheaf of papers in Lars' face. "Here are the eviction notices. You are allowed to go in and get essential items like clothing and toiletries. Please be quick. Take no valuables. The court will decide upon dispensation of those later."

Lars put a hand on Toby's shoulder and they went up to their rooms together. As in a dream, Toby opened the suitcase that had been packed for the Bahamas—he wouldn't need all that summer wear, but what should he pack? Where was Duffin? He turned around just in time to see the butler heading downstairs.

"Duffin! You need to re-pack this suitcase," he ordered.

"I don't work for you or your father anymore, you spoiled little brat," he spat by way of reply, and hurried down the stairs. Bewildered, Toby stood rooted to the spot and watched through an upper window as their late butler left the house and got into the waiting limo. He had never liked Duffin much, but hadn't they treated him well? Did he have some hand in this disastrous situation?

Like wading through deep water, Toby went to his huge dresser, struggling to think what he might need. He had never looked much through his dresser drawers, since his clothes were laid out for him every morning. *Definition of irony* was a phrase that floated into his mind, as he delved through the dresser for the first and last time.

"Toby, it's time to go." His father appeared in the doorway.

"Yeah, well you didn't give me much time," Toby muttered bitterly, flinging beachwear out of the suitcase. His father retreated to the hall and Toby hurriedly re-stuffed it with whatever he could grab. He looked around his spacious bedroom for the last time, taking in the dark oak paneling and feeling the luxurious thick carpeting underfoot, as if for the first time.

Toby gulped as he looked out his large window over their expansive grounds. The old forest beyond the graceful gardens, the familiar pathways he had walked, coaxing birds to land on his arms. He saw the tell-tale swoop of a swallow, finally returning from the south—he would miss out on their busy nest-building. A robin pair searched the grass. Toby had his own names for them. A tribe of juncos flitted by noisily. Soon warblers would join the resident nuthatches, sparrows and chickadees. He would miss the return of the hummingbirds.

Walter stood on the patio below, looking up at him with a stricken face. Toby shrugged, tried to give a reassuring smile and waved. He turned to go.

In the hallway his father handed him his newest tennis racket, which they had bought together.

"Will they let me take it?"

"Let them try to stop us." His father's voice was grim. He carried one of his old sets of golf clubs along with a medium-sized suitcase. As the two walked out of the mansion, a heavy-set man emerged from the limousine. His bushy black eyebrows contrasted with sparse white hair, almost hiding the darting, dark eyes. He moved like a walrus.

"Suchno Whenge! I might have known you'd be here gloating," said Lars.

"The order says you're not to take anything other than a suitcase," the man sneered with a shake of his heavy jowls. He turned to the warrant officer. "Take those golf clubs and that tennis racket."

"How are you so familiar with what the order says, Whenge? And why are these police officers allowing you to be here at all?" Lars turned to the warrant officer, who was now mopping his brow. "He has no right to be here."

"Ha!" the man barked. "That's where you're wrong, Myers. I own this mansion now, and those golf clubs and that tennis racket are mine, too!" His eyes gleamed darkly. "That'll teach you to interfere in my business dealings…"

Then it happened.

A great blue heron appeared overhead and let go of a giant plop, which struck the side of the limousine closest to Whenge, splattering onto his face and down his expensive suit. Toby gaped in surprise and then burst out laughing. His father quickly covered up a laugh, too.

"Shoot that bird!" screamed Whenge at the police officers. They gave him a startled look.

"Shoot it now, damn you! It desecrated my property."

Herons do not fly fast under the best of circumstances but this one had circled back for a look at the commotion below. Wild with worry, Toby was sure that it was Beogall.

One of the police officers looked uncomfortably from Suchno Whenge to the warrant officer to the Myers. The other, with the name "Cnst. Backer" on his lapel, slowly drew out his weapon and aimed it upwards.

What followed seemed to happen in slow motion. Toby's hand holding the tennis racket, swung around and knocked the gun out of the policeman's hand.

The man shrieked in pain. "Chow, arrest that boy!"

The other officer grabbed the racket from Toby and put handcuffs on him. Constable Backer rubbed his hand, glaring at Toby, while his father looked on in dismay. Whenge's expression turned from anger to triumph. "Your son is as stupid and impulsive as you, Myers."

"No Dad!" Toby pleaded, as Lars made a move to grab the man by his expensive lapels. Duffin emerged from the limo to assist, but Suchno hissed at him, "Get back in the car, you fool. They'll both be arrested if he lays a hand on me."

Seeing his butler now taking orders from Suchno Whenge acted like a splash of cold water. Lars abruptly stepped back and turned to Duffin. "So you're in on this too, are you Wint? Proud of yourself? I hope you come to realize what a monster you're now working for," he said in a steely calm voice.

He turned to the policemen. "Officers, I'm sorry for what my son has done. He loves all birds and I'm sure just reacted without thinking. If you take him in for questioning, I'll follow you to the station, or you can release him to my custody and I assure you this matter will be dealt with. He has never been in any trouble before."

G.G. Neilson

Constable Chow was prepared to release Toby but Constable Backer was not.

"There's no point arresting him; he's underage—he's only fifteen," said Lars.

"Dad, I'm only fourteen. I won't be fifteen till the summer."

"I stand corrected." Having to be corrected about his son's age seemed to relieve the tension a bit because the warrant officer chuckled.

"I'm sorry, Officer Backer. My father is right—I didn't mean to. I hope your hand is alright," Toby said in what he hoped was a sincere tone, which he didn't exactly feel, since he was still upset that the heron had come so close to being shot.

Suchno Whenge was fuming. He had taken a silk handkerchief from his suit pocket and was wiping heron splat from his face and sleeve. "I won't press charges this time. But don't ever be caught around my property, or even in my neighbourhood, either of you," he snarled.

"With respect sir," said Constable Chow, "you were not assaulted or even touched by either of these people. We live in a free society so they are allowed to come to this area, but not onto your private property, of course." Chow did not appear to like this assignment.

Constable Backer abruptly said, "Give me the details of your whereabouts and we'll release the boy into your custody, as long as he doesn't cause any more problems." He had his notebook out.

"Yes officer, I'll give you that information, but not here," said Lars pointedly. "Perhaps we should come down to the station after all. I'll follow you."

Without a backward glance, Lars got into the Prius to leave their fine home. The two officers put Toby in the backseat of their cruiser for his first ride in a police car.

Whenge stood watching their departure, an inscrutable look on his face. Then he stalked into his new mansion.

Later, driving from the police station, Lars and Toby sat in grim silence. They were headed to their new home in a condo complex east of downtown. It was now rush-hour and they were snarled in traffic.

Toby, awash in anxiety, finally asked, "Who is that horrible Suchno Whenge anyway and why does he hate you?"

His dad told him briefly about how Whenge or "Lord Whenge," as he preferred to be called, arrived at their firm from Toronto. There had been rumours about the man, who had started off first in real estate and then had gotten into land development, making a killing in Wattasaga, Ontario. He had branched out into investment banking. When he moved to Vancouver and the firm Lars worked for, his father had questioned some of the wealthy man's business practices and even raised it with higher-ups.

"Suchno found out and had it in for me from then on," Lars continued, "but I had no inkling of the lengths to which the man would go. I discovered too late that he was undermining me to the point of bankruptcy. By that time, I wasn't able to take steps to avoid it."

"I didn't know we had lords in Canada, Dad. Why is he *Lord* Whenge?" asked Toby. The traffic had started moving again.

"Well, there's an arcane law that allows for it. A large donation makes it easier to be considered. There are one or two other lords I believe. Maybe their egos are as big as his." His father's voice took on a cold edge. "You know, Toby, to get rich, you often do things that aren't necessarily good for others. Maybe this situation is for the best."

He added that he was just one of many who had been victimized by Whenge. "There's no way I was going to give out our new address in front of him," he muttered bitterly.

They were discussing the ramifications of Toby now having a juvenile record when they arrived at their new neighbourhood, Cypress Gardens. Constable Backer had made it clear that he would be keeping tabs on Toby. Constable Chow at least had showed some sympathy, and told them their new address was in his regular precinct.

"There are the tennis courts," his father pointed out hopefully, slowing down. The golf clubs had stayed behind at the mansion, and the tennis racket was being kept at the station for evidence. Toby noticed a lot of people waiting their turn at the courts.

The sun was out and the weather had warmed up considerably. A nearby skateboard bowl was crowded with skaters doing their daring stunts. It was ringed by a huge green space scattered with benches, a lot of them occupied. There had been so few young people living near their mansion that Toby found himself wondering what it would be like to have so many potential friends nearby. There were lots of young families as well. On the way up to their apartment, number 505, they shared the elevator with a mother pushing a stroller and a middle-aged man with a big dog.

"Do they allow dogs in here?" Toby asked in amazement, after they got off at the fifth floor. He had always wanted a dog, but his mother didn't like the idea of shedding fur, dog smells and messes in the yard.

"Apparently so—I've seen lots of people with them in this building."

His father did not divulge how they came to have this apartment, and Toby didn't ask. He felt a combination of pity and seething anger toward him for having been put out of their accustomed way of life.

"Well, here we are," announced his father, opening the door to their new home.

They entered a tiny hall with a cramped kitchen off to one side and stepped directly into a sparsely furnished living area; a dining room and living room combined. Toby had never been camping, but imagined it might be something like this.

His father pointed to a door leading off one side of the living room. "That's your room."

It took only a few steps for Toby to cross the living area and step into a room no bigger than his closet back at the mansion. His second-best tennis racket lay on the bed. His father had managed to put a few other things of his in the room already—his violin and flute in their cases along with some other prized items.

"How long did you know we'd be coming to live here?" he asked, turning to his father who was studying him anxiously.

"I didn't have much time, but I've been making arrangements for a few weeks. There are laws in this country; neither Whenge nor Duffin Wint will be able to get anything from here, and the police would need a search warrant."

"Did you know that Duffin was in cahoots with Lord Whenge?"

"Only belatedly."

"Does Mom know that we're here?"

"She knows that we were going to have to move. I didn't give her the details. I'll let her know where we are. She isn't ready to visit yet, but she will be, Toby. I know she will be."

Well then, that was that. It was the most he had gotten out of his dad on the topic.

A door on the other side of the living room led into his father's room. Toby went to check it out and as he entered, let out a hoot. There were his father's newest, prized golf clubs. The older set was obviously a ruse.

"How did you get these in here?"

"It didn't take much really—I've had them in my office for a while."

Toby noticed two late model, ultra-thin laptops on the desk. "One of these is for you, Toby. Gladys helped me to pick them out. I'll miss her." Gladys was his dad's middle-aged, plump and efficient secretary.

A sliding glass door from his father's bedroom led onto a balcony. Toby opened it and stepped out. To his surprise, the balcony was quite spacious and overlooked a pleasant terrace filled with gardens, shrubs and trees. He heard a robin singing over the noise of traffic and shouts of children, and saw juncos and towhees flitting about. And wasn't that a Steller's jay in the giant dogwood tree below their balcony? His black mood lifted a little—maybe it wouldn't be so bad living here. Cramped, but exciting. Not that he would admit it to his father.

The balcony was also accessible through a door off the living room, which his dad unlocked to go back inside. The two bedrooms, one small bathroom, kitchen, and dining-living room, could have fit comfortably into his parent's bedroom at the mansion.

"Well, I'm afraid that's all there is," said Lars. "There's a storage locker downstairs and I'll show you the garbage room."

"Garbage room? What's that?"

"Let's check it out and we'll go over how the keys and swipe cards work."

The garbage room was on the first underground floor. It had a smell that made Toby retch—probably rotting meat, he thought disgustedly. He realized that he was pretty naïve about where garbage goes as his father pointed out the house-hold waste container, and the various recycling containers.

"You know, your grandmother would be pleased to hear that you will be recycling," his dad said. "I always told Duffin to recycle but I don't think he did."

They returned to their apartment and his dad asked, "Do you want to explore the neighbourhood?"

"Okay." It wouldn't hurt to check out the place.

His father gave him his own set of keys and a swipe card. "Don't be longer than half an hour. I'll order in."

"What does that mean—'order in'?"

"Ordering in some supper. I bought a few groceries, but tonight I'll just order Chinese." Lars showed him the stocked cupboards and fridge.

"Who will cook for us?"

"Why, we will cook for ourselves. I used to be a decent cook—you'll see."

Toby was aghast. His way of life had abruptly changed. They were now living in a closet. And they would have to do everything for themselves that had once been done by servants.

Without another word, he checked the time on his phone and left the condo, slamming the door on his way out.

Toby emerged from their apartment building and surveyed his surroundings—a forest of high-rises. But there were also abundant green spaces—lawns, shrubs and well-tended gardens with trees just beginning to bud forth. The first really warm, spring-like day had turned into a pleasant early evening, and people were drawn outside.

As he went to cross the street, a young man in a wheel-chair whizzed by without looking—he seemed to have an attitude. People of all shapes, colours, sizes, were out enjoying the evening around the wide green belt that was dotted with benches and paved areas for strollers and roller-bladers.

Multi-cultural was a term Toby had learned in school and now here he was, surrounded by people of all cultures. Some were wearing clothing he had only seen in pictures. He found himself wondering about the lives of these people. Where were they born, what were they thinking, how did they live?

There were families, singles, couples, and people of all ages—walking, running, cycling, sitting, chatting. Some were just loitering. Then he realized that he had put his own troubles out of his mind briefly.

What a grand adventure!

As in a dream, Toby continued to explore. Once he had read a book, where you didn't know until near the end that the people were living in a black and white world, but a few people had the gift of seeing in colour. Toby felt like he had suddenly been reborn into a world of colour. Here was diversity that he had not yet experienced.

Like a revelation, it hit him that this was what nature was like: a profusion, a confusion of thriving diversity, organisms sharing the same ecological space, claiming their own niches. All going about their business with purpose. And now he was part of it. Like Mr. Getty's science project, he was the organism he was studying in this small, teeming eco-system. He was the one trying to fit in. The thought of submitting such a paper to Mr. Getty made him laugh out loud. He looked around but nobody had noticed.

Except maybe that Steller's jay on a nearby bush. *But that was too weird.*

For the entirety of his short years, Toby had lived a rather dull life. There were his parents, servants who would come and go, and the occasional visiting relative. He didn't have close friends, but those whose houses he had been to, lived like him. There had been occasional, exciting visits to his grandmother on Truewind Island. And of course their family trips, where they stayed in fabulous resorts. But except for servants and waiters, they saw mainly other tourists, wealthy like themselves.

Here at Cypress Gardens, Toby felt as if he had been suddenly shoved into the light of reality—a bustling, brimming world of people as diverse as the creatures of the earth. And now he was part of it. A rebirth, *a Renaissance*, like he had learned about in Socials.

"What're you staring at?"

His reverie was broken abruptly. A boy, maybe around his age, maybe a little older, skateboarded toward him. He was tall and slim, dark-skinned with long, black dreadlocks. He wore baggy pants and a brightly patterned hoodie. Dark, shining eyes drilled into Toby.

With a start, Toby realized he had wandered over to the skateboard bowl and was now surrounded by a group of teens glaring at him.

"Well, uh… I'm new here and I—I just wanted to check out the place."

"Yeah, well you look like a tourist. Comin' over to see how the other side lives?" Toby looked down at his pressed slacks and polished shoes—he was still wearing the St. Zallo's 'casual Fridays' outfit. Probably clothes none of these guys would ever be caught dead in. He realized he would have to come up with something fast.

"No, really, I live here now. And… and I noticed this skateboard bowl. Thought I might like to try it out." This last part was fabricated on the spot, since he didn't even own a skateboard.

"Yeah, what kind do you have?" asked another boy stepping forward. He had sandy hair gelled into spikes and was about Toby's height but with a stocky build. He gave Toby a belligerent stare.

"It's a um, a Silver Tornado," Toby spouted out the name of his tennis racket. Wouldn't makers of sports equipment make all kinds?

They all looked blankly, first at him and then at each other, then shrugged.

"A Silver Tornado—well, I sure would like to see that one," said the first boy again. "Make sure to come back here with it." Toby knew that he was being dismissed, but was only too glad to leave.

"And fo' sure don't wear those geeky clothes," jeered the sandy-haired boy, accompanied by laughter. As he walked away, Toby drew himself up, shoulders back, exuding a confidence he didn't feel. Years of private school had taught him how to carry himself so as not to be picked on. Striding away deliberately, he headed toward the tennis courts, realizing he would have to get appropriate clothing, and fast. None of the skaters appeared to be tailing him. *Whew, that was a close call.*

The courts were full, but he stayed to watch and check out the potential competition. He looked around to see if he could figure out the system of court usage—but there was no chart. Then he took a circuitous route back to his apartment, just in case.

Was it only his imagination or was that Steller's jay following him?

His senses, especially his hearing, were on full alert. In addition to traffic noises there was the sound of occasional gusts of wind mixed with something else. Then he realized he was hearing the Skytrain stirring the air as it passed. Other than the chatter of wheels rolling over the tracks, the electric trains were quiet. He had once ridden the Skytrain, but hadn't registered its distinctive hum, surprising since he was so sensitive to sounds. Now, he realized, he would be hearing it a lot.

When he arrived back at the condo, his Dad had made a salad to accompany some heavenly-smelling pizza. "Olives, mushrooms and green peppers," he told Toby. "After you left I made a unilateral decision for pizza instead of Chinese."

Toby nodded his approval as he dug in. Lunch seemed like a lifetime ago. "I have to get some different clothes," he announced between mouthfuls.

"I guess we both have to," his dad replied. "We'll see what we can find tomorrow—we have some shopping to do anyway."

After they ate, his dad said he would clean up. Toby had never helped clean up in his life and had no intention of starting now. He disappeared into his room.

It was almost claustrophobic and he wondered how he would get used to it. There was a tiny closet, which didn't matter since he had brought so few things, a small dresser and a pint-sized desk that held his own desk-lamp from home.

He saw with surprise that his father had secreted out a painting, one that his mother had bought and one of his favourites. It was a Robert Bateman numbered print of a wading heron. Again it occurred to him that his father must have had some advance warning in order to set up this place. *No wonder he was never home.* He thought about his mother—when would he see her again?

His new room's one window did not look over the terrace, but instead over the front entry of their building and onto another apartment building across the street. He could see the Skytrain whizzing by in the distance. He checked his phone—no messages. It didn't take much time to organize his few things in the room before he flopped onto his bed and listened to music.

Now that he had such full-time access to his father, Toby found that he didn't know what to say to him. He could hear his dad moving around restlessly, but didn't want to go out to say good night.

Around midnight he awoke, still in his clothes. He had fallen asleep listening to music. Looking around, he wondered where he was. Then with a lurch in his stomach, remembered. His father was still up.

"Toby." There was a quiet knock and his father opened the door a crack. "I'm sorry, sorry about everything. I'll... I'll make it up to you."

As his father stepped into the room, Toby suspected he had been drinking. "Um, it's okay, Dad. It sure wasn't my finest hour when I hit that cop with my tennis racket."

"And that bird splatter on Whenge's face—" his dad began and then chortled.

Toby began shaking with laughter. Pretty soon his dad was doubled over, dissolved in stitches. After everything they had been through that day, it sure felt good.

"Hey Dad, you should go to bed," Toby said at last. "We'll get by… and don't drink anymore, okay?"

Later that night, Toby was startled to see a dark form swoop past his window. Then he heard a shriek. He rushed to the window, to see Beogall toppling to the ground and there was Lord Suchno Whenge holding a weapon, which emitted a screaming sound. Beogall lay unmoving in a crumpled heap. Suchno looked up at Toby with a triumphant leer.

Toby awoke in a cold sweat and realized that the noise was just a siren going by. He tried to calm his mind by breathing deeply. When that didn't work, he reached for the feather. It seemed to glisten in the dull light from the surrounding buildings.

As he listened to traffic noises, Toby thought about the possibilities of his new life. He would have to ask his dad about school. Surely he couldn't go back to St. Zallo's. And if he was going to school around here, wouldn't they have to check it out before the end of spring break? How did Beogall and Mr. Getty know that his life would be changing?

He would miss Dalton for sure and probably Thompson too. But he would really miss Walter. What would become of him now? And what of their plans for the garden—a bird bath, more feeders… Would Suchno Whenge keep Walter on, or would he hire a new gardener?

Still clutching the feather, his many questions subsided as he recalled the delicious feeling he had experienced exploring his new neighbourhood. He let that feeling of rebirth, of being part of the wide, curious world wash over him as the Skytrain's wind-like *whoosh* lulled him back to sleep.

Chapter 3

A Steep Learning Curve

Toby awoke in his new room, trying to get his bearings. He remembered the previous morning, the tingling, the sense of anticipation. It was gone.

In its place was anger. How could his father have let this happen? And Suchno Whenge—what right did he have taking away their home?

He realized anger wouldn't help but... He could hear the songs of these new birds over traffic noises. There was that strange new register, airy, subtle. What he used to hear as one note, he now heard as many—complicated and elusive. You had to listen extra hard. Was that the key to understanding them?

Robins chirped happily about the rain that had brought worms to the surface. A crow perched nearby, cackling testily. Toby's keen hearing picked out the sounds from a distance. Wait! Was that the sound of warblers? He leapt out of bed, but couldn't see the terrace from his window.

He loped out to the little dining room, ravenous, to wait for his meal. Then he realized his father was not there. He fought down a surge of panic—maybe his dad had gone out to do the shopping without him.

It occurred to him he just might have to prepare his own breakfast, so he went to the fridge to have a look. The pizza from last night was all gone. Checking through the rest of the food, he noticed some yogurt and pulled that out.

Then he recognized a toaster and figured out how it worked and sat down to enjoy a bowl of yogurt. He didn't notice the toast burning until smoke filled up the place. A fire alarm shrilled throughout the small apartment.

"Damn, Damn!!" he yelled as the noise screamed through his head. He had just enough wits about him to unplug the toaster. Lars rushed in then and quickly turned off the smoke alarm. The relief was immediate.

"Here's how you turn off and reset the alarm," his father instructed.

"Where were you?" Toby asked accusingly. He now had a slight headache.

By way of answer, Lars set a large cup of Starbucks coffee and a medium cup of tea on the counter. "The first priority for shopping will be a coffee maker," he commented. "I bought some fair trade coffee, but forgot about something to make it in."

His dad had to have his coffee in the morning, that much Toby knew. "I saw a movie once where they made camp coffee, Dad. They just boiled it in a pot."

"Then you won't mind if we don't get a kettle either? You could just boil water for your tea in a pot too," his father quipped.

Toby grinned. He had noticed the nice selection of teas his father had bought. "Looks like you got a lot of stuff for the kitchen already," Toby said in a conciliatory tone. Actually he had no idea what you were supposed to have in a kitchen.

Lars nodded. "After breakfast we'll go over our shopping list."

The list included hardware items and clothing and they drove around the neighbourhood to see the whereabouts of shops they would need. Starbucks and the grocery store were within walking distance, but the hardware store where they bought a coffee maker, a kettle and a few other items, was further away.

But where would they go for clothes? "We won't be able to have a tailor make our clothes anymore," his father said ruefully.

"But do tailors even make skater shorts?" Toby replied and his dad chuckled.

"Here's a store that looks promising." Lars parked nearby.

They surprised a plump saleslady with their request for poorer quality clothing, as she eyed their obviously expensive clothes. After a lot of try-ons because there were no alterations offered in that store, they found a few things more suitable to their new lifestyle.

"Do we have enough money to live on?" Toby asked on the way home. He was beginning to realize how much he had always taken for granted.

"We'll be fine. I put a bit away. Especially for your phone plan." He winked at Toby. "I think I'll go to a golf course that I played at when I was younger. My membership at Hope Highlands is still good, but I probably won't be going back there."

"Don't we have more than golfing to think about?" Toby asked accusingly. His father was an avid golfer and a very good one too, but surely they needed to get on with their new life.

"I mean to try and get a job there. I did some groundskeeping work as a kid. Maybe I could get on there again. Work my way up."

Toby stifled a groan—his father a groundskeeper like Walter? Maybe he would need to get a job, too.

When he mentioned that, his father declared, "No Toby, you need to focus on your studies. There'll be plenty of time for work later on and now you'll have to get used to a new school. There's a public high-school in the neighbourhood."

Well, that was that. He wouldn't be going back to St. Zallo's. And did those belligerent skate-boarders attend this new school? He would be ready for them.

Maybe there was a tennis program. Anyway, he had his flute and violin. Would his practising disturb the neighbours now that they were living on top of, and next door to so many people? He asked his dad about it.

"It should be fine as long as you don't practise late at night. I hope you keep up your music studies—I enjoy your playing."

His dad made him help make sandwiches for lunch and they ate out on the balcony. Then his dad organized the few items they had bought into the kitchen cupboards, while Toby watched. It was amazing what you had to have in a kitchen.

"What is this thing anyway?" Toby asked, holding up a strange gizmo with two handles.

"That's a can opener. Here, I'll show you how it works." His dad grabbed a can of tomato sauce and showed him how to place and turn the apparatus.

"Cool!" declared Toby as he tried it out.

"Now we'll have to use this tomato sauce for supper. I'll make spaghetti. Maybe add black olives, parsley and mushrooms."

"So you're going to cook and are you going to do all the cleaning too?" Toby couldn't keep the sarcasm out of his voice.

"It's just you and me, Toby. No more servants."

Disgusted, Toby retreated into his bedroom and went on the computer. He didn't feel like going outside again and besides, it was pouring rain. After practicing both flute and violin for a long time, losing himself in the music, he started to feel better.

Along with the spaghetti for supper, his father had prepared a Greek salad and set out some fragrant garlic bread. Toby had to admit that his dad was a good cook. He wondered if he should learn to cook something himself, then quickly dismissed the idea. Still, later on, he decided to check out a few pasta recipes on the Net.

The next day, they went out to the golf course Lars had once worked at. It was a long way from the Hope Highlands, but still, Toby hoped they wouldn't come across anyone they knew from their previous life—a life they were quickly leaving behind.

Trout Creek Links, on the North Shore, had a smallish, somewhat dingy clubhouse. It turned out that the manager, an older man, remembered Lars from years before when he played there as a junior, and was surprised that he was looking for work.

"I thought that you were a big shot now, Lars. Why do you need a job here?"

"Things change. I'd like to introduce you to my son, Toby, Mr. Frobisher. He plays golf too, but he's a formidable tennis player."

"Are you now? Are you looking for work too?" inquired Mr. Frobisher.

"Sure," said Toby at the same time as Lars said, "No. He has school work to concentrate on."

"Well, I better let you two sort that out, but there's always a part time job for an enterprising and responsible young man." Then he continued, "Your timing is good, Lars. The season is just getting underway and our grounds marshal quit yesterday to go work at the Hope Highlands." Toby and his father exchanged a quick, nervous glance. "Come with me and I'll introduce you to Anna Feathers. She's the office manager here."

They followed him into a smaller office where an attractive woman in dark slacks and a casual suit jacket sat behind a cluttered desk.

"Ms. Feathers, I'd like to introduce you to Lars Myers. He's an excellent golfer and he's come looking for work. I'm thinking of him for the grounds marshal position."

Ms. Feathers turned and rose. She was tall and with lovely green eyes and reddish hair tied back stylishly, reminded Toby of an exotic bird. Her ears were adorned with earrings made of tiny feathers. "Well, that is good news since we were going to have to advertise immediately," she remarked in a melodic voice. "Our previous marshal left with little notice and we're starting to get busy."

She looked at Lars. "Are you familiar with our golf course, Mr. Myers?"

"Familiar! He practically lived here as a young man!" declared Mr. Frobisher before Lars had a chance to respond. "He was so good, he should have gone pro. Had to give it up to… What was it you were doing, Myers?'

"Investment banking. Turns out you can lose your shirt doing that. Like anything, I suppose." Lars shrugged. "I think I could do a good job for you here."

"Well, if we hire you Myers, I'll need you to commit for at least the season. Don't want to have to fill the position twice in one year."

While his dad and Mr. Frobisher went next door to fill in some papers and work out a timetable, Ms. Feathers spoke with Toby. He was no judge of women's ages, but thought she might be around his mother's age, possibly a little younger. She was kind and he felt so comfortable talking with her that he didn't notice when his dad returned.

Ms. Feathers looked up suddenly. "Well, it's been a pleasure meeting you both. When will we see you again, Mr. Myers?"

"Call me Lars. Mr. Frobisher wants me to start tomorrow."

She bid them goodbye, with a final, "Don't forget what I told you, Toby."

As they drove away, his father asked what she had said to him.

"What if I told you that she thinks you're hot?" he snapped.

His father reddened and Toby regretted saying it—but he wondered if sparks were flying in that short introduction to Ms. Feathers. *No way*, he thought. Mom will come back. I know she will…

Who am I kidding? There is exactly zero chance of her coming to live in that tiny condo.

After an early supper, his father said he had to go out. Toby wondered if it was because they were not used to living in such close quarters. He took his phone out onto the balcony. There were no new messages—Dalton was probably too busy on his holiday. He thought about calling Thompson, but what could he say? He'd have to admit that they had lost everything; that he wasn't returning to St. Zallo's. Instead he sent a short text just to say hi.

He stared over their balcony and into the terrace, looking for the birds he knew were there. He was considering phoning his grandmother when he became aware of a lovely, lilting voice. Peering over the balcony for the source of this enchanting sound, he saw a girl emerging from beneath the huge dogwood tree, which was just coming into leaf.

"Bibbi, Shasta, come back here!" Two small, white dogs raced ahead with the girl behind them, laughing at their antics. They returned excitedly when she called them. She looked about his age with straight, long brown hair. Tall and slender, she moved gracefully. He couldn't take his eyes off her.

Suddenly she looked up, straight at him and she wasn't smiling. Toby was mortified to be caught staring. He gave a feeble wave then smiled. What else could he do? He was only five floors up—should he call down and ask if she would introduce him to her dogs? Going to a private boys' school had not given Toby much experience with girls.

While he was hesitating, she picked up her two dogs and stalked away. *Damn, I should have said something,* he thought. In case she looked up to see him still staring, he retreated inside.

He watched television for the rest of the evening, striving to keep his mind off how he had bungled the interaction with the girl with the heavenly voice. Finally he went to bed and was almost asleep when his father came in. As Lars poked his head into the room, Toby pretended to be asleep. He could sense his father standing there, gazing at him for a few moments before he quietly left. Then he heard him getting ready for bed.

Toby woke up much later. Someone was shouting in a nearby apartment. Someone else hushed them up. He thought about Beogall as he listened to the traffic noises. Once again he held the feather and fell asleep to the windy *whoosh* of the Skytrain.

Chapter 4
An Unlikely Alliance

"Where were you last night?"

"I have lots of things to arrange still, Toby," his dad chided. Then he added in a gentler tone, "Sorry I was late. Next time I'll call. I hope you weren't lonely. What did you do?"

"Computer stuff," said Toby. He wasn't about to mention the girl. "But I'm going to check out the tennis courts this morning. They shouldn't be too busy at this hour, even if it is spring break."

It was Monday morning and his dad was getting ready to go to Trout Creek Links—his first day on the job. While he made himself a lunch, they discussed their plans.

"I think my work schedule is pretty flexible so we can check out the school sometime this week. We have to get you registered," said his father on his way out.

When Toby got to the tennis courts, he was surprised to find them completely empty. Being spring break, he figured there might be at least a few people there. He hit off the back-board for a while and noticed the Steller's jay watching him from a nearby tree. It cocked its head and made long, low, clicking noises.

He thought about approaching the bird, when a man, probably in his twenties, showed up. "Looking for a game?" the man asked.

They played a few fast-paced sets. "Wow, you're good!" said the man, who had worked up a sweat. "I can't win a point against you." He was getting ready to leave. "I'll bring a friend of mine over. He'll give you a run for your money."

Looking around for the jay, Toby noticed with a start that the dread-locked kid was on the other side of the fence, watching.

"Not bad, man." He sounded almost friendly.

"Thanks."

"Is that racket a Silver Tornado?" the boy asked with a grin.

"Yeah," Toby groaned, remembering the name he had spouted out at the skate bowl.

"I thought so. I went on line and found out that they make high-end tennis rackets. And guess what? They don't make skateboards. Why the story?"

"I guess to fit in," Toby decided to go for honesty. "Do you play tennis?" It was worth a try.

The kid laughed. "Hey, are you skipping school too?"

"Skipping school? No way! It's… it's spring break," said Toby.

"Not in this part of town. Spring break isn't till next week. Where are you from anyway?"

Toby ignored the question. "Well, I wasn't planning on skipping, but it sounds as if you were. How come *you're* not in school then?"

"I have to go visit my dad. I'm smart enough to miss a few classes." He winked. "What's your name?"

"Toby." He wasn't about to give out more than that. "What's yours?"

"Well Toby, I'm Chester. I see you've changed your clothes."

"Yeah, well, it looked like I had to, if I ever went near you and your crowd again."

"Hey man, sorry about that, but if I hadn't approached you before JB did his usual… Well, you never know what that guy is going to do or say. I softened things for you."

"Thanks, I guess. I'm really in transition here. I could use an ally."

"I'll back you, man. Just don't mess with me."

"Heaven forbid." They both laughed and the alliance was sealed with a high five.

"Want to hang for a bit before I have to go? I'll show you around."

Chester took him first to the local community centre. "They have courses for adults and stuff. There's a games room for kids and they don't mind if you, like, just hang out."

Next, they checked out the basketball court. "Now this place is really busy when there's no school. There's some guys who spend, like, every waking minute here. Maybe think they're going to be the next LeBron James or something."

"Do you play basketball?"

"Are you kidding? Don't you?"

"Well, I do in gym class of course. I'm okay, not great."

"Other than acing tennis, what do you do, Toby?"

Toby felt comfortable enough to tell Chester about his love of music, his interest in science in general and birds in particular.

"Ornithology, huh?"

Toby realized that Chester was pretty sharp. The memory of the warm glow—his epiphany about his new neighbourhood hit him. He decided to take a chance. "I guess you know all the kids around here?"

"You could say."

"There's a girl that walks two little white dogs. She has long brown hair, about our age…" As he pointed in the direction of his building, a thought struck him—what if she lived in his own building?

"That'll be Alyssa. You're interested, I can see. Well Alyssa's a little aloof. But she's okay. She likes music too. Don't get your hopes up though. I think she goes for Seymour Gregory, but then all the girls do."

Toby made up his mind right then to not like this Seymour kid.

"Have you been over to the school yet?"

"Not yet. My dad and I are going later this week. Where is it?"

"Well, I gotta go soon but I'll point you in the direction first. I can't go near—for obvious reasons. I try not to skip out, drives my mom crazy, but seeing my old man is important."

"You live with just your mom?"

"You could say that. How about you?"

"Just me and my dad."

Toby wondered if his emotions showed because Chester asked, "Pretty recent that your mom's gone?"

"Yep." He didn't want to talk about it to an almost stranger, but Chester seemed to figure that out. They walked in silence along a busy street that formed the boundary of Cypress Gardens.

Now it was Toby's turn to figure something out. "What's that building?" he asked.

They were passing a large, ramshackle old house, and outside were people who looked like beggars, just hanging out. Chester had picked up the pace and didn't answer until they were well past it.

"That's a place where the homeless can get something to eat, wash up, hang out, even sleep there. They run some programs for street people. On really cold nights they bring in extra cots."

Toby had never seen homeless people before and wondered why Chester seemed to know so much about the place, and why they had to hurry by, but he didn't ask.

"Okay, just follow this street down two more blocks," said Chester, pointing down the intersecting street, Willow Street, they had now reached. "Then turn right. You'll be able to see the school field from there. Be careful, though. They'll think you're skipping."

"But I don't go there yet."

"The teachers there are cool, but they mostly don't know all the nearly nine hundred students."

"Oh, okay," Toby gulped. That was more than three times the student population of St. Zallo's. "Hey, thanks for showing me around. I guess I'll be seeing you."

"No worries. Looks like I know where to find you—the tennis courts, right?"

Toby took a chance and told him his building.

"Awesome! That's my building, man. What number are you?"

"We're number 505."

"No way! We're 405, so we must be right below you. That's one quiet condo up there. We hardly ever hear anyone, but I thought I heard some music the other day—nice stuff too," Chester paused. "Yeah, we figured someone new must be in there now. But you sure aren't noisy. Not like the people beside us—wow, they go at it sometimes!"

He stuck his hand out. "Welcome to the neighbourhood," he said before he turned to go.

Toby continued on, approaching the school grounds warily. He could see that there were some classes out playing soccer. The school was large but nondescript and looked like it had been thrown together out of several rambling buildings. It was one level mostly, but two levels here and there. There was some brick, but most of it was a kind of garish green stucco. A far cry from the well-kept grandeur of his old school.

There was an immense field with a track, presided over at either end by goal posts. A few straggly trees and bushes were scattered around the edges. Toby drew closer.

A boy who was sitting out came over to the fence. "Hey you!" he shouted.

It was the sandy-haired skateboarder. Toby approached him—it couldn't hurt his credibility that he was skipping. "What?"

"You're skipping. I could tell on you."

"Hey, you're JB, aren't you?" Toby asked, using the same tone of voice.

"What's it to you? I see you at least got out of those geeky clothes."

"Well JB, I don't actually go to this school yet, so you just go ahead and tell. You'll look like a fool, but I guess that's normal for you." Toby turned and left. He knew enough to establish right off that he wouldn't be pushed around by the likes of JB.

On the way back to his building, there was the same Steller's jay. It seemed to be following him, flapping from tree to tree, but keeping its distance. He thought again about Beogall—would he ever see the heron again? At the thought, he touched the feather, which now hung from a cord under his shirt so it wouldn't get tattered.

Toby decided to explore his new building. The keys his dad gave him let him into the bike room, the storage area, the garbage room and even the garage. He checked out the amenity area, too. There was a small meeting room on one side, leading out to the terrace he could see from their balcony. On the other side was an exercise room with a treadmill, a stationary bike and some weight machines. He resolved to try them out, but first raced up the stairs, right to the top floor—there were twenty of them. On the way down he passed by his own floor and entered the fourth.

Number 405 was unmistakable. The door was intricately painted with an idyllic scene of forest, woodland animals and a small waterfall dropping into a pool. Mesmerized, Toby felt pulled toward it for a closer look—the scene was somehow familiar. He noticed a small Steller's jay, perfectly painted, perched in a tree, and reached out to touch it.

Just then the door opened.

"May I help you?" The voice was warm but strong, emanating from a tall woman with dark brown hair. Her skin was a lot lighter than Chester's. Toby wondered if this was his mom. Since Chester was supposed to be in school, he knew enough not to bring it up.

"I… I was just admiring your door. It's incredible. Who painted it?"

"Thank you. Two of us worked on it. Are you from around here?" As she spoke, Toby caught a glimpse inside the apartment, which looked, even with his quick glance, like a veritable jungle of plants.

"I am now. We just moved into the building." Toby quickly added, "But I haven't started at the school yet."

"Would that be Willow Heights?"

"Is that the closest one?" She nodded, so he said, "I guess I'll have to get registered soon."

"You should do that this week, since the school will be closed for spring break next week."

"Thanks. Uh, I better get going."

"Wait, what's your name? My son Chester seems to know everyone around here."

"I'm Toby, Toby Myers," he admitted and then added, "We live right above you." She seemed like a woman you could trust.

"Well, now I know, in case you make too much noise," she smiled and it was as if the sun had come out. "But I'm sure you won't." Then, echoing Chester's words, she said,

"Welcome to the neighbourhood, Toby. It's a great school, but get signed up soon."

And so it was that Toby and his father ended up at Willow Heights Secondary the very next morning. The name seemed a bit of a misnomer since Willow Street didn't climb much where the school was built. Classes had already started as they made their way past the glum exterior and into a surprisingly spacious foyer. It featured a large mandala of multi-coloured tiles embedded in the floor. On closer inspection, it looked like each small tile had been made by a student. Each one had three small initials in the lower right hand corner. There were lots with nature designs.

"May I help you?" A stern-faced woman peered at them from behind a glass enclosure. A sign above said "Office" and below that, "Mrs. Nasino".

"We're here to register my son for school," said Lars. "We've just moved into the neighbourhood."

The secretary eyed Toby up and down. "I'll try to get a counselor out here," she said curtly, turning to pick up her phone. A few moments later she reported, "They're both in meetings. I'll see if the principal is available."

She disappeared and a few minutes later, a strange little man approached and briskly introduced himself, "I'm Principal Standing. Why don't you come into my office?"

The offices were sparsely furnished with small windows to the outside, hung with dowdy blinds. By contrast, there was lots of glass toward the inside hallways, probably to keep an eye on the students.

Toby stifled a chuckle about the principal's name. He didn't look as if he were standing even though he was. At that, Principal Standing swung around and it seemed as if he were reading Toby's mind, who quickly regained a serious look. It wouldn't do to start off badly with a principal.

G.G. Neilson

"Have a seat. A counselor will be along soon," said Mr. Standing, sitting down. As he did, his chair rose up, automatically and silently, allowing him to peer sternly over the desk at Toby. "Where are you from and why are you hoping to register this far into the school year?"

His father explained without going into too much detail. Mr. Standing seemed surprised that he was transferring from St. Zallo's.

"You'll find this school quite different, but it is a good school. The counselor will want to know your interests for scheduling purposes, as well as the courses you've been taking this year. Here he comes now. Mr. McFru, meet Toby Myers and his father."

"How do you do. Sorry, so busy today. Meetings. Can't use the counseling office." Mr. McFru smiled as he bustled in and shook their hands. "Things piling up before spring break. What brings you here so late in the year, Toby?"

As his father briefly outlined what he had already told the principal, Toby studied the nodding counselor. He looked more Asian than Scottish, as his name implied—or did it? He was in constant motion, nodding his head and shrugging his shoulders.

"St. Zallo's," he repeated to himself as his dark eyebrows darted skyward. "I'll get in touch with your counselor…" He tapped his index finger to pursed lips, "Mr. Forger." He and Toby said the name together, and then both laughed. McFru had a high and melodic laugh.

"Do you know him?"

"Of course." The man positively beamed at Toby. "We've been at workshops together. Conferences, the like. Excellent fellow."

The connection suddenly made Toby feel a little less like a stranger here.

"Now. Any special interests, Toby?" As the question was asked, both the principal and counselor peered at him intently.

"Uh, er, like, vocational interests?"

"Well, I suppose so, yes. Often one's interests end up becoming one's life's work," said Mr. McFru, waving a hand dramatically. "We pride ourselves on scheduling our students into just the right classes. For them."

Since it looked like his father was bursting to tell them all about his interests, Toby quickly said, "I play the violin...and the flute. I enjoy tennis. I'm interested in ornithology. Do you have a music program?"

"Whoa, now. Those sound like good interests," said the counselor, studying him. "We have an excellent music program. We'll schedule you for band. Do tell about your interest in birds." The man leaned forward.

"I, um, like to go bird-watching. Well, I like to study them. Well, I guess it's because I used to go with my grandmother. She lives on Truewind Island," he blurted out in a rush.

A glance passed between the two men. Then they noticed that he had noticed and they studied him a little more before Principal Standing said, "A candidate for Odd S, Mr. McFru?"

"Perhaps," the counselor cleared his throat. "Toby, you don't have to answer this, but are you by any chance vegetarian?" It didn't seem that unusual a question. Lots of people talked about eating preferences. Toby looked at his dad who nodded, so he answered that he was.

Another glance passed between the two school officials. "I could prepare an Odd S schedule," Mr. McFru suggested. "There is that vacancy now—" Then he recited solemnly, "The courses in that rotation, in addition to French, Music and Science include a vegetarian cooking class—four Foods credits. How does that sound to you?"

"Great!" Toby agreed eagerly. He would like to learn to cook, especially now. Foods wasn't offered at St. Zallo's. It was assumed the boys would never need to do any of their own meal preparation—ever. Maybe he could even help with the cooking. His dad looked pleased at his interest.

Mr. McFru went on to explain the school's eight-day rotation. Students went to half of their classes on days 1, 3, 5, and 7 but in a different order each day. The other half, on days 2, 4, 6 and 8, were also in a different order each of those days. Toby was familiar with a rotating schedule and only half listened. He had noticed the large sign as they entered the school, saying "Odd – Day 5". Odd S was probably one of their class groupings, similar to St. Zallo's.

"Can't get to your schedule at this point, Toby. Can you come back in two days? Give me a chance to speak with St. Zallo's." With that Mr. McFru hurried out and Mr. Standing led them to the main office to fill in forms.

As they walked home, his father mused, "Funny little principal. I think that counselor is gay. Maybe this Odd S cohort will be good, Toby—students with similar interests as you."

"Nothing wrong with being gay," Toby defended the man. That was the mantra his teachers always used when the boys called things gay, and then would add, "Just don't use it in a derogatory way." The boys thought they knew which ones were gay and some suspected Toby too, because of his love of the flute and his interest in birds. "Don't stereotype. It makes you look ignorant," he would retort, so they stopped bothering him, except Milton.

"Dad, do you think Mr. Standing is a midget?"

"I don't know if that's the right term, Toby. He seems okay—he's proud of his school, that's obvious. Well, let's just see what kind of a schedule they come up with for you. After lunch, I have to head over to the golf course. Do you want to come?"

It was a good chance to improve his game, so he readily agreed. A side benefit of his Dad now working at the golf course was that they both got to golf for free. He also wanted to check out the pileated woodpecker at the 8th hole that Ms. Feathers had told him about.

"It's no big deal," was all he had said when his Dad bugged him again, wanting to know what Anna Feathers had said to him the day they had met. He could have a secret too.

Sure enough, the bird was there pounding away on an old snag.

Toby spent the afternoon on the golf course and was pleased with his low score, which he bragged about to his dad on their way home. They discussed plans for the following week—the real spring break. St. Zallo's private school was quickly being relegated in Toby's mind, as not the real world.

His father asked, "Would you like to go to Truewind Island for spring break? I'm sure your grandmother would enjoy having you visit. Of course, you're welcome to hang out at the golf course with me."

Toby hadn't been to Truewind for a while. Usually they vacationed in other parts of the world and he was pretty sure that his mother didn't like going there—too rustic for her tastes. But he had always jumped at the chance to go. "Yeah, I'd like to go there. I want to see Grams!"

The more he thought about it, the happier he felt. Better than some resort in the Caribbean any day. He was still thinking about it when they arrived home.

Waiting for them at the front entrance of the building was their ex-gardener, Walter. He was pale and trembling. "Mr. Myers, Toby! Something terrible is going on at the mansion."

Chapter 5

Trouble at the Mansion

"Come up with us, Walter," said Lars, ushering him into the lobby and onto the elevator. They got off at the fifth floor and led him into their apartment. Lars asked Toby to fetch the man a glass of water.

"What has happened, Walter?" he asked solicitously.

"Well, after you two moved out, Mr. Wint got very mean with me and said Lord Whenge would not want me to stay on. I had started looking up some old employers anyway. It just wouldn't be the same without you. I've been with you since Toby was small. Longer than him."

Lars nodded, encouraging him to continue.

"The next day, Lord Whenge told me I had to be out by Monday—that was yesterday. Said they had a new gardener lined up. No gardener, if you ask me. More like a butcher." Walter took a huge gulp of water before he could continue.

"Duffin taunted me. Told me they would be chopping down trees and taking out bushes. 'Why?' I asked. 'Don't want any birds coming around. We'll just make it all gravel and patios,' is what he said."

Toby turned pale—what about all their efforts to preserve the beautiful grounds? "Why that's outrageous, Walter!" he exclaimed. "I hope it wasn't because of what Be—the heron did."

"I sure heard about that. They ranted on about it half the night and right cursed you, Toby. They seemed to think you brought it about somehow. Well, I did leave Monday morning. The new guy just breezed in, didn't want to know anything about the gardens or grounds, and brought a chainsaw with him. I went back today for something I had left there and... and there were trees already chopped down. The hydrangeas were all dug up along with the new bulb beds."

Walter's eyes welled up as he said, "They saw me looking and told me to come see their handiwork. They killed a pair of robins, Toby, and a swallow too—they said they would kill any birds that bothered them. I didn't know what to do! Mr. Myers, since you had given me your new address, I just had to come tell you."

"You did the right thing coming to us," said Lars and invited their ex-gardener to stay for lunch. Over pasta salad, he told Walter he would give him an excellent reference. He even insisted that Walter call him 'Lars' then said, "I'll look into this, Walter. Give us your new address and phone number so we can keep in touch."

Walter gave the information and added, "I'm sorry for what's happened to you. It doesn't seem to be a bad place you've got here."

"Quite comfortable really," replied Lars charitably.

After Walter left, looking considerably better, they talked over the situation. But his father didn't think there was much they could do.

Badly shaken, Toby went to his room to do some Internet research. Even though it was now Whenge's property, maybe there were laws that could be used to stop the carnage.

Then he had an idea.

The next day was Wednesday. Toby spent some time working out in the weight room. He practiced the flute and violin,

G.G. Neilson

which always put him in a good mood. When he figured school would be out, he went looking for Chester at the skateboard park. He watched the throng of boys (and was that one a girl?) going through their moves.

JB was there, sailing along the railings and flying up and down the two bowls, adding in fancy flips. Toby had to admit that he was good. He caught some big air in the closest bowl, spiraled around in the air like a bird and swept toward Toby, landing in front of him. JB came to a full stop and with a confident leap off his board, flipped it over neatly and leaned on it.

"What do you want? How come you're lurking over here?"

"Hey man, you're an awesome skater. Ever thought of doing it professionally?" Toby asked with genuine admiration.

Somewhat grudgingly, JB said, "Yeah–I've been looking into sponsorships. You looking for Chester?" Toby nodded—how did he know? "He's over at the basketball court."

"Thanks man. See you around," said Toby over his shoulder as he headed to the courts. It couldn't hurt to be friendly—give the guy a chance.

As soon as Chester spotted him, he extricated himself from a pick-up game and came over.

"S'up?"

Toby told him what had happened. Chester's eyes grew large as he described his plan. His jaw dropped, "Oh man, I'm going to have to think about that," he said finally.

"Sure, no problem," replied Toby. "Could you let me know by tomorrow? Maybe come by my place after school? Say three-thirty?"

Supper was somber that evening as they talked again about the situation at the mansion. Then Lars phoned Walter but there was no answer. "I'm going out, Toby. I won't be long."

In his room, Toby went on the computer and began formulating some plans. When he finally got up to stretch at his little window, he couldn't believe his eyes.

There was Alyssa on a balcony in the building across from his—one floor up. She was playing with her two little dogs. He couldn't help but look and memorize her apartment. He was just about to turn away and close his blinds so she wouldn't think he was a stalker, when she caught him staring. She froze.

Oh God. She'll hate me forever, thought Toby. He pretended he hadn't seen her and immediately closed his blinds. What was the good of having her live practically opposite, if she detested him?

His dad, true to his word, wasn't late. They had a brief conversation about getting his schedule at Willow Heights the following morning.

That night, Toby woke up again and listened for the whoosh of the Skytrain, waiting to be lulled to sleep. But there were only faint traffic noises. He stared at the time: 3:00 a.m. The Skytrain had probably stopped running. He tossed and turned, thinking first about the mansion and then how he had totally blown things with Alyssa and they hadn't even met. He took out the feather and was holding it when he fell asleep.

It was raining the next morning when they walked to the school, this time with umbrellas. The stern secretary greeted them, and again they had to wait for Mr. McFru in the principal's office. Mr. Standing wasn't there—according to Mrs. Nasino he was supervising.

Mr. McFru hurried in, waving several sheets of paper. "We could have emailed this to you. But better to make sure you understand your schedule. Now. The day you come to school after spring break is an even day. See, you'll be starting with English, then Math." The counselor pointed as he read off each block. "After lunch you'll have Phys Ed and Socials. I was able to speak to Mr. Forger—the secretary at St. Zallo's had him phone me. Very nice of him since he was on holiday. He was sorry you wouldn't be returning to St. Zallo's."

Toby's eyes studied the floor.

"He wished you well," Mr. McFru continued cheerily. "I've gone ahead and enrolled you in the Odd S rotation, Toby. It's a unique group of students. But I think you'll fit in just fine." Mr. McFru eyed him intently as he said this last bit.

Toby wondered what it all meant, but figured he would find out soon enough. Just then the bell sounded and Mr. McFru rushed out leaving them to fend for themselves. Hordes of teens pushed and jostled through the halls. The place buzzed with conversation and a general air of excitement.

Toby was used to a smaller, more orderly school. These halls here were pure mayhem. Some students towered over them. Others eyed them with curious looks. He couldn't help but gape at what appeared to be many under-clad girls. Chester appeared from around a corner and gave him a high five.

"Hey man, did you get registered?" Several students stopped nearby to take in the new kid Chester was speaking with.

"Yep. All set to come here after spring break." Toby introduced him to his dad, relieved when Chester didn't say anything about them getting together later on that day.

As they left, Lars remarked how the halls of Willow Heights took him right back to his own school days. Then he said, "Chester seems okay. How did you meet him?"

"Just around—you know Dad, he lives right below us."

His dad's eyes widened. "Apartment 405! I've heard about it. Well, I've seen the door. Caused quite a stir around the building when they painted it. It's very beautiful... " He added in a puzzled tone, "Some people worried they were breaking the rules, but others didn't even seem to be aware of the door. Strange, but they weren't made to paint over it."

His dad was full of surprise information. Toby asked, "Have you met his mother?"

"Not really, but I've seen her around. Seems nice."

They stopped at Starbucks for a latte and a muffin on their way back to the apartment. Then his dad had to leave for work. "If this rain keeps up," he muttered, "I might be back earlier than usual."

Toby hoped not. Otherwise he and Chester would have to talk somewhere else. He couldn't chance his dad finding out about his plans.

With time to kill, Toby decided to try out his new Skytrain pass and rode around the different lines for a couple of hours. When a security guard began to notice him, he ended his explorations, remembering that it wasn't yet spring break for most students.

By the time the school day was finished, the rain had cleared up so his dad had not come back. There was a knock on the door at exactly 3:30 p.m. as planned, and there stood Chester. He looked around and said, "Yep, exactly the same layout as our apartment. This your bedroom over here?" Toby nodded and he asked, "Mind if I take a look?"

As they entered, it occurred to Toby that their place was spartan compared to the Oldwin's—with just a few things smuggled from the mansion. Chester noticed the important things: his flute and violin, and the Robert Bateman print.

"What a great painting. That Bateman, he's the best."

"Chester, I saw your apartment door. Did you paint that?"

"Yeah, my mom told me you'd been snooping around," Chester chuckled. Then he admitted, "I painted some of it. It was mostly my mom though. She's real artistic."

"She doesn't look much like you. Pardon me for asking, but are you adopted?"

"Oh man, do you ever stereotype. Ever heard of a black man and a white woman getting married? Actually one of my grandfathers on her side was black, too."

"Sorry, I guess I was just being nosy. Actually I have, like, native blood on my grandmother's side."

"Yeah, well, we're all a pretty multi-cultural mix nowadays." Chester looked out his window and said, "I guess we have the same view, too." He turned to Toby, his eyebrows raised. "Did you see our neighbour?"

"I have to keep my blinds permanently shut," Toby admitted, shoulders slumped.

"Yeah, I know what you mean. Look Toby, there's lots of nice girls at our school. Didn't you notice?" Toby cursed himself as he reddened. Chester grinned, then changed the subject. "Your dad seems cool. What's he do anyway?"

Toby went for the same abbreviated story that he heard his dad give and told about him working at Trout Creek Links. Then he remarked, "You have a fabulous balcony. I can see some of your plants from ours."

"Thanks, we actually grow some of our meals on it. Are you vegetarian?"

It turned out they both were although Chester ate some seafood. Then Toby launched into his plans for the next day.

Chester responded slowly, "I wouldn't have to skip, since tomorrow is a professional development day for the teachers."

"That's good. So are you in?"

"I'm in," said Chester, and he added, "but you owe me big time."

Toby had no way of knowing just how big he would owe him, in spite of his careful planning.

Friday morning arrived sunny and warm. "You're up early," his dad commented. "I have a long day at the golf course today. Have you made up your mind about spring break?"

"I'd like to go to Truewind Island. Have you talked to Grams?"

"Yes, and she said you're welcome anytime. She's looking forward to having you. I'll check with Mr. Frobisher to find out what day I can take you up there–probably not till after the weekend. I'll stay over one night, since I haven't spent much time with your grandmother in the last few years." He paused then asked, "What are you up to today?"

"Little of this, little of that. I should do some practising on the flute and violin." This last part wasn't a lie.

"Okay, call me at noon." They had started connecting at noon and again at 4 p.m. if his father was working longer hours.

"Dad, I'm almost fifteen, remember?"

"It's a new life, Toby," said his dad as he turned to leave.

Toby had the jitters and went over his plans for the fourth time. He phoned Chester who was already at the tennis courts. They went by Skytrain to the station nearest Toby's old neighbourhood then transferred to a bus. That took them within walking distance of the street Toby used to live on.

They were both going to take video of the destruction; their phones were charged and Toby had a camera, another item his father had managed to secrete out of the mansion.

Chester had thought to pack a water bottle and snacks as well as a poncho to sit on if needed. "This place is amazing," he said as they walked up the street approaching Toby's old home. "You guys must have been really rich."

"Didn't do us much good though, did it?" Toby replied bitterly. "Since it's rich boy spring break, as you like to call it, we won't look out of place walking around here, but still— act natural."

They were approaching their old grounds from the back, where Toby knew a path led to a small opening in their back fence. He and Chester walked casually toward the path. There was no one around; probably everyone was off holidaying elsewhere. But it also meant that alarm systems would be activated.

"This is where we have to be careful," said Toby as they approached the tall wrought iron fence. "It's wired with an alarm, but I know a place where we can get in."

They could already see some felled trees. Several alders were down and some hemlock trees had been cut as well as a giant old Douglas fir. Toby choked when he saw that their oldest trees, two giant yellow cedars near the back of the property had been chopped down. Huge chunks lay scattered in a colossal, cast-off heap. A wave of silent rage swept over him.

He heard Chester gasp. "What a totally senseless thing to do," his friend whispered grimly.

Seeing the massive trees lying in pieces strengthened Toby's resolve. He climbed carefully through the opening in the fence and into the mess that used to be forest. He began to video the carnage with his camera.

Chester followed, avoiding places that Toby pointed out. "I've got a bad feeling about this," he muttered softly as he pulled out his phone and began filming too.

Toby spoke quietly about the damage as they filmed.

Just then a shadowy form appeared beside them out of nowhere. They both stifled an urge to yell out.

It was Beogall. The heron began making excited noises to Toby, "You're here!" Toby was able to make out. "I told Walter you would know what to do. Bofu is dead."

"Whoa there, Beogall. You scared us out of a year's worth of growth. We have to keep it down. Who is Bofu?" Toby was amazed at how well he could understand. Chester looked on with curiosity.

"Bofu, the woodpecker—you know, the pileated one."

Toby suddenly felt sick. He remembered the boisterous bird very well and enjoyed his visits. He always made a huge racket whenever he found a nice rotten snag to pound into.

"They killed that mother and father robin and I think their eggs have been eaten. Some swallows were killed too. The nuthatches are safe."

"Well, they are fast," said Toby. As if to punctuate this last point, several nuthatches flitted over to land on a nearby spindly tree still standing. They peered from their upside down position.

"Toby, who is your friend?" asked Beogall, but Chester had disappeared behind a large stump.

A familiar voice boomed out, "Aha – I thought it might be the arrogant *Master* Toby. Come down in the world have you? Now all you can do is sneak around the old property. I hope you like what we've done with the place." Duffin Wint was approaching from about 40 feet away and had a gun pointed at Toby's chest.

"I can't believe you like this desecration, Duffin. These grounds were home to a lot of wildlife. It looks awful now," said Toby. His heart was pounding with anger and fear.

"I like the more open look. I see you've got your friend with you." Duffin now waved the gun towards Beogall. "Is this intruder the same one that dirtied Lord Whenge's car? That's going to cost you." He spat out the last sentence as he trained the gun on Beogall.

"You kill him and the world will be watching." Toby had his camera up and resumed filming. "I'm hooked into UsLive right now and people are watching. Great blue herons are on the protected list and it'll be jail time for you if you kill him."

"I don't believe you," said Duffin.

"Don't keep up much with stuff, Duff? D'you think I'd come here without a plan? I'm streaming live right now."

"Well, if that's the case then your audience should know that you are trespassing. This is private property and I'm about to remove you. You have ten seconds to get out, or I'll call the police."

"Yes I'll leave, but people should know that you have chopped down protected trees." Toby pointed to the hunks of ancient yellow cedar littering the ground. "That's a bigger crime than trespassing."

"Get out now, you hooligan!" Duffin snarled. "And don't come back again."

"Yeah, well if I hear that you're killing birds or cutting down any more protected trees, it'll be my turn to bring the police." Toby's knees felt like putty as he backed away slowly. "Don't you know that Walter got a special designation for rare trees and species on these grounds? Your new boss was a bit too quick to fire him."

Toby's hands were trembling as he inched backwards, hoping to buy time for Chester to do the same. "Walter would have told you about it if you had kept him around. Even for a day."

Toby waved for Beogall to fly off. He could sense that Duffin was just itching to shoot the bird. He fought back terror. He wanted to turn and run, but forced himself to continue facing the big man as he felt his way back, hoping not to trip over the debris.

Duffin had moved threateningly forward during the exchange. Suddenly he lunged forward and made a wild grab for Toby's camera. He was surprisingly quick for such a large man and caught Toby unawares.

Toby tried in vain to block himself. But in one fluid motion, Duffin crunched the camera in one big fist and punched Toby with the other. He saw stars and then blackness.

Chapter 6
A Minor Celebrity

Toby awoke groggily, to see his father and Chester peering anxiously down at him. They looked blurry—what was it with his eyes?

"Thank god! I was so worried about you," his father exclaimed, leaning so close Toby could feel his breath.

"Dad. Chester. Where am I?" Toby tried to look around and then groaned with pain. His head was pounding and there were bandages over his throbbing nose. He realized that his left eye would not open.

"You're in the hospital, Toby. Do you remember anything about what happened?" asked his father.

Toby nodded then groaned again. His dad would know by now what he and Chester had done. "You okay, Chester?" His friend nodded. "How did I get here? Where is Duffin?" He looked around, half expecting the big man to be lurking nearby, ready to pounce again.

"No, he's not here," Chester assured him. "What a monster that guy is."

"What happened back there anyway?" asked Toby.

"What do you remember?"

"Everything up to when Duffin punched me. He did punch me, didn't he?"

"Yeah, and good," said Chester shaking his head. "Well, your old butler hadn't seen me. I got behind a big stump but

I was still filming. A back-up, just like we planned. When Duffin attacked you, I went for his gun. He had dropped it, so I just walked over and picked it up. Man, was I scared, but I aimed it at him." Lars stared at Chester as if he had sprouted an extra head. "Then I yelled for him to stop."

Toby pictured Duffin whirling around to see the dreadlocked Chester training his own gun on him. "Wow," was all he could say.

"Do you have any experience with firearms?" Lars asked, incredulous.

"My dad taught me a little about them," he answered and then continued, "That great blue heron—you should have seen him! He just flew up into the air and then swooped down and charged right into Duffin."

Toby grinned at this image.

Chester went on, "Some other herons came too and some gulls screeched in and started dive-bombing him. All hell broke loose. Other birds got in on the action too. You should have seen them—flying around him, scolding like crazy, and like, totally carrying-on. Then this woodpecker came in and just a-pecked away on that butler. I actually felt sorry for him."

"Don't be. That would be Bofu's mate," said Toby grimly as Chester and his dad regarded him strangely. "They killed Bofu. Walter will be happy to hear all this."

"I'm not so sure," Lars responded, "but I will let him know. It sounds like you kept your cool, Chester. I'm glad you were there. How did Toby get to hospital?"

"When things settled down a bit, I called 9-1-1. An ambulance arrived pretty fast. And the cops too."

"That was good thinking." Then Lars turned grimly to Toby, "I can't believe what you did, but I'm glad to finally learn all the details."

"That's quite the address you folks had." Chester was shaking his head. "One of the officers seemed to know you. They called your dad."

Toby groaned again and hoped his dad would think it was from the pain.

"Yes, well you are in a bit of trouble with Officer Backer again, Toby," said Lars lowering his voice. "He wanted to speak with you as soon as you woke up. You were trespassing after being specifically warned not to."

"You were in trouble before?" Chester asked, mouth agape. Lars filled him in about the tennis racket incident. "Wow man, you surprise me."

Toby wondered why communicating with birds didn't surprise Chester, but violence with a tennis racket did.

"They took Duffin away," Lars said almost to himself. "Whenge wasn't home at the time of the attack, but no doubt he'll get a good lawyer. He'll probably even post bail for his new employee," he added bitterly.

"What happened to the stuff you recorded?" Toby suddenly remembered to ask Chester.

"I posted it to the Net—UsLive, just like we planned." His friend grinned, "I checked to make sure what I recorded was okay. Right up to where he punched you."

Lars gasped, spluttered, then cleared his throat. "Well, I'm just happy that you're both safe. I won't go into what a stupid thing that was, Toby." His dad's eyes drilled into him. "And dragging Chester into it as well! I have a lot of questions about it all, like… well, forget that for now. I think Backer is just outside the room—he might be listening in."

Just then, the door opened.

It wasn't Constable Backer though. It was Barbara Myers.

"Tobias! Darling. You're safe! I heard you had been shot." His mother rushed over and hugged him gently but he still winced. She threw an accusatory glance at Lars with blue eyes that perfectly matched her sky-blue dress. Her blonde hair was immaculate as always.

"Mom!" Toby's voice came out part squawk and part sob. "I wasn't shot, but I am hurting. Why didn't you call?" He couldn't keep resentment out of his voice. "I didn't know where you were." His eyes welled up, even the one that wouldn't open.

Chester excused himself, saying he had to get something to eat.

"Why, your father knew where I've been staying. He even came over to see me once."

Toby stared at his father.

"You know that I thought it would be better if you made the first move, Barbara." Lars gripped the chair as if it was an effort to stay seated. "You could have contacted him anytime. And besides…" He stopped.

There was an awkward silence.

"Well, I… I just didn't know what to do or say myself," Toby's mother finally admitted. "But I'm here now and I'll make it up to you." She touched his bandages gently. "Are you going to be okay dear? Tell me what happened." She perched lightly on the edge of the bed.

He gave a brief rendition of the events, leaving out the role of the birds, while his father added in a few details.

"You shouldn't have gone there, Tobias. How could you?"

Lars gave her a steely look. Then he asked, "How did you find out what had happened?"

"Why, it's on the news. They didn't name Toby, but I recognized his voice of course and our old grounds."

Toby and Lars looked at each other. There was a television set in the room. Lars immediately turned it on. As he fiddled with it, Barbara continued, "There was footage from UsLive. That dreadful Duffin Wint has been arrested. Is it true that he attacked you, Toby?"

"It's true. And here's the result," he answered gingerly touching the bandages.

"That's ghastly. How could he? He was with us for years."

Lars had managed to pull up an all-news channel. "Why don't hospitals provide computers instead of T.V. sets," he grumbled as they all studied the screen.

"The camera is toast, Toby, but Chester had your phone." His father pulled it out of his pocket and started to hand it over. Then he seemed to think better of it and put it back. He asked, "When did you guys plan all this?"

"Dad, do you remember when Walter and I catalogued the valuable trees on the property and got the yellow cedars and some nesting sites and stuff registered?"

His father looked at him blankly so he continued, "I thought that if I recorded what was happening, it would convince Suchno Whenge to stop destroying it. I didn't know how bent Duffin could be." Toby shook his head sadly but then stopped when he realized how much it hurt.

"Who's the boy who was here?" his mother asked, but there was no time for an answer. The news item appeared on the television. They watched, astonished, as their previously beautiful grounds came into view, looking like a disaster zone, with Toby's voice talking quietly about yellow cedars being cut illegally. Then they saw Duffin approaching. The audio was indistinct but the threat was clear. Toby's mother gasped as Duffin lunged. Then the picture went black.

The announcer said, "Duffin Wint has been charged with assault. The minor cannot be named, but trespassing charges are pending. Neighbours called 9-1-1 and the boy was taken to hospital but his injuries are not life threatening. Mr. Wint's employer, Lord Suchno Whenge, said 'no comment,' but our news team has found out that a lawyer has been hired and bail was arranged."

As the announcer went on to another news item, Constable Backer entered the room. With a frown, he rubbed his hand and asked to speak to Toby alone.

"No. He's a minor, so I will stay," Lars insisted. His mother stated that she would stay also and reached for Toby's hand.

"Okay then. You were trespassing, Toby. You were told not to. I'm afraid we'll have to charge you for that." Backer seemed to relish the last bit.

"But Officer Backer, there are protected species and trees on that property," Toby protested. "They were, like, registered and everything. Destroying them is a bigger crime than trespassing! I've researched similar cases." Toby began to reel off precedent-setting cases.

Constable Backer stopped him. "You'll have a chance to go over all of that in court. I'm here about the trespassing charge. Why didn't you leave it up to the authorities to go after them?"

"There wasn't time! Who knows what other damage they would have done? They fired the gardener who could have told them about it." Lars put a restraining hand on Toby's shoulder but he carried on, "I happen to know every tree and most of the bird species there, and according to legal precedent, they have rights, too."

Backer ignored this and proceeded to ask for Toby's official statement. Then he announced, "This will be added to your juvenile record. And I need a statement from the other boy. Where is he?"

"He left. And besides, this was totally my idea. I talked him into it. I just needed someone to help me with the equipment and for back-up."

"What equipment?" asked the policeman.

"I brought a video camera and had it connected to the Internet through the phone. I wanted to record the destruction and live-stream it to the Net." Toby had an idea. "I will be charging Mr. Wint with wrecking my video camera. It was quite expensive."

"And we will be pursuing an assault charge. Isn't that worse than trespassing, Officer?" Lars asked.

Constable Backer shifted uncomfortably. "Well, of course we're looking into that," he admitted. "How did you manage to get it onto the Net?" he asked turning to Toby. "You were being attacked—I mean, you were busy with Duffin Wint."

"Well Officer, I guess all of that will come out in court," interrupted Lars. "Toby is in pain and very tired. You've got your statement. I will come down to the station later to press charges about the destroyed video camera. And I want to make sure that Duffin Wint is held responsible for the outrageous assault on my son," he said in a tightly controlled voice. "Forget your little trespassing charge. Can't you see what that man did?" said Lars pointing to Toby's bandages.

Without another word, Constable Backer turned and strode out.

They all looked at each other.

"I think he realizes that his pal Wint doesn't stand a chance," said Lars sourly. "Good deflection off your friend, Toby. Chester doesn't need to be dragged any further into this. I'll give him a ride home if he's still around. I better make sure Backer doesn't find him."

"You look worn out, dear," said his mother tenderly. "I'll ask them at the desk to give you something to help you to sleep."

"Get some rest now," said his dad. "I'll be back tomorrow."

His mother rose and leaned over to kiss the top of his head. Just like old times. "Yes dear, get some rest. I'll call you soon."

His parents left together. As Toby drifted back to sleep, he wondered whether they might get back together. They could be a family again. They could go to the Bahamas.

G.G. Neilson

Then he realized he didn't want to go there. What he wanted more than anything was to go to Truewind Island and see his grandmother.

As soon as possible.

Part 2 –
Truewind Island

There's no reason to be ignorant about nature. We are no different than the birds and animals of the forest. If you watch with your eyes, hear with your ears, smell with your nose and feel with your hands, as well as your heart, you can learn everything about the world around you.

Mary Ellen Paull

Chapter 7
Grams

It was late morning the next day when Toby again woke up to the anxious regard of his father. His nose was throbbing and his head ached. He was aware of other tender places, too.

"Dad, how long have you been here? Aren't you supposed to be at work?"

"I haven't been here long. I got a few days off work on the promise that I'll make up the time on weekends. Things are working out well there—they like me. Guess I'm meant to be a groundskeeper."

"When can I leave the hospital?"

"After the doctor sees you today, you're allowed to go home. I've spoken to your grandmother and she's expecting us at Truewind Island tomorrow. I told her you're supposed to rest."

Two hours later, Toby was discharged. He hadn't realized he could be so happy to see their little apartment. While his dad packed for their trip, Toby checked his messages. Chester had left two, and an email from Dalton Butter startled him. "Toby—saw a weird thing on UsLive—sure sounded like your voice and looked like your property. Are you okay? What's going on? I'm having a good time in Mexico. Check my messages often. Text me, Dalton"

Toby texted him right away, giving a very abbreviated version of events, adding that he had now moved.

What could he say to Chester? How could he apologize for dragging him into this whole mess? He was still sitting with his phone in hand, when there was a knock on the door. His father ushered Chester into his room.

"Hey Toby, you're still looking kinda rough. How you feeling?"

"Hey, Chester. Just saw your messages. I'm feeling better than the last time I saw you, but the doctor says I have to take it easy."

"Yeah, you should. Thought I heard noises up here, so I decided to see if you were back. Here—my mom sent along these home-made cookies." He handed over a fragrant package.

Toby stuck his nose in the bag and inhaled deeply. "Hmmm," he said breathing in fresh-baked cookie. "Thanks! Are these chocolate chip?"

"Yeah. Looks like you still have your sense of smell."

"Yep, but not as good as it normally is. Look Chester, I'm real sorry I dragged you into all this. It wasn't fair. I just wanted to get some footage of the damage then leave."

"Well 'the best laid plans of mice and men' and all that. No worries. Looks like it was a good thing I was there. Your dad told me how you kept my name out of that policeman's report. Thanks for that."

"Least I could do. Besides, I don't trust that guy."

There was an awkward silence and then Chester's eyes lit up, "Hey, you're famous now! Well not exactly you, but your voice. They're calling it 'the mystery boy's' voice and showing that clip of your old mansion. They're like, even doing special reports about protected trees and species around the city. All the stations are doing that."

"Wow, that's great! Maybe there won't be any more cutting down trees or killing birds over there."

"Speaking of birds… that's quite the friend you've got there. Beogall, is that his name? How did you get to know him?"

Toby told Chester about meeting the great blue heron at St. Zallo's.

"Can you communicate with other birds?" Chester asked this so straightforwardly that Toby went for the straightforward reply. Besides, he had already trusted Chester with his life.

"I didn't know I could but I've always been able to, like, sense stuff about them," Toby related, glad to be able to talk about it. "I can understand Beogall pretty well, but when we were there," he recalled, "I sensed some other bird communication going on around us. That's why I wasn't too surprised when you said more came to help…"

"It'll be strange to see your old butler bring all that up in court."

They both laughed and Chester asked, "Do you know when that will be?"

"My dad says the wheels of justice turn slowly and all that—it might be months. He just wants me to get better. We're going up to Truewind Island for spring break."

"That's a great place. Well, I better let you get some more rest."

"Wait, what are you up to for spring break?"

"After all this excitement, I think I'll just do something low key. There's some things I can help my mom with, spend time with my dad. Skateboarding, basketball. No shortage of things to do around here." He turned to go.

"Have a good one, eh. And, and thanks again, Chester." It was on the tip of his tongue to invite Chester to Truewind Island, but it wouldn't be much fun for his friend, watching him lie around.

"Later alligator."

The next afternoon found Toby and his father sitting on the ferry to Truewind Island. Toby felt self-conscious about his bandaged nose, but at least his head wasn't aching as much. They found seats in an out-of-the-way corner of the ferry, but still with a good view.

"It's been too long," said Lars gazing out over the rippling ocean. With a backdrop of jagged, snow-capped mountain peaks layered in the distance, it was like a scene from one of Barbara's Mark Graff prints.

Toby realized how much he had missed this trip.

His father was quoting a poem. "*Beyond the ocean, the mountains stand; shoulder to shoulder, crouched on the land.*" Toby looked at him. "Those are the first two lines from a poem by your Aunt Heather. They always pop into my head when I'm on this ferry. I don't know if that one was ever published. Some of hers were. One was in the high school yearbook—Grams and Gramps were very proud."

Toby really liked his aunt—two years earlier he had flown out to Toronto and spent a week with her. She was a lot of fun. He hadn't seen her since—he would be sure to ask Grams about her.

They were "driving on" so Grams wouldn't have to pick them up on the other side. The ferry held a surprising number of cars but it was expensive to drive versus walking. Toby looked at the receipt after his father paid and quickly calculated how many hours he'd have to work at a minimum wage job to cover the cost. A lot.

He had never thought much about money before, but now realized they would have to be careful with their spending.

"You know Dad, we could always take the bus out to Horseshoe Bay so we wouldn't have to pay for the car. Grams could meet us on the other side."

"Good idea, Toby." His father looked at him gratefully. "If we come over more often, we'll have to do that. I had forgotten how expensive it is to take a car."

More like he never had to worry about it before, thought Toby.

"I don't think your grandmother would mind picking us up from the landing," added his dad after a while. "She has the old station wagon, but I think she still rides her bike around—even to get groceries sometimes." He sighed and observed, almost to himself, "After Gramps died, she's become even more independent, if that's possible."

Toby had a vague memory of his grandfather, a kindly man with tired eyes. "There it is!" he cried as Truewind Island came into view.

The island first appeared as an emerald slope of land rising out of the ocean. Small mountains rose up from the northern end of the island, sporting a light dusting of snow on their upper reaches. The town of Fairwind was coming into view, but they wouldn't be driving through it. The ferry terminal was a few kilometers from the town.

The ferry docking announcement piped up—"sixteen, sixteen" followed by a polite request to return to the cardeck. Dutifully they followed the other passengers down and within a few minutes had joined a line of cars driving up the bypass. Being a school holiday, there was a lot of traffic.

"There's the bus," commented Toby, and he could see foot passengers trooping toward it. "I wonder how close it goes to Grams' place? I think I'll google it."

Grams was waiting as they turned from Berry Farm Road into her driveway. Carol Myers was dressed in her usual garb, an old shirt over a blouse and serviceable jeans. Pure white hair formed a brilliant halo around her head. Half-moon reading glasses dangled from a cord around her neck. In this small, slightly plump form, resided an energetic woman. She rushed out to meet them when the car came into view.

"Lars, Toby! So wonderful to see you!" She gave Toby a light hug avoiding the bandages. "Come in, come in. You must be hungry." Grams first order of business was always to feed people. Even though they declared they were not hungry—it was mid-afternoon—she insisted they have tea, and served a selection of cheeses and a platter of muffins. "There's nothing much in the garden yet, but the blackberries in the muffins are from last year's crop." Grams had a deep-freeze that she kept well stocked.

Toby and Lars sat drinking in their surroundings while Grams caught them up on island news. She lived in a rustic post and beam cabin that she had helped Toby's grandfather build almost forty years earlier. Lars was a toddler when they moved there from the city, but his sister, Heather, was born on the island. Carl Myers continued to commute to the city for work until he retired. Carol Myers had found work at the local post office.

They had purchased their first ten acres and used logs and lumber from trees milled on their own property to build the cabin. The open living-room and country kitchen featured a lot of wood and large windows. There was also a small den, a bathroom, a laundry room, and a mud room downstairs. Upstairs were three smallish bedrooms and a second bathroom. The upper hallway overlooked the open area on the main floor. Until now, Toby had forgotten about the wonderful recycling closet, where everything from paper to plastics were "kept out of the landfill" as Grams announced cheerfully whenever he explored. He breathed in the lavish scent of lavender—and then noticed stalks of them tied together with ribbons on the sideboard.

A few years after moving in, a neighbouring ten acres had been put up for sale. The Myers dipped heavily into their savings to buy the adjoining property. "Our twenty acres of paradise," Grams declared now as she often did. Most of it was still in a natural state. The windows all had remarkable views—trees, shrubs, meadows and two small areas of tended garden. A south-facing slope had been cleared at one time, when the plan was to plant grapevines and operate a small vineyard as extra income in their retirement. Gramps got sick soon after, so it never happened.

Now flocks of birds enjoyed the wild blackberries, huckleberries, elderberries and other plants that the meadow freely offered. Grams still jokingly called it "the vineyard" and it was this view that the three sat enjoying at the kitchen table on that Sunday in March.

"So tell me about what happened, Toby," said Grams gravely, as she poured them all a second cup of her mint tea.

Toby told her the story and answered her questions. Even his father hadn't heard some details and twice Lars and his mother exchanged worried glances.

When he was finished she said, "Beogall. I've heard of him—young and impulsive."

"You've heard of Beogall?" Toby was incredulous. She nodded and Toby took a deep breath, "Grams, can you communicate with birds?"

Lars gave her an inscrutable look as she paused. "Toby, I've known for a long time that you can sense things. And I wondered if you'd be able to communicate with birds." His dad sat stiffly as she continued, "It's a rare gift, but I thought you might be blessed with it. People who can communicate with the bird kingdom, or the animal kingdom for that matter, are reluctant to let others know. Only my closest friends know I can communicate with birds."

Toby sat on the edge of his chair while she continued, "As you know Toby, it takes a lot of focus and an intuitive ear. It seems that we can hear outside the normal human range, where birds do a lot of their communication." Grams continued thoughtfully, "I've heard it said there may be some who can communicate with birds, animals and plants. Such an ability would be rare, and the knowledge protected. I have been hoping all my life to meet such a person. I've also been hoping that some brave person would come forward to be a real voice for the birds and pave the way for others. Since that hasn't happened yet and because I'm old now, I'm willing to do it myself."

Her son and grandson looked at her in alarm. "No, Mom, it would be too risky," said Lars.

"I could do it," stated Toby.

"No, Toby, your life is just beginning." But she looked at him with a fierce pride. "I'm sure you will help when the time comes. I'm an old woman. It would not be a hardship for me, except as it affects you two. After all these years, I'm thinking of changing my name back to 'Forest', my maiden name. What do you think?"

"Nothing wrong with Myers if you ask me. I'm going to go look around the property," Lars said and abruptly left.

Grams looked after him with a worried look and then turned to Toby. "He just needs more time to get used to the idea of talking to birds. I wasn't much good at it myself until later in life. Toby, you look tired. I've set up a lounge chair out on the patio if you'd like to lie down out there."

Toby fell asleep lulled by soft, rejuvenating breezes. He awoke much later, listening to a song sparrow singing nearby. She cocked her head and twittered, "Are you the boy injured by that bad man over in the city?"

Toby haltingly admitted he was and she seemed to understand him. The sparrow chattered briefly in sympathy and then flew off. He thought about how his ability to communicate with birds was growing stronger. It required great concentration since birds pack so much into their sounds. His grandmother was right—it was partly intuitive and some things were just sensed. It hadn't occurred to him that he could hear sounds others couldn't, like she suggested. Dozing off again, he wondered if his grandmother had ever tried to teach his dad.

Much later, Toby awoke and realized that someone had put a blanket over him. He could feel his wounds healing rapidly in the soft spring air—what was it about Truewind Island?

Staring up into the deepening blue of the sky, he indulged in his childhood game of imagining shapes in the clouds. As sleep caught up with him again, a great blue heron shape formed in the billowy clouds high overhead.

The sun was low in the western sky when Lars woke him. "You really needed that rest. Grams has supper ready."

There was a delicious vegetable chowder and fragrant buns, which Toby slathered with butter then ate three in a row while Grams smiled her approval. Dessert was a fruit cobbler drizzled with honey. After serving blackberry tea, Grams removed his bandages and clucked, "Your poor nose!"

Actually Toby thought it looked much better and his eye wasn't nearly so swollen. "I can see just fine now."

"I think you might be ready to go on a walk tomorrow," Grams declared. "There's a place I want you to see and someone I'd like you to meet."

The next morning was brisk and windy with a slight threat of rain in the air. After breakfast Lars announced that he had to return to the city. "Can't afford any more time off!"

"So soon?" said Grams, disappointed.

"I'm the new guy, so... But I'll be back up in a few days to fetch Toby." He gave them each a quick hug and said,

"Gotta go—if I miss this ferry, the next one won't be along for another two hours."

A sense of anticipation gripped Toby as they set out in Grams' car, heading to a part of the island unfamiliar to him. They passed fewer and fewer homes the further west they drove, to a remote section of island. The silence of the forest closed in around them as the highway narrowed to a road and finally to a dirt track. Grams parked the car off to one side and they continued on foot into the woods. She told Toby that they were in a large tract of crown land that the islanders wanted set aside as a protected area.

The woods were dark and hushed; Toby breathed in the pungent smell of pine, fir and cedar—kind of a cinnamon aroma. Their feet sank slightly as they stepped quietly over soft beds of moss and needles. Toby's grandmother pointed out the ferns growing in profusion – sword, deer and the occasional maidenhead fern along with bracken. There were mosses, salal and patches of Oregon grape.

Silence enveloped them like a blanket although Toby could sense the presence of birds. The forest gradually gave way to a meadow, graced with shrubs, grasses and wildflowers. Large boulders emerged from the earth here and there. A puff of wind made Toby shiver.

"This is known as the glade," said Grams.

He realized they were near the water as he caught glimpses of slate grey ocean in the distance, through a thin fringe of trees.

Insects buzzed tranquilly, but with no birdsong, the hush felt weird. Grams looked up and began singing a haunting tune.

> *Grandmother Eagle floats on high*
> *Grandmother Eagle floats on high*
> *See how she dances on the wind*

See how she dances on the wind
O-lee-o oh-oh-oh lee-ohh
See how she dances on the wind

Soaring high above their heads Toby could see the out-spread wings of an eagle who began a slow majestic spiral down toward them. Toby was enthralled.

The bird gracefully flapped its great wings and alit on an old Douglas fir tree; Toby held his breath. He had never been this close to a bald eagle, although he had spotted them before, high overhead.

"So, you've finally brought the young one," uttered a raspy, contralto voice, as the eagle settled onto a large branch. Her giant head bent low, piercing eyes appraised him. "You're the boy I've heard so much about. Welcome to Westwind, sanctuary for birds."

Suddenly the glade erupted into bird sounds—a chorus, then a full symphony of songs, twittering, chirruping and trilling. As wave upon primeval wave of sound rose and fell and rose again, Toby was overcome with delight. Was this how it sounded at the dawn of time, before there were even humans? He didn't want it to end.

"Enough," commanded the eagle, silencing the orchestra as abruptly as it had started.

Grams introduced the bird to Toby as Grandmother Eagle. With a nod of her regal head, she asked him about the events at the mansion. It seemed that the birds of Westwind Bird Sanctuary knew all about Walter's efforts to preserve the place for birds, and its subsequent destruction.

"We're very grateful to him," a swallow sang out, "and you too Toby, for putting a stop to it."

"Do you know Beogall?" he blurted out, trying to deflect the praise.

"Of course, of course," came a chorus of replies.

Grandmother Eagle said that the heron flew in sometimes to report on happenings, but that he mostly divided his time between the grounds of an old school, which had been built on the ancestral home of his family, and the heronry at Stanley Park. Toby was amazed to find that he understood much of the bird chatter. "Do you understand everything they're saying, Grams?"

"It took me many years to learn to communicate with birds, Toby, and I still cannot get the hang of it with a great many of them," she replied.

"Very few of you humans can speak with us," stated Grandmother Eagle, "and many birds cannot understand humans. Why, we often can't even communicate among ourselves. Especially with hummingbirds." There was a chittering round of agreement.

"You have a rare gift, Toby," she continued. "Your abilities are developing early and quickly. We hope you will use this gift well."

Toby was not at all sure about this—he suddenly felt nervous about the faith they placed in him. His uneasiness grew when other birds chimed in about areas crying out to be saved from destruction. Grandmother Eagle cut them off. "He is too young yet, but he will be ready to help in the fullness of time. Such conservation campaigns need many to help out," she said.

"We have our scouts," cawed a crow. "Don't most have some? Like Beogall. They help find people who can communicate with us."

"Caw, caw. Yes, scouts," another crow bobbed its head in agreement. "Find good people—ones who can communicate with us. They respect—"

"Most people don't seem bent on destroying us and our habitats," Grandmother cut them off, "but those who do, seem to have a lot of power and cause such havoc! We are afraid for our very survival."

The old eagle flapped down to a lower branch and said, "The memories handed down by our ancestors show that our numbers used to be much greater before mankind's numbers exploded and people moved everywhere, into all of our places."

As the birds chimed in their agreement, Toby knew she spoke the truth and felt ashamed about what was happening to them.

"We had to learn to reach out to the humans who care and can help. But you need us too." Then the eagle lowered her head still further and said in a low rumble, "We have recently heard about a threat to this place. To Westwind."

The birds flapped about angrily at this and the two crows cawed in unison, "No, not Westwind!"

"I, too, have heard a rumour about a development," said Grams finally. "I belong to a group that's trying to preserve this place as a park and bird sanctuary."

The assembled birds chattered excitedly about those who could help. Toby didn't understand it all but thought he heard his science teacher, Mr. Getty named as well as Walter. Was it possible that he heard Willow Heights mentioned? He immediately dismissed the idea.

A politician was named who had gotten into office specifically to help save natural habitat and they twittered excitedly about this. Toby was so engrossed that he didn't realize that the wind had been picking up.

Suddenly several gulls flew in. "Take cover!" they warned in raucous shrills. "There's a storm sweeping toward us from the ocean. It's rough out there!" They said this hurriedly then flapped toward the interior of the island.

Grams and Toby looked in the direction the gulls had come from and sure enough, dark clouds were approaching ominously, scudding quickly from the west.

"Yes, you must leave at once," said the old eagle, "but Toby, you are to come back here again before you leave Truewind Island. Your grandmother tells me that you are only here for a few days. There is someone I want you to meet."

Toby promised to come back by the end of the week.

"Farewell, Grandmother Eagle," said Grams and then turned to Toby. "We must get going. The wind and those rain clouds are making me nervous."

And indeed, the winds had increased drastically in just a few minutes.

Chapter 8

Stormy Dreams

As Toby and Grams hurried down the trail, rain whipped at their faces. It was a struggle to walk. Birds flew off to the security of forests and nests, shrilling out warnings as they went. By the time the two reached the car, the wind was so violent, they fought to open the doors.

Toby finally managed to pry the driver's side door open for Grams then he scrambled around to the passenger side. As he did, a loud crack made him look over. A violent gust of wind had blown the door against Gram's head. He raced back and wrenched the car door away from her. There were tears in her eyes as he helped her into the driver's seat.

"Grams! Are you okay? I don't think you should drive."

She held her head in her hands. "Just give me a minute. I'll be okay," she said, her voice wavering.

Toby worked his way around to the passenger side again, guilt hanging like a blanket over him—why hadn't he stayed to hold the door open for her? He sat anxiously while the wind whipped up harder than ever.

"I think we should go," Grams said finally, and turned on the engine. Toby watched closely as she drove slowly and erratically up the trail.

"Um, Grams," Toby spoke gently, "I think we need to back down to the turn-around."

He wasn't sure if she heard him because she continued, white-knuckled hands clutching the wheel. He grew alarmed. Tree branches slapped at the car.

She brought it to a halt. "I can't drive right now, Toby," she finally said. "Maybe we should wait out the storm."

"You know, Grams, Dad has been teaching me how to drive. I practiced on the driveway at the mansion—it's very long, you know. I could drive."

Adrenalin pumping, he got out and fought with the wind to open her door. He coaxed her into the back seat, carefully ensuring the door didn't suddenly shut on them. He folded his jacket into a pillow for her. Battling the wind again, he struggled into the driver's seat. It had been a while since his Dad's lesson on their driveway, but he had been watching his Dad and Duffin drive for years.

The hardest part was backing down the narrow trail. He finally maneuvered to the turn- around and had them pointed in the right direction. He thought the worst was over, but by this time, trees were swaying dangerously over the old dirt trail. What if one came down on them?

Toby drove cautiously to the main road and onto the highway. His heart thumped loudly in his chest as they crept along. But there was little other traffic and noone noticed the under-age boy behind the wheel.

What felt like a lifetime later, Toby drove up Grams' drive-way. He helped her into the house and into her old armchair. Should he take her to the small island hospital? It would be hard with the storm still raging. His father would know what to do. But he couldn't get through to his dad, even to leave a message.

Grams' landline was out so he called the medical clinic on his cell phone. Because of the storm they were exceptionally busy. It took ages to get through to a nurse practitioner who assured him it was a good sign that Grams was conscious.

She told him what to look for that would require bringing her to the hospital. Reassured, Toby applied a cold compress and kept a close eye on her.

He heated up some left-over soup and watched with pleasure as Grams finished the whole bowl. When she joked about the two of them now being invalids, Toby felt more reassured.

"You need some rest, Grams. Can I help you lie down?"

"I can manage," she declared wearily. "Toby, I'll live. I've just got a bit of an egg and a giant headache. Now let me be." But her face was white so he decided to keep looking in on her.

Violent winds rattled the house and Toby heard branches cracking. He hoped all the birds had found safe shelter. He tried to call his dad again but realized that his phone was dead and quickly plugged it in. How could he have forgotten to charge it? They were now totally cut off! Was the storm affecting the whole coast? What if they suddenly lost power?

He raced around looking for candles and then built a fire in the woodstove in the kitchen, glad that Grams had once showed him how—he finally got it going. Just when he tried the radio to get some news, the power went out.

Pleased with his roaring fire, Toby made tea on the stove. He carried a cup of steaming tea in to his grandmother, but she was sound asleep. Carefully he set the cup on her bedside table in case she woke up. Then he noticed the feather. It was grey and smaller than his, and it looked old and tattered. Grams' wrinkled hand, sticking out from her blanket was just barely touching it.

Toby was restless. It was unsettling to be completely out of touch with the outside world. By the flickering light of a candle, he looked around the bedroom he always slept in when he came to visit—Aunt Heather's room. Other than a framed copy of one of her poems, *The Runner*, and some pictures on the walls, he had never really explored it. He came across a folder of her poems and read through them. Then he came across a map she had drawn of Truewind Island—it looked like a school project. Toby studied it for a long time, paying particular attention to Westwind sanctuary before finally dropping off into a fitful slumber.

Wind lashed at the bird sanctuary where a giant bulldozer crushed the trees and the meadow he had been a few hours earlier. The tree that Grandmother Eagle perched in, blew over in the wind and she flew off to the Trout Creek Links. Toby drove his father's car around the grounds—his dad running behind shouting at him to stop. But he drove right into the clubhouse, coming to rest in Ms. Feathers' office.

"Toby, nice of you to drop in, but I have to fly," she said. And then she did, turning into a sparrow and flying out through the open window.

He ran over to the window to look for her, but instead, saw his grandmother lying on the ground, his father bent over her. "What happened to her, Toby? I thought you would take care of her," he said accusingly.

The phone on the office desk was ringing and Toby answered it.

"Toby, where are you? What happened to you? Why have we drifted apart?" It was his mother's voice. He didn't know what to say to her, but then another phone started to ring. He looked on the desk; there were three phones, all ringing. As he tried to decide which one to pick up, he awoke.

It was still dark and the phone really was ringing. He looked at the time—6:50 am, and jumped out of bed.

"Toby, are you okay?" It was his dad. "I tried phoning last night but couldn't get through. I heard that the storm hit there really badly."

Toby told him what had happened to Grams and then about the power.

G.G. Neilson

"I better go back up there. I'll let them know I can't come in to work today."

"It's okay Dad—the power's back on and I'm taking care of Grams. The nurse told me what to do. I don't think Grams has a serious concussion."

"Well, let me speak to her."

"I'll get her to call you back." Toby thought his grandmother should wake up gradually. He also felt guilty about not checking on her overnight. After hanging up, he knocked quietly on Grams' door.

"Come in, Toby." Her voice sounded stronger. "Was that your dad phoning?"

"Yes, but I didn't want to disturb your sleep. How are you feeling?"

"That was nice of you dear, but I'm fine. I have a bit of a headache. I'd like to talk to your Dad though." He plugged his own phone into its charger, punched in the number and handed it to her.

He heard her talk his father out of returning to Truewind. "He told me there was a lot of damage at the golf course, so it's really better if he stayed there to help out," said Grams after she hung up. Then she noticed him looking at the feather. "That was from Susu—from the day we first communicated. She's been gone four years now, but I think about her every day. Do you have a feather of Beogall's?" Toby nodded. "I thought so."

He made his grandmother some hot oatmeal, glad that he had looked up the recipe on the net. Then they sat looking out at the remnants of the storm over a cup of chamomile tea he had prepared and talked over the events of the previous day. Toby went outside to check for damage. Birds were flitting about in an agitated state. Some had lost nests in the storm.

"There are quite a few branches down, Grams," he reported back. "Two old alders came down—one barely missed landing on the shed. But no major damage."

His grandmother patted his hand, relieved.

For the rest of the day Toby waited on her. She commented on how much he had learned about getting around a kitchen, but in truth, he was learning as he went. He had never thought of Grams as old before, but now she did seem, well, a little elderly and he found himself wondering about how that was for her. Did she have aches and pains? He recalled her mentioning arthritis in her fingers one time, and realized he should pay her more attention. She had never been a complainer, so it was guesswork to figure out how she was doing.

In his worries about his grandmother, Toby had completely forgotten about his own injuries and was gratified later on to see very little evidence of them when he stopped to look in the mirror.

He was outside cleaning up broken branches when the same song sparrow flew up and asked about Grams. "The birds have been worried about her. Especially Grandmother Eagle."

"Tell Grandmother Eagle and the others that she is fine. I'm taking care of her," Toby proudly assured the bird. Rio, her name was, flew away with the news.

That evening, his grandmother was feeling much better. "I think I'm up for a trip to town tomorrow," she told him. "We need some supplies."

After a game of cribbage, they decided to turn in early.

The next morning was cloudy with only a light breeze as they made their way to the town of Fairwind, this time his grandmother driving. She couldn't recall much about their trip from Westwind, but did remember that Grandmother Eagle had asked Toby to return in a few days.

"But don't think you're going to drive out there," she clucked. "That was a risky thing to do, Toby. And you are not insured."

"But I had to, Grams. I needed to get you home."

She patted his arm. "I guess it's just as well that your dad gave you a few driving lessons. Sometimes people just have to take risks. Think of the risks birds take all the time when they migrate."

Grams gave Toby some money in case he saw something he needed for school, while she picked up groceries. Small as it was, Fairwind had a London Drugs, which Toby went to check out. Heading down the stationery aisle, he stopped short. There at the end of the aisle, looking at birthday cards, was Alyssa. He was about to turn tail, when he decided that it would be better to just face her and get it over with. His stomach was doing somersaults as he approached. It didn't help that she was taller than him.

"Hi Alyssa. What brings you to Truewind Island?" He tried to sound casual.

She whirled around and stared. "How do you know my name?" she demanded in the voice like golden honey that had first attracted Toby's attention. Up close, she was just as beautiful as he imagined, with deep dark eyes and rosy lips.

"I'm getting to know lots of people at Cypress Gardens. I only just moved in, but I've made friends."

"And is one of your friends Chester, by any chance?" The lovely voice now had more than a hint of sarcasm.

"As a matter of fact, yes. Why do you ask?"

"He's a lurker just like you. He also lives below you, as I'm sure you know. But I have to admit that he or his mom or something have good taste in décor. Well, you better tell me your name so I can report you to the cops if I have to."

"Well, Alyssa, my name is Toby Myers and it seems you've been lurking too if you know all about the décor in Chester's apartment."

"It's pretty hard not to know, if you live in an apartment right opposite."

"Well then, I rest my case. It's been nice talking to you, Alyssa, but I've got to meet someone."

"Wait a minute," she said and he stopped. "Are you related to Carol Myers?"

"As it happens, she's my grandmother. I've been coming to Truewind for years. How about you?"

"I'm visiting my Aunt Fern and my cousins. I think they live pretty close to your grandmother."

Just then Grams spotted them, "Well, here you are, Toby. I see you've met Alyssa. My dear, would you like to join us for scones and a smoothie at Claude's Café?"

"Thanks for the offer, Mrs. Myers, but I have to go catch up to my aunt and cousins. Oh, here's Holly now." A dark-haired beauty came rushing up and Alyssa grudgingly introduced her cousin to Toby. Holly's dark, almond-shaped eyes opened wide as she took him in. She glanced meaningfully at Alyssa, who fidgeted uncomfortably.

"Mom's just going through the check-out now, Alyssa. We're to join her there," said Holly after acknowledging Mrs. Myers.

As Grams had a purchase (headache pills and vitamins, Toby noticed), they also had to wait in line.

Speaking to an attractive, dark-haired woman, Grams said, "Fern, did you ever meet Toby, Lars' son?"

"My, my, Toby," the woman replied, her dark eyes twinkling. "I last saw you when you were little, but here you are, all grown up. And I see you've met Holly and my niece, Alyssa." Fern introduced him to her three other daughters. Gemmie the toddler, and Judy and Jeanie, twins of about eleven or twelve, Toby figured. They gawked at him, whispered to each other and giggled.

"Girls," said Fern sternly, before she turned to Carol Myers, "Wasn't that a storm the other day?"

Grams told her about the car door incident and Fern gasped. "I thought you looked a little pale. How are you doing now?"

Much to Toby's embarrassment, Grams told her about his heroic efforts while the girls inspected him as if he were a strange new life form. With an inward groan, he realized that anyone Grams knew would have heard of him. But he knew she would never have told about the trouble at the mansion. Only his voice could be heard on the video clip, which had been played surprisingly often, quietly describing the destruction.

"Hey Toby, why don't you come over to visit us tomorrow?" invited Holly, interrupting his thoughts.

"Yes, why don't you?" Fern urged. "It's close by your grandmother's place—a nice walk—especially in good weather."

Toby looked at Grams who nodded, so he readily agreed.

At Claude's Café, Grams introduced him to half the people there. On the way home, she told him about the people he had met, what they did and which ones belonged to the same groups as her. Toby wondered what it would be like to be part of such a small community, where everyone knew all about you.

"Are you still with the Ranting Grannies?" he inquired. It was one of the more bizarre of Grams' groups—elderly women who attended rallies, wearing funny hats and singing songs of protest about this or that cause. Toby was incredibly embarrassed when he was dragged along to an event once, but also a little proud of his grandmother. His father called her "a force to be reckoned with."

"Some of our group are in poor health but we still get together from time to time. Things have been quiet lately, but recently someone was elected who's been promoting some large developments here on the island. So I may just have to dust off my old flowered hat."

After supper, Grams retired early. Toby restlessly checked his mail and the Internet news. Like a magnet, he was pulled outside and stared up at the clear night sky. Here, away from the bright lights of the city, he marveled at the millions (or was it billions or trillions maybe?) of stars. A verse from Aunt Heather's poem, *The Runner*, popped into his mind.

> *Heartbeat pervades and swells*
> *up the hill's ascent.*
> *Earth's darkening side*
> *now turns into a window*
> *onto the universe of stars.*

It made him wonder about life on earth and if there was life out there in the far-flung universe. A faint breeze wafted over his bare arms and it was almost as if it spoke to him— *use your gift*. What was he meant to do with it? Weird, he thought.

Then he got to thinking about spending the next day with Alyssa and Holly and found himself assailed with a case of the butterflies. Just before he turned in for the night, an owl swooped silently overhead, a black form blotting out the stars for an instant. On its busy night-time hunt, it was too preoccupied to do more than acknowledge Toby.

But then again, barred owls aren't very talkative.

Chapter 9
The Stronghold

The next day proved to be as clear as the previous night promised and Grams sent Toby off with a bag of home-baking "for all those girls". His hopeful anticipation propelled him quickly along Berry Farm road to the Strong's place.

They lived in a rambling old farmhouse that Grams said had been in the family for three generations. It had been added onto haphazardly and was badly in need of a paint job. A sprawling, fenced garden, complete with gangly scarecrow, nestled up to a meadow where an old horse grazed. A stream gurgled beside the road and turned, babbling down one side of the Strong's meadow, which Toby now crossed to get to the porch.

"Toby's here!" he heard Holly yell to the others as she peered through the side door. Then she turned back to call to him, "Welcome to the Stronghold! Come through this way. We're just finishing the dishes."

He followed her through the family room where a dog greeted him excitedly. "Come here, Taz!" Holly commanded the exuberant hound, which had launched himself onto Toby's chest, licking furiously at his face and hands. She led the dog away, tail still wagging hopefully.

Toby noticed some striking native art on the walls. One was a print with strong black, red and white design features, a raven as the focal point. Then his eye was drawn to an intricately carved mask of an eagle. Toby thought that his mother would like this art, especially a stone carving of a bear, which occupied its own specially built shelf.

Fern Strong noticed him admiring the art. "I come from a family of artists," she remarked. "Although that bear was given to me as a gift many years ago."

She invited him into a large sunny kitchen that overlooked a deck and a large vegetable garden. As she thanked him for the baked goodies, Toby realized that he was the only male surrounded by females of all ages. Besides Fern Strong, there were her four daughters, Alyssa, and an old woman seated at the table. Mrs. Strong seemed to read his thoughts as she said, "You're probably not used to being surrounded by so many females." If only she knew, he thought. "My husband Jack complains about it all the time, but he gets away from us every weekday since he commutes into Vancouver."

She introduced her mother, Granny Renie. She was older than Grams, maybe a lot older, but there wasn't much grey in the black hair pulled back into a tight braid hanging down her back. Piercing ebony eyes studied him closely.

"So you're Toby," she said as he sat down. Her old hand reached out and touched the cheek on the side that had been injured. He resisted the urge to flinch and discovered her hand was surprisingly soft. "Ah," was all she said.

As they talked about their plans for the day, little Gemmie crawled onto his lap and asked about the "boo-boo" on his face. There was a faint bruise near his eye and his nose was still slightly discoloured from the injury.

"Just an accident, Gemmie," he said as she reached up her chubby hand.

"Granny Renie make better," she told him somberly.

After tea, Alyssa and Holly invited him on a hike up the small mountain nearby. Toby had a vague recollection of going there once with his dad. As they scrambled along the path, he discovered that Alyssa and Holly were a wealth of information about plant life. Toby recognized huckleberry and salal, a rich source of berries for the birds. But he didn't know near as many plants and mushrooms as they did.

"There's Oregon grape and here's a nice patch of bleeding heart," said Holly.

"Wait, isn't that devil's club?" asked Alyssa and the two ventured into the underbrush, very excited. They soon emerged with scraped arms, carrying leaves and berries of an ugly-looking plant.

"Granny will be happy about this," said Alyssa, beaming. "She was, like, teaching us about devil's club yesterday."

"She knows all the plants and their healing properties," Holly confided. "She is known as a great healer by the Oyster Narrows people—my mother's people."

"Does she live with you?" asked Toby.

"No. She has a home on the reserve, but she likes to visit the Stronghold. We're always happy when she stays for a few days, like now," Holly replied.

It was Toby's turn to surprise them with his knowledge of birds. A couple of times they looked at him strangely as he listened intently, trying not to let on that he understood them.

At the summit of the Thumb, as the locals called it, were stunning vistas of almost 360 degrees around. They sat atop a giant rock, perfect for picnics. They could see deep green forests punctuated by lighter green deciduous trees, adorned in their spring finery. Far below, was a patchwork quilt of fields stitched together by roads and streams. Toby breathed in deeply—the air had a warm orangey tang.

Alyssa pointed to the Stronghold and the Myers' place to the south, looking like doll houses. Far to the east lay the town of Fairwind and even further away they could just make out the ferry terminal. A ferry was pulling away from the dock. "That'll be the 12:30," Holly observed.

Over lunch Toby asked what they knew about Westwind.

"Why, that's the land the islanders want kept as a nature preserve and a bird sanctuary," said Holly. "It's beyond the little mountains." In the direction she pointed, Toby could see dense forest covering small, rounded mountains. "My mother's people want it to be kept in its natural state."

"Are there other plans then?" asked Toby, remembering how anxious the birds were.

"Well," Holly's voice lowered conspiratorially, "I heard my parents talking about some businessman who wants to buy it up for a posh housing development. We won't let that happen though."

Toby was thinking that he used to live in a posh area himself, and that most of those places were well treed. But then, you had to trust the people who lived there to keep the area habitable for wildlife. That was a lesson he had learned the hard way.

As the two girls munched cheese and sprout sandwiches, Toby discovered that they were both vegetarians. He asked Holly about going to school on Truewind and she complained about how small it was. He told them about St. Zallo's and his favourite teachers there and then asked Alyssa about Willow Heights.

"It's okay, I guess," she replied warily. "Do you have your schedule yet?"

"Yeah. It looks pretty good. I've been put in something called the Odd S rotation."

"Oh!" she exclaimed. "Well, it's a good group. I'm in it too." There was a long pause. "There are some unusual things about it. Our school's probably a lot different than St. Zallo's."

She didn't say any more and he didn't ask. Holly mentioned plans to go to the beach the next day. "Why don't you come, Toby? It won't be warm enough to swim, but there will probably be some other island kids there. We could all hang out."

G.G. Neilson

"I would really like to go, but... well, I have to do something with Grams," he said, remembering his promise to Grandmother Eagle. And the day after that his father would be coming to get him, and after that—school. "I can't this visit, but I wanna return to Truewind soon. Maybe I could go to the beach with you then."

"Sure, that'll be good." Holly sounded disappointed. But was Alyssa?

On the way back they ran recklessly down the steep slope of the Thumb. At the bottom the girls laughed and panted, hanging on to each other. Toby looked on awkwardly.

The rest of the way home, Toby listened to their chatter about the island kids and what they were up to. Alyssa seemed to know a lot of them. He imagined living here full time—there was a golf course on Truewind and he toyed with the idea of his father getting a job... But he was starting to get used to living at Cypress Gardens. His dream was to play tennis professionally and now that they couldn't afford tennis lessons anymore, he had to rely on competitive partners at the courts there.

Back at the Stronghold, Granny Renie was sitting out on the deck. She didn't hear them come up, and Toby distinctly heard her say to a Steller's jay, "Well, we'll just have to wait and see."

"Talking to the birds again, Granny?" Holly asked, with a wink.

"Here's that boy," said the jay, tilting her head toward Toby with a cocky stare. "Grandmother Eagle is expecting you tomorrow." And with that she flew off.

"Jays are a little abrupt, but easy to understand," said Granny Renie. "Holly, you just have to be more patient."

"Granny, you know I prefer plants. Alyssa, did you understand what that jay said? You're better at it than me."

Toby's jaw dropped as Alyssa admitted, "I understood a little. Jay talk is easier than most birds."

"How about you, Toby? Can you communicate with birds?" asked Holly. Toby stifled a splutter.

"Sure he can," interrupted Granny Renie. "I knew as soon as I saw him. He has a rare gift."

Was Alyssa looking at him with new respect?

"It's okay, Toby, your secret is safe with us," said Holly. "I thought you were listening in on the birds on our walk. In my family, we're mostly into plants, not that they communicate like birds, mind you. Granny is hoping the other girls will be able to communicate with, well anything—but they're still too young. We know it's not common…"

Granny Renie stopped her. "You have to seek out others who can also understand," she said. "Now run along, Holly and Alyssa—Fern needs you." They left reluctantly.

"Toby," she began seriously after they had gone, "I've known your grandmother all her life—I remember when she was born. I knew she would have the gift, just like I knew your dad wouldn't. It broke her heart when Lars and you stopped coming to visit. A big shot, your dad was.

"But now he's doing what he should be doing. Sometimes it just takes people a while. Use your gift for good, boy. Don't waste it." Her voice was wavery but clear. "And be sure to do right by the birds—they seem to have high hopes for you. Do you have your feather?"

Toby pulled out the feather that he always kept close, hidden under his shirt. She reached out a gnarled old finger and touched it. "Ahh," she murmured. The feather almost seemed to glow. "There's trouble ahead, Toby, but there are people who can help. You heard what the jay said, you need to go back to Westwind tomorrow."

She leaned back and closed her eyes. Toby knew the conversation was over.

He was deep in thought as he walked home from the Stronghold. That evening reminded Grams that he had to return to Westwind the next day.

"I know you do," she declared, then added, "and I feel perfectly well enough to take you there, Toby. I spoke to your Dad today and he's planning to come over the day after that to fetch you."

"So soon! I wish I could stay longer."

"I'm so glad you feel that way, dear! Come up any time you want—I'd love to see you more often." Were those tears glistening in his grandmother's eyes?

There was no better place to spend spring break he realized later that night, lying in bed in the room he had slept in as a small child, his aunt's room.

Chapter 10

Chosen

Toby was up before Grams the next day, surprising, since she was an early riser. He went for a walk around the property, marveling at the work she and Gramps had put into the place, wondering how long Grams could keep it up. She had hinted to him that he could be a real help with yard work and tending the garden if he came to visit in the summer. Toby liked the idea, especially when he discovered that there was a well-used tennis court in the town of Fairwind. And he thought eagerly of visits to the Stronghold.

When he got back to the house, Grams was up and had made blueberry pancakes. "From last year's crop," she told him. "And the honey is from a local beekeeper." After breakfast, she packed a lunch and a thermos of tea and they headed out once more to Westwind.

This time, they heard birds chirping all around as they approached Grandmother Eagle's tree. But she wasn't there. Instead, a very old man, with long grey hair flowing down his back, waited for them, seated under the tree.

"Greetings, Carol Forest," he said formally, using her maiden name. He got up slowly from his sitting position.

"Greetings, George Rocky Ground," replied Grams. "It has been a long time. I hope you are keeping well."

"Yes, too long. I see the years are treating you well. And here is the grandson I have been hearing about," he said, turning dark, penetrating eyes on Toby. He was surprisingly upright for such an old man and stood a couple of inches taller than Toby.

"Are you the person Grandmother Eagle wanted me to meet?" asked Toby.

"Maybe, but there's also another – old Windrunner."

"I'm pleased to meet you, Grandfather Rocky Ground," said Toby, wanting to show respect. "Who is Windrunner, and where's Grandmother Eagle?" Toby knew he was being impatient, and that all would be revealed "in the fullness of time" as the old ones liked to say.

By way of reply, the old man chuckled and pointed up. Arcing toward them in slow circles was the eagle. She came at last to alight on a branch of the same fir tree with a few flaps of her enormous wings.

"It does a body good to get out and about early, and I saw you were out early this morning too, Toby," said the eagle. "Before I take you to see old Windrunner, I wanted you to meet George Rocky Ground. He was chosen by Windrunner's father."

The man bowed his head.

"Chosen? What does that mean?"

"I didn't tell you about it, Toby," said Grams, "because I thought that it would be better coming from elder Martin. Besides, I still feel the grief of my own loss…"

"Beogall has chosen you, Toby," Grandmother Eagle began. "He would like you to be his bird-human bond. He thought it over and discussed it with his elders. But the final choice is the bird's alone."

"Beogall can be hot-headed sometimes," George Martin took up the thread. "We heard about that incident of his, how should I put it—lack of control, the day you moved out of that mansion. However he was not impulsive in his choice of you."

"When a bird chooses a human to communicate with for the first time, a special bond develops, that is, if the human is able to respond," said the old eagle. "If you formalize the bond, it will last as long as you both live. And it can never be made again with another bird."

At these words, Toby noticed that Grams had tears in her eyes.

"Your grandmother's bird bond never returned from migration a few years back and we learned that she had been shot by a duck hunter on her flight north," said George somberly. "The human will always have a special connection with the first bird he or she communicates with. But the bond ceremony carries a deeper connection—and a deeper responsibility."

"Do you wish to proceed in a bond ceremony with Beogall?" asked Grandmother Eagle.

"Yes!" Toby quickly blurted out.

The others nodded and George said, "Toby, there is a special way you can call your bird partner. If the bird is anywhere in the area, he will do everything possible to come. But no-one should use the call unless the situation is serious."

"Please teach me the call," begged Toby.

"First, you will meet Windrunner," said the eagle.

"I like to come up here from time to time to visit him," said George Martin as he led them to the other side of the glade. "He doesn't leave here much any more. Windrunner is ancient in gull terms, and he has asked for you Toby. A great honour."

They stopped at an arbutus grove at the far edge of the clearing. Toby could see that just beyond the trees, the land gave way to a sloping cliff ending on a rocky beach and beyond that, the ocean. The island was narrow enough here to afford a view of the water on three sides. The oldest and largest arbutus tree Toby had ever seen clung to the edge of the slope. One giant branch leaned over the cliff. Underneath the tree, on a large boulder, sat a grizzled gull.

"So you've come," croaked Windrunner. "You're the one that young Beogall chose. I hope you know what that means, boy."

"Not really, your honour," said Toby, not knowing what else to say.

The old gull cackled, "Just call me Grandfather Gull— everyone else does. I'm not much of a windrunner anymore but my heir carries on. Living for a long time doesn't give you honour—it's your actions that do that, boy. But I have been around long enough to know the old stories. Sometimes the young ones don't want to hear them, but it's important to tell them."

Then in a rasping voice, Grandfather Gull told him the story of how gulls learned to communicate with people. His great-grandfather, the first Windrunner, had been lost at sea, run off course by a storm he could not out-fly, in spite of his amazing flying abilities. He was at death's door when he fell into the raging waters and was spotted by a sailor on a small fishing boat also caught in the storm. The man, Dewitt by name, risked his own life as he leaned over the rails with a long-poled fishing net. He was able to snag Windrunner on the first try, just as the boat lurched away from the high wave that the gull was foundering on. Toby listened, hardly daring to breathe.

The other sailors derided Dewitt for his efforts to resuscitate the bird, but his persistence paid off. Great-grandfather Windrunner, in addition to his superb flying abilities, could understand humans. He came from a family of gulls who were developing the skill, but he himself was the most adept.

"A lot of crows could too, but chose not to," interjected Grandmother Eagle disdainfully. "Parrots and other tropical birds have long been able to, as you well know. *(Actually,*

Toby didn't know.) But most of us learned from the Windrunner line of gulls."

The ancestor gull was able to teach the sailor how to communicate with him, and they developed the first known human-bird bond. Both Windrunner and Dewitt would spend long periods away from each other, but they re-connected from time to time using a special call. This call was taught by certain people, one of whom was George Rocky Ground.

"So you see how important it is to remember the old stories, Toby?" croaked the old bird.

Toby nodded slowly. "Can you teach me the call?"

"Why do you think you're here, boy? A social visit?" chuckled George Martin. He put Toby through a series of breathing exercises and then demonstrated the call. It had an unsettling effect on all the birds at Westwind and they twittered nervously in the trees, some flapping up into the air. But it agitated Windrunner most of all.

"You should never do it unless there is real need," George said seriously. "Your bird partner will be willing to put himself at great risk to get to you if you make that call. My bird-bond, Windrunner's father, is now gone and it is my duty to pass along the call. Did you bring the feather?" Toby took it out and the old man reached for it reverently.

He showed Toby how it must be held, "Now you try the call."

Toby tried and waited. Nothing happened. The birds all seemed indifferent to his attempt. The elder put his hand on Toby's shoulder and told him to close his eyes, "Think of the first time you touched the feather—the tingling you felt."

The image of when he met Beogall combined with other images. He could see George Rocky Ground with a young gull and was that Grams and Susu? Toby shivered and a tingling wave began and grew from the bottom to the top of his spine. He took a deep breath and made the call again.

This time it felt right. Birds chirped fretfully from the trees.

Grams sighed and George nodded and spoke. "Now we wait."

And they did.

In the distance, flapping slowly toward them, a large heron approached. An exhausted Beogall finally landed with a plop on a rock nearby.

"You did it," he gasped. "I was waiting on Deadman Island for your signal. It was very clear."

Toby wore a wide grin. He touched the bird's head gently. "Does this mean that we're partners?" The great blue heron nodded and pressed his beak against Toby's cheek.

"I'm so proud of you, Toby," Grams was beaming. "I feel as happy as I did when Susu and I became partners."

"So Beogall, what is Toby's name in bird language to be?" George asked.

Toby waited impatiently, for the heron took a long time to reply. "Your bird-bond name is Beorand," he finally said. The others nodded slowly and repeated the name softly.

Grandfather Gull seemed especially moved. "Very apt," he said in a voice that sounded like beach gravel. "The name in heron is similar to the name in gull language and it means 'one who hears'. You all know that Beogall means 'one who seeks'."

"Now hear me." The attempt to raise his voice caused the gull to splutter. Finally he said, "You are witnesses to this sacred bird-human bond. You are entrusted with this boy's name in bird tongue, but it is not to be used except on special occasions. And never with people who cannot communicate with birds."

"Give me the feather, Toby," said George and as Toby handed it to him, the elder leaned over and plucked out a strand of Toby's hair. He wrapped the hair around the feather and voiced a solemn blessing.

"The ancient language of the Oyster Narrows people," Grams whispered quietly.

After the blessing, his new name was used by everyone in unison. As they said "Beorand" then "Beogall", the hair-wrapped feather was touched to both Toby's and Beogall's brows. It gave Toby a jolt.

"This feather is entrusted to you, Toby. We don't really understand it, but birds who are part of a bird-human bond outlive other birds, sometimes by many years," George continued. "The bond is for life and you must always strive to support the other."

"I promise," said Toby and Beogall said something to him, in what he later found out was the ancient language.

It felt strange to chat and visit after the seriousness of the ceremony. The afternoon was sunny, if a little windy, and as they watched sailboats and flotillas of marine birds on the ocean, stories were shared. But the afternoon wasn't all pleasant. There was some chittering about unsettling rumours—of plans afoot for Westwind.

"What can be done?" asked old Windrunner plaintively.

"We must look into it," Grandmother Eagle answered.

"Carol Forest, can you find out if this threat is real?" Elder Martin suggested.

"Why, yes…"

"I can help too," said Toby.

Grams looked at him proudly. "I'm sure you can," she said. "We'll put the word out on the bird-human network. But it's getting late and we must be going. Beogall, why don't you come back to our place? The fields are comfortable and you are welcome to stay overnight," she encouraged. "You could meet Toby's father who will be coming up tomorrow."

"Yes, would you come?" Toby asked, his eyes shining.

"Of course," the young heron agreed and added, "Beorand."

"Farewell then, Carol Forest, Toby-Beorand and Beogall," said George as they made their goodbyes. "I'm staying on here for a while. Windrunner and I seldom have a chance to visit."

The next morning when Toby raced out of the cabin, he felt his heart would burst on seeing the great blue heron circling overhead.

"I've had my breakfast," Beogall said, landing near him.

Toby was too polite to tell him that his breath smelled like fish and offered him a bite of Grams' homemade muffin, which he reluctantly tried. Then he had a second piece.

"Grams has asked me to help out with some yard work," said Toby after a bit. "I should get to it before my dad arrives. He'll be here soon."

"I'll come back then, Beorand."

Lars didn't arrive on the 10:30 ferry as planned. He phoned to let them know he would be on the next one for sure. Grams held lunch and was pacing back and forth until he arrived. "You seem in good spirits," she said, greeting him with a hug.

"So do you."

"It's been lovely to have Toby here!" she exclaimed.

Over lunch they told him about visiting the birds at Westwind Sanctuary, leaving out the bird bond ceremony.

Lars frowned and said, "I don't put much stock in all that communicating with birds stuff."

"But Lars, you know that I can. And so can Toby."

"Dad, you remember the great blue heron from the mansion? Well he came to visit. Would you like to meet him?" asked Toby.

"Uh, okay."

When Beogall returned, Toby nervously introduced him to his father.

"Greetings," said Lars stiffly and Toby translated. "Ask him if he knows how things are at our old mansion."

Beogall reported through Toby that there was no more cutting of trees and the birds were cautiously carrying on. "Walter applied at other mansions in the area and I heard that he might get on at the Butter's."

Toby grinned, since he had been emailing Dalton about what a great gardener Walter was. He wasn't sure his dad believed the news as he had a bit of a scowl.

"Well, I must be getting back," said the heron abruptly and he flew off. Toby watched him flap away, feeling an immediate sense of loss.

They were repairing a fence, when to Toby's delight, Beogall returned. "Ferry traffic is building up. You should go early to whichever ferry you're catching," said the bird.

"Thanks for letting us know. When will I see you again?"

"Maybe I'll come visit you at Willow Heights. Isn't that where you'll be going to school?" As he flew away, Toby's mouth dropped in amazement. He hadn't seen much sign of bird life around the school.

Grams convinced them to stay for supper, so he and his dad spent the afternoon cutting up the two alders that had come down in the storm. Later, they walked around the grounds.

"It's as beautiful as the mansion grounds here," said Toby. "I'd like to come back soon."

"Sure, good," said his dad. "Look Toby, I've never understood this trick of talking to birds. I know your grandmother says she can and now apparently, you can too. But she wasn't talking to birds when I was growing up."

"It's not a trick, Dad. We really can."

"When I listen to you, I don't hear much of anything. Well, maybe it sounds like birdsongs."

"I think what happens is that, like, birds have these complicated registers that they communicate in. And each tone a person can hear is actually broken up into all different

G.G. Neilson

bits," Toby tried to explain. "To me, it's almost like listening to music."

"How can you possibly understand all the different birds?"

"I can't. I'm just starting and some are clearer than others." Toby was glad they hadn't told him anything about the bonding ceremony. His dad was looking more and more troubled and besides, wasn't even allowed to know his bird language name. It's so complicated, he thought.

Grams wanted them to stay over another night but Lars declared that no, that Toby had to get ready for school. "Don't worry Mom, we'll be back anon if not sooner."

That got a laugh and his mother remarked, "Just like your dad always said."

"Besides," said Lars, "the ferry traffic will be impossible tomorrow since it's the last day of spring break."

Toby and his grandmother shared a long hug and her throat had a catch in it as she whispered, "You've made your old Grams very happy."

They arrived early and the ferry was indeed packed. They managed to find an empty table in the cafeteria. Toby with a mug of hot chocolate and Lars with his coffee, each took a section of the local newspaper to read. But Toby couldn't concentrate. When he looked up, he suppressed a strangled gasp. He quietly got his father's attention and pointed. Several tables over, sat Suchno Whenge and Duffin Wint.

Dismayed, they hid behind their newspapers, craning to hear the conversation.

Even with his excellent hearing—there was a lot of background noise and Whenge and Duffin were speaking in low voices—all Toby could make out were certain words.

"I'm sure I heard the words 'money', 'development', and 'idiot'," he told his father later. They had stealthily left and returned early to the car deck, long before the docking announcement. "I think I might have even heard the word

'Westwind'. Do you know if they've been to Truewind Island before, Dad?"

"Not that I've heard of, but Whenge has dealings all over the country. He loves his mega-housing developments and often uses his name on them. There's a real monstrosity called Whengewood in Wattasaga. I sure hope he doesn't have those kinds of plans for Truewind. Maybe it was just a holiday," he added without conviction. "I'll tell your grandmother to keep her ears open."

"It isn't fair," Toby complained. "I had such a great time on Truewind Island, and now I find out that Whenge and Duffin were there too. What a downer."

He was deep in thought as they drove off the ferry.

Chapter 11
Unsettling Developments

It was late by the time they arrived at the condo. Because it was Saturday, Toby still had another day before he had to start at his new school. He wanted to contact his friends, Dalton, Thompson and, of course, Chester.

As they entered the condo, Toby sensed a difference. Then he spotted a pink hair elastic on the counter dividing the kitchen from the dining room. It had several strands of reddish hairs clinging to it. Lars saw him staring.

"Dad, did you have someone over while I was away?" Toby tried to keep the anger out of his voice.

"Er, yes. Um, Ms. Feathers, Anna, came for supper. Toby, I'm an adult—I can have another adult over sometimes," said Lars defensively.

"What about Mom?" Toby's voice rose. "Have you made any attempt to contact her?"

"I speak regularly to your mother, but there's no chance of reconciliation." His father paused. "Toby, it's probably time to tell you that when your mother moved out, she moved in with another man. A very wealthy man as it turns out. I didn't think it would last, but I guess it has. She won't be coming back and certainly not now that we're in reduced circumstances."

"You just never tried!" Toby fought to keep calm, but how could he? "Just like you don't try to understand birds. All you cared about was work!" He couldn't stifle his growing anger.

His father said very calmly, "It's time for me to move on and it turns out that Anna Feathers and I have a lot in common. She seems to like you." Toby frowned and Lars quickly added, "I know that your mother loves you. She'll stay in touch." He tousled Toby's hair and said jokingly, "Hey, we're doing pretty well here, aren't we?"

Toby wrenched away and disappeared into his room. He saw the truth of his father's words, but still—a woman here while he was gone! He wanted to ask if she had stayed overnight, but was afraid to hear the answer. He heard his father speaking on the phone and had a feeling it was to Anna Feathers.

He texted his friends, then lay on the bed, listening to music. Much later, he was startled by a knock at their door. It was his mother. As she stepped into their living room, Anna Feathers was just emerging from his father's bedroom. His mother screeched at her and Anna turned into a sparrow and flew out their open door to the balcony and then into the courtyard.

"Now look what you've done!" yelled his father. "It isn't enough that you had to leave us, but you've destroyed any chance I have of happiness."

"I'm sorry Lars, but you cared more for work than for me," said his mother. Then she reached into her fur coat and drew out two blue robin's eggs, which she handed to Toby. "These are for you. I know how much you love birds."

As Toby took the eggs from her, they turned into robins and also flew out into the courtyard. They all leaned over the balcony to watch the birds and there in the courtyard was a darkened limousine. Suchno Whenge got out and leered up at them. Duffin Wint got out the other side of the car. He had a gun and pointed it up at the robins. The sparrow suddenly flew in between the robins.

"Stop!" Toby and Lars screamed at the same time.

G.G. Neilson

Toby woke up with a siren screaming and his heart racing. He wondered if he had called out in his dream. After the ambulance—or was it a fire truck?—had ebbed away into the night, a sense of stillness reigned. Toby listened for the reassuring *whoosh* of the skytrain, but it didn't come. He looked at the time—1:50 am. Wasn't it still running? Finally he heard it, and realized that fewer trains ran late at night as he dropped off to sleep.

The next morning, Toby lay in bed late—it was his last chance to sleep in before school the next day. Plus he didn't feel like facing his dad. Lars tapped on his door and said he was leaving for work. Then he asked somewhat hesitantly through the closed door, "How would you feel about Anna, er… Ms. Feathers, coming to dinner tonight?"

"You're the adult. Do what you want," Toby muttered. He heard his father sigh and then heard him leave, locking the door behind him.

After checking his phone, Toby had a leisurely breakfast. He got dressed and crept down one floor to knock quietly on apt. 405. If there was no answer, he would leave. The painting looked a little different to him as he waited. Part of it now reminded him of Westwind.

Just as he was turning to go, the door flung open and there stood Chester's mom. "Come in Toby. We thought you had come back last night."

Toby looked around their condo in amazement. Although it was the exact same layout as theirs, the Oldwin's apartment was filled with plants of every type. It was a veritable jungle of plants, crawling up the walls from pots on the floor and sitting on every available surface.

"They clean the air," Chester's mom said when she saw him looking. The walls were adorned with pictures of plants, and on some surfaces, intricate, woodsy scenes were painted. It struck Toby that his own condo was like a desert by comparison.

"Hey man, welcome to 405," said Chester, shrugging into a hoodie as he emerged from his room. He went to the kitchen and poured himself some juice and then sat down to a bowl of cereal, offering some to Toby, who declined. "How was Truewind?"

"It was just great. I... I met some new people."

Chester looked up at him. "Hey, you look good—I can't even see any signs of your injury."

"Yeah, I feel good. Almost ready for school tomorrow. How was your break?"

"It was okay. I hear your friend Alyssa was at Truewind too. Did you see her?"

Toby admitted that he had and Chester gave him a wide grin.

"You'd like Holly," he said after he gave a brief outline of the day spent with Holly and Alyssa. Then he took a deep breath. "My dad had a woman over when I was away. Do you know if she stayed overnight?"

Chester and his mom gave each other a startled look.

"Toby, good neighbours don't interfere in other neighbour's lives," Marion Oldwin said gently. "Well, unless it's a matter of safety. It must be hard to think about sharing his time."

"You got that right. He's always been so busy with work. And now, with this new job, it seems like, like, he's met someone," said Toby in a rush. "Just when we were finally starting to spend time together."

Marion Oldwin nodded sympathetically.

Toby continued pensively, "I've met Ms. Feathers and she's nice, but my mom hasn't been gone that long. Maybe she'll come back."

"Do you think that's going to happen, Toby?" Marion asked quietly.

"No..., no." There was a catch in his throat. "I don't think they'll ever get back together. But I guess I keep hoping."

"Ms. Feathers. What an interesting name," said Chester's mom after a while. "What's she like?"

"Anna Feathers—she runs the office at the golf course where my dad works. I've only met her a couple of times. The first time we met, she told me to watch out for a pileated woodpecker at the 8th hole—and I did see her."

"Her?" Chester remarked. "Yeah, I guess male and female birds look different."

"Have you spoken with her?" asked Marion. "I mean the woodpecker."

Toby stared at her and then at Chester. "Sorry man, I told her, but my mom's cool. She understands these things. I had to tell someone and I trust my mom more than pretty much anyone else. Except for my dad."

"No, I haven't really spoken to her—she was busy at the time, but I'm pretty sure her name is Wonger. They don't really have much to say... I guess with all the bashing they put their heads through." They shared a laugh.

"What about at Truewind, Toby? I've heard there is a special place that birds congregate – Westwind it's called. Did you talk to any birds up there?" inquired Marion.

Sitting amid the plants in the Oldwin's apartment with it's unusual door, it didn't seem a strange question. Toby told them what had happened, except for the part about his bonding ceremony with Beogall. Then he told them of the birds' fears that the place would be sold for some sort of development. He finished by telling them about seeing Lord Whenge and Duffin on the ferry.

Marion Oldwin wore a worried frown. "Well, maybe it was just coincidence," she said unconvincingly.

Chester and Toby decided to head out and shoot a few hoops. They hadn't gotten very far when Chester nudged him. A darkened limousine nosed up the road leading into the condo complex. Both boys stood watching while it approached slowly. Toby made out the familiar outline of Duffin behind the wheel and knew that Whenge would be in the back. He resisted the urge to pick up a rock and chuck it. Plus he knew Chester would have stopped him. They watched as the car retreated down the street, speeding up as it left the complex.

"Looks like they found out where I live now. I sure hope they don't try to make trouble for you, Chester. Good thing I never gave out your name."

"That was ominous. Maybe they're trying to send you a message. Any chance they saw you on the ferry?"

"I'm pretty sure they didn't."

They discussed it a bit more as they made their way over to the basketball courts. A pick-up game was in progress and Toby was overjoyed to recognize Thompson Coyote. His friend from St. Zallo's saw him and came over while Chester took his spot on the court.

"Thompson! Hey. What brings you over to my new neighbourhood?"

"Hey Toby. I got your text that you had moved. This where you live? Awesome. I've been here for spring break—my auntie lives over here," he said pointing.

Toby discovered that Thompson knew a lot of kids at Cypress Gardens and that his aunt lived in the same building as Alyssa—in fact, their mothers were cousins. They joined the pick-up game, but soon Thompson had to get packed up and head back to St. Zallo's.

"I'm gonna miss you, Toby. I don't have too many friends at that school. I asked my auntie if I could move here and go to Willow Heights, but she says it's a great honour to get a scholarship to St. Zallo's."

"You know, Thompson, Dalton Butter is cool. He's not like some of the others. Hang out with him. Anyway, maybe we'll see you some weekends. Could you say hi to Mr. Getty for me?"

That evening, his father did invite Anna Feathers for supper. She asked Toby about his spring break. "Did you ever check out the pileated woodpecker at hole eight, Toby?" she asked after supper.

"Wonger? Yeah, I saw her."

"So you know her name?" asked Anna. His father gave her an indecipherable look.

Toby had answered the question automatically, but now something struck him. "I guess you do too. Can you communicate with birds, Ms. Feathers?"

"Call me Anna. I can a bit." She glanced at Lars who was holding his head in his hands. "But it's taken me a long time to learn and… and I can't at all with some species. You seem to have more of a gift. Wonger isn't very communicative and it took me ages to learn her name."

"Well, woodpeckers are a little dense—all that pounding."

She laughed, "I know. We have to leave up a certain number of snags for them at the golf course. I'm hopeful that she's got a nest somewhere."

"She does. It's over by the 9th hole, but really well hidden."

Toby wanted to talk to her more about birds, but his dad seemed upset. Instead he excused himself. "I have to some practicing to do," and disappeared into his room.

He missed his music. He hadn't played the flute since getting his face punched in, but decided to try it out now. Once he blew out the rust, he had a pretty good sound going.

He didn't even know Ms. Feathers had left when there was a quiet knock on his door.

"Anna enjoyed your playing, Toby," said Lars, poking his head in.

"She's okay, Dad. I guess I was getting used to it being just you and me—hanging out together. But I… I don't mind her coming over sometimes." He decided not to add how great it was she could communicate with birds too.

"I thought you two might get along. Anna's a really nice person and she likes you. Don't stay up too late. Big day tomorrow."

As he got ready for bed, Toby thought maybe he should tell his dad about seeing Whenge and Duffin in their neighbourhood, but didn't want to worry him. If it happened again though, he definitely would.

For now, he had his first day at the new school to think about.

Had he known what the next day would bring, Toby might not have had such a sound sleep that night.

Part 3 –
Willow Heights
Secondary

The only choice we don't have is whether to change the
world:
Every choice we make sends out ripples.
Frances Moore Lappé

Chapter 12

Day 8 - Even

The day dawned overcast with a threat of rain. Toby stretched at his window and wondered about Alyssa—would she be back from Truewind yet? He resisted the urge to look over at her apartment and instead, quickly got his school supplies ready.

His dad made him hot cereal and had packed him a bag lunch.

"You can see what kind of a cafeteria they have, then I can give you money for lunch if you like," he said.

"Well, they asked me if I was vegetarian back at that meeting, so wouldn't they have vegetarian options?" The meeting with Mr. McFru and Principal Standing now seemed like a lifetime ago.

He had arranged to walk to school with Chester who was going to show him where his classes were. On even days, like today, they had only one class together, Phys Ed, which was after lunch. Chester hurriedly showed him around and then to their lockers.

"See, we're neighbours," he announced. Sure enough, their lockers were near each other. "But today's classes aren't in this wing."

Toby tried his lock combination and stowed his stuff.

"Alyssa's is down here too," Chester added, "but word is that she didn't get back from Truewind yesterday. She's supposed to catch an early ferry this morning."

Toby nodded. He knew how busy the ferries could get on a holiday Sunday.

Since their classes were in opposite ends of the school, Chester gave him a few directions and they parted company. Toby was early for English, so he waited outside the door, watching the stream of students who were watching him back. A group of girls passed, checked him out, and he heard snatches of "the new boy" as they continued on down the hall.

Finally, an ancient man hobbled up and unlocked the door. Toby had never seen such an old teacher, but he was with it enough to know that Toby was new, and demanded his name.

"You're the one McFru told me about. Have a seat. We're starting *Romeo and Juliet* today."

Toby shuffled to the back and sat down. He watched the others file in. Included in the throng was JB, who saw him and grinned. Was that a good sign or bad?

Mr. Draper droned on about Shakespeare—what a brilliant playwright he was and why he's still studied today— then handed out copies of the play. They had to read the first act and answer questions which the teacher scrawled on the board in a spidery hand. He then sat down and promptly fell asleep. Toby couldn't make out his writing and whispered a question to the boy in the adjoining desk. Mr. Draper immediately opened his eyes and asked for silence. When the bell rang at last, Toby asked the same boy again about the questions.

"Yeah, you can't talk in his class. Interferes with his nap time." The boy grinned and introduced himself as Glen. He was also heading to Math next so they walked together. "Where you from anyway?"

"St. Zallo's," Toby replied a bit warily.

"I've heard of it. Hey, what's it like?"

Toby was happy to tell him about it and even happier that Glen seemed so interested.

By the time they reached Math class, Toby had become a minor celebrity. It seemed like they didn't get many mid-year students at this school.

Glen pulled him along to a spot near the back where he kicked someone out of his seat to offer it to Toby, and popped into the empty seat next to it himself. Toby was relieved to be at the back, especially in a weak subject. "Thanks," he said and looked around.

A boy seated near the front seemed to be getting the lion's share of attention from the girls. He was tall and well-built with curling, dark blond hair. Toby overheard one of the girls call him Seymour. Who else could it be other than the Seymour Gregory that Chester had told him was the one Alyssa liked?

The bell rang and in rushed Alyssa, grabbing the last available seat in the front, closest to Seymour. Toby watched as she flashed the popular boy a brilliant smile. Even though they had by now shared several hours together, he hadn't received a smile like that. And how about their connection to Truewind Island?

Such thoughts were going nowhere, so it was just as well that the teacher demanded silence and began a lesson on trigonometry. His accent was hard to understand and Toby had to ask Glen a couple of times what the teacher said.

Soon he got mired in sine, cosine and tangent—he should have taken up his Dad's offer of a tutor! He hoped that the Math teacher wouldn't call on him. But then, of course he did. Maybe he wasn't being mean; maybe he was just trying to assess what Toby knew, but whatever, it wasn't his finest hour.

Alyssa threw him a pitying glance. A boy with an unpleasant sneer, named Harsten, answered in his stead and then sniggered. Toby decided right there and then to study like crazy before the next class.

Seymour could answer all the questions put to him in what Toby detected as an Australian accent. Finally the hour was up and the bell for lunch rang. With great relief, he got up to leave. Immediately a few girls came up to him and asked him where he was from. Grinning like a hunter with a prized trophy, Glen dragged him off to the cafeteria where Chester was waiting for him with a seat.

"He's sitting with me, Oldwin," stated Glen.

"Uh… Glen, Chester and I arranged earlier to meet for lunch," said Toby. "Why don't you join us?"

"Sorry man, but my buddies are over there," said Glen, pointing to a nearby table. Seymour was already seated there along with Harsten and a whole group of girls. Toby was torn, but Chester was his friend. Even if JB was just then approaching their table to sit down.

"Hey Toby—if you want to sit with them, that's okay by me," said Chester.

"Thanks Chester," he said, "but hey, we've got to catch up."

Besides JB, another familiar-looking boy joined them and they talked about their mornings. Everyone found it hard to get back into schoolwork after spring break. Toby didn't mind admitting his math disaster, but blamed the teacher's accent more than his own failings.

"Pang's a good math teacher though. You'll get used to his accent—knows his stuff but he really moves along. Gotta do your homework in that class," advised Chester.

"Hmmm," JB mumbled, practically inhaling his lasagna.

Toby noticed that he had the meat one and that Chester had the vegetarian version.

G.G. Neilson

"They've got a great cafeteria here," said Chester digging in, "and not too pricey."

Toby was suddenly less than enthusiastic about his bag lunch. "Those cookies smell delicious," he said, pointing to JB's hoard.

"I found out that they bury healthy stuff in these cookies," announced JB, downing the last of his lasagna and waving a cookie under Toby's nose. "But I don't mind. They're still good. Besides, the cafeteria doesn't sell chips." He proceeded to stuff down a whole cookie.

"JB needs his energy for after school at the skate bowl," grinned Chester.

"Well, if that's what helps you do all those terrific stunts, I'll have to try out those cookies too," said Toby.

"Hey man, I'm still waiting to see your skateboard," said JB between mouthfuls. "What was the name of it again?"

"Toby here is not the skateboard aficionado you are, JB," said Chester with wink at Toby. "But I've seen him play tennis and he's good. Plays like a silver tornado!"

The warning bell sounded for the first class of the afternoon and they headed toward the gymnasium. Toby was glad he had had a light lunch. Phys Ed on a full stomach was not fun.

Their gym teacher was young—a short, dark-haired dynamo. "Let's go!" she shouted to the stragglers from the change rooms. She made everyone sit on the floor while she talked a mile a minute.

"Now people, we're going to play that Australian football game today. You all remember the one that we tried out before the break?" To the blank stares she said, "You know. The one Gregory showed us." She gave Seymour a grin and a thumbs up. "Great game—fast-moving. Eighteen per side, so we all get to play. I picked up this ball"—she held up what resembled a giant orange egg—"over spring break. Refresh the rules for us, Gregory."

She was obviously one of those teachers who use last names only. She didn't seem to even notice that she had a new student in her class. Chester whispered her name as Ms. Koh.

"Well, you move the ball any way you can down the field—kicking or running it or even bashing it with your hand," said Seymour. "Only thing you can't do is throw it." Heads were nodding now. "But Miss, there's supposed to be four goalposts at either end."

Several girls were gazing at him, hanging on his every Australian-accented word. Toby was glad that Alyssa wasn't in this class.

"Improvise, Gregory! We'll just use the goalposts we have. Any more rules they should know about? Be quick—we gotta go."

Seymour just managed to add, "Well, if you snag the ball when the other side's kicked it, you're awarded a free kick. It's called a mark…"

No-one was sure if she heard, as she was by then running them out of the building, ahead of even the fastest in the class.

"The game is known as footy," said Seymour to several rapturous girls, practically clinging to him as they jogged outside.

"I looked it up on UsLive," Chester told Toby. "They play it on a field shaped like a giant egg. Totally awesome, man."

Toby was swept onto Chester and Seymour's team and they began racing around after the orange ball. It was pure mayhem.

JB, Glen and Harsten were on the opposing team; other students were starting to look familiar. As they all flew around the field after the ball, Toby was fleetingly grateful that he had done some working out at the condo. The scoring was fast and furious, but the teams were well matched. Chester managed to snag the ball once from JB's kick and so made two extra points for their team, evening the score.

On the next play, Glen climbed up Toby like a ladder to capture the ball. As Toby toppled over, Glen used him a launching pad to kick the orange missile even before he landed again. It was the game-winning goal for his side.

"Sorry, man," panted Glen as they headed off the field. Toby, sides heaving, couldn't speak. Their teacher, who had raced all over the field for the full period, had not yet broken a sweat as she lined them all up to say "Good game" to one another.

"You, you're new," she said, jabbing a finger in Toby's direction as they trooped off to the change-rooms. "You're the private school kid, Myers, aren't you?"

"Yes, ma'am."

"Thought so. In this class, you have to bring your gym strip or points off, and main marks are for participation."

Finally—something the same as at St. Zallo's. He was sweaty and muddy as he got to the change-rooms and stripped down to get into the shower. He discovered too late, that not one other boy was doing so. At St. Zallo's it was mandatory to have a shower after Phys Ed.

Toby had become the centre of attention. Some stared, others made rude comments as he struggled valiantly with the dysfunctional shower faucet. Finally he managed to get a trickle of water going and bravely splattered his body.

Chester started talking loudly about Australian footy. Seymour gamely joined in. Toby used the distraction to quickly shut off the water and make a mad dash for his pile of clothes. By now, wetted down, he skidded and went flying into the bench. He landed in a naked heap between Chester and JB who stared down at him, mouths agape. The change-room erupted into laughter.

"Hey, what's going on in there!" Ms. Koh yelled through the door. "Let's get a move-on. Warning bell has gone."

The shrieks of laughter died down to snickers.

Beet red, Toby struggled to pull pants on over his damp legs.

With great bravado, Chester said, "You know man, I don't think anyone's ever tried having a shower in there. Who knew that water even came out of those old pipes? You don't even look rusty."

Amid the chuckles, Toby shot him a grateful look. He mumbled, "They were big on hygiene at St. Zallo's. Even supplied us with fresh towels."

The change-room went suddenly silent and people stared at Toby as if he had just announced he was a space alien. He quickly continued, "How do you get clean after Phys Ed anyway?"

This proved to be a redundant question as they resumed spraying or rolling on copious amounts of deodorant.

Toby used his new hoodie as a towel for his wet hair. Ms. Koh banged on the door again and those already dressed trooped out. Toby could hear the refrain of "shower boy" to sniggers as they left.

"Umm… I should go to class now," said Chester after the last one, Harsten, closed the door behind him, jeering, "Fresh towels!"

"You doing okay, man?"

"I'll live. I guess. And thanks, Chester. I made a first class fool of myself."

"That must have been quite the school you used to go to. Fresh towels. Were they heated too?" asked Chester with a grin as he left. Toby grinned back.

He reminded himself to never, ever, admit that they were.

Alone in the change-room, he managed to blot the remaining water on his upper body with a piece of notepaper he found lying on the floor, the paper towel dispenser being empty. He was still damp as he hurried off to his last class of the day, Socials.

It was so late by now that he didn't want to go to class. But the thought of his father getting a call home for him skipping on his first day, made him force himself into the room. All eyes turned toward him as he looked around wildly for an empty desk. There wasn't one.

Some were sympathetic, others snickered. It hadn't taken long for news of the shower incident to get around. He heard whispers of *shower boy* and *fresh towels* as he stood fighting off growing panic. Pulling himself together, he turned to the Socials teacher. "Where should I sit?"

She looked at him with a kindly face ensconced in the largest body he had ever seen. "Are you the new boy?" She had a pleasant, lilting voice.

He nodded and waited for instructions, trying to exude a confidence that he did not feel. "I'm Miss Shepherd and welcome to Socials class. You can sit on the window ledge for now." She waved a gigantic arm in the direction of the windows. "I'll see about getting you a desk as soon as I can."

Toby couldn't see where one could possibly fit, but headed resolutely over to the window and perched thankfully on a wide ledge, as far to the back as possible.

He thought about Beogall, towering over the other birds and felt that in this situation, being tall would not be an asset. Thinking about his friend, made him suddenly feel better and he looked out the window, half expecting the heron to appear.

He didn't see the bird, but did see an enormous patch of lush gardens and trees—why hadn't he noticed it before? Just then Miss Shepherd announced that she would be the Teacher-on-call for the next few days and began a discussion about current events.

Toby was practically sitting on top of a strange boy with long greasy hair sticking from under a baseball cap with the word "Skull" in bold letters. He took pity on Toby, and whispered, "The real Socials teacher doesn't show up much. Shepherd is always here. But she's cool," he added.

When one of the students brought up the curious case of a grown man beating up a boy, Toby experienced an anxious few minutes. "See, this kid had trespassed onto his property. It was in that rich community—out by Gold Beach," explained the student.

"Yes, I heard about that," said Miss Shepherd. "What else can you tell us?"

"According to the report, the boy, was like, trying to stop the destruction of trees and stuff. They were, like, registered or something. It was all caught on video."

Toby's stomach lurched as Miss Shepherd nodded and added, "Yes, I heard about it too—the boy cannot be identified since he is a minor." As she continued, Toby's senses were on red alert. "Do you think a person has the right to go onto private property if a law is being broken?"

The students were divided on the issue. One student, a gangly girl with a raggedy fringe of reddish hair declared that the boy was brave. "I think more people should stand up for nature—those trees can't speak for themselves," she declared.

"Good point, Robin," remarked Miss Shepherd and then to Toby's relief, she called on the next presenter who talked about a bad car accident in the interior. He looked gratefully toward Robin, who looked back at him with large blue eyes.

When it was time to read over the textbook selection for the day and answer the assigned questions, Ms. Shepherd waddled out, saying she'd be back soon, "and please be quiet." The instant she was gone, a loud buzz of conversation began.

"Is it true that you tried to have a shower?" someone asked.

"How did you get it to work?" Skull Boy questioned.

Toby shrugged.

"Here, take this," said Robin, handing him a paper serviette. "I saved it from the cafeteria at lunch. You're still damp."

Toby reddened as she plucked a scrap of note-paper still stuck to his arm. "Thanks," he said dabbing at his wet shirt. "Umm—I agree with you about that current event."

They were still talking about it and amid the other chatter, didn't notice that Miss Shepherd had returned. Behind her was a massive woman with closely-cropped hair, wearing a suit and carrying a desk in one arm and a chair in the other. The class was instantly silent.

"Vice-principal," whispered Skull Boy, as the muscular official expertly got the new furniture through the door. Ms. Shepherd pointed Toby out and she strode up the aisle and crammed the desk and chair in beside Skull Boy with a quick nod to Toby. As soon as she left, the chatter began again which Miss Shepherd soon gave up on trying to control.

"Free time for the last 15 minutes of the day," she called out and proceeded to check on the work of students near the front. She cast an appraising glance at Toby, but they both knew she wouldn't be able to squeeze through the cramped aisles to speak to him at the back of the room.

After the bell, Robin walked with him as they were pushed and jostled through the hall. The bedlam was even worse at the front foyer. Chester was easy to spot, and as soon as Toby arrived, they headed out to the skateboard bowl. Everyone seemed to have heard of the change-room incident and some thought it was a terrific joke to continue calling him *Shower Boy*.

"You're famous, man. Enjoy it," advised Chester.

JB was there and others were starting to look familiar. Robin was a shaky skateboarder, but another girl was terrific.

Toby heard her referred to as "Freddie" and she was almost as good a skater as JB. With a baseball cap on backwards and dressed in the loose garb and canvas sneakers of the other skaters, she sported nose and eyebrow piercings and her short hair was dyed pink on one side. She and JB seemed to have a little competition going.

After watching for a bit, he and Chester wandered over to the busy basketball courts.

"I'm going to see if I can get onto the tennis courts," Toby said.

"Catch you later," Chester replied, expertly snagging the ball and dribbling it toward the basket.

Toby was once again followed by the Steller's jay. He was dying to communicate with the bird, but couldn't risk attracting attention. When he got to the courts, someone was looking for a partner. The jay perched on the branch of a nearby tree and watched as Toby easily clobbered his first and second opponent. Someone else was watching too. A young man stepped forward and introduced himself as Chi Li.

"I heard there was a new tennis player who was ace," the man said as the others made way for him. "Care for a game?"

Chi proved tough competition. When they finally had to give others a turn, he stuck out his hand to Toby, "Very nice to have such a strong competitor. Same time tomorrow?"

Invigorated by the work-out, Toby was in a better mood when he got home to find his dad already there. "It was pretty slow at the golf course," Lars offered by way of explanation. "How was your first day of school?"

"Uh… alright. The classes sure are big—there wasn't even a desk for me in Socials." No way was Toby going to tell him about the shower incident, but he did add, "And no-one takes showers after Phys Ed."

"Well, it's going to be different from St. Zallo's. Do you like your teachers?"

"They're okay I guess. One's ancient and I can't understand the Math teacher."

"Toby, remember to be respectful! Meet any new students?"

"Yeah, of course. I guess it'll be alright." Actually, his day was a total disaster. "But, I really could use some help with trigonometry. Are you any good at it, Dad?"

"Are you kidding? I was the best in my class. Let's get at it."

They went over the basics, then while he made supper, Lars had Toby work through some problems on tangents. After supper, they did a lesson on sine.

"I think you're getting it," his dad finally said. "We've done enough for now. We'll save cosine 'till tomorrow."

Toby was happy to just zone out in front of the television for the rest of the evening. His dad went to his room and Toby could hear him talking on the phone, probably to Anna.

He was so tired that he fell into to bed early and was still dead-to-the-world when his dad tapped on the door the next morning to get him up for his second day of school.

Chapter 13
Day 1 – Odd S

"It's okay. I'm awake."

As Toby pulled himself out of bed painfully, he noticed bruises—oh yeah, getting knocked around in that game. He groaned—well at least he didn't have to face Phys Ed today.

"I'm leaving now, Toby," his dad called out. "I'm, um, I'll be going out later with Anna. Do you have plans this evening?"

"Other than boring old math homework, no. Bring her over if you want."

"I might do that. I left some cereal and fruit out. There's lunch money on the counter. See you later."

"Bye, Dad."

Toby dressed gingerly, hoping odd days would be an improvement over the evens—how could they be any worse? He heard a bird chorus outside and suddenly experienced a tingling running up his spine. He gulped down his breakfast and headed out into the spring sunshine. Chester had an early basketball practise so Toby had to walk to school on his own. He resolved to find out if the school had a tennis club, but from what he had seen, he had his doubts.

The Steller's jay was perched on a nearby tree.

"Hi guy—nice day, isn't it?" Did it nod its head? If so, it didn't communicate back. Why was it following him? Maybe he had become an object of interest in the bird community.

When he got to school, the schedule was listed as *Day 1*. As he looked at the notice, he could make out a faint *Odd S* beside it, or did it say *Old S*? It seemed to waver a bit. Then he felt the same slight tingling. Weird.

Toby studied his schedule. Chester had told him where his classes were. First up was Foods—his vegetarian cooking class—then French. After lunch there was Science and finally Music. He already preferred this schedule.

After stopping for directions twice, he still arrived at the Foods room early enough to look around. There were six kitchen units, each painted a different, garish colour. A stout teacher, her brown hair streaked with purple, looked up from her desk. She was middle-aged but was that a stud in her nose?

"Are you Toby Myers?"

"Yes." Toby wondered what she had been told.

"I'm Mrs. Polley. Welcome to vegetarian cooking class. Have you had much cooking experience?"

"Um… not really." If only she knew, he thought.

"Doesn't matter—attitude is everything. Well Toby, we'll put you in the orange kitchen as a student has recently left that group." She turned to greet other students now filing in.

A boy on crutches, with some sort of physical ailment, was followed by the boy Toby recognized from the previous day as *Skull Boy*. Today he was wearing a black hoodie covered in white skulls. With a look from Mrs. Polley he removed his baseball cap which was adorned with some sort of werewolf.

Behind them was a dark-haired girl. The teacher introduced them to Toby: Michael on the crutches, Skull Boy was Robert, and the girl was Raven, an easy name to remember, given her hair colour, thought Toby.

Students had to sit with their kitchen groups and Toby was pleased when Robin plopped herself down beside him and Michael in the brilliant orange kitchen. Chester arrived, still sweaty from basketball practise, and filled the fourth chair in their unit.

"You should have had a shower," Toby joked.

Chester gave him a friendly poke.

Alyssa entered just then, and she nodded to Toby. She sat down in the royal purple kitchen beside Raven. Then she looked around and graced Seymour, in the lime green kitchen, with a smile.

"Attention please," began Mrs. Polley. "Today we'll learn to make vegetarian lasagna." She proceeded to explain the intricacies of perfect pasta noodle preparation, adding, "We'll be making this next class."

Everyone paid full attention to the cooking demonstration. The mysterious purple object in front of her turned out to be an eggplant. Toby had only ever known it as a cooked vegetable.

Finally Mrs. Polley pointed to the recipe written on the board, which looked as complicated as a lab experiment. "Use the rest of the time to write out the recipe. Take out your books now, please."

There were scattered groans. "Do we have to?" someone asked.

"You young people are forgetting how to write," Mrs. Polley responded. "And besides, you never get the measurements correct unless you write them out by hand."

She didn't use a smart board like most other teachers, but had an old-fashioned blackboard, like the English teacher, Mr. Draper.

Michael had a fancy little computer that typed and formatted the recipe perfectly as he spoke to it. "I have cerebral palsy," he said when he noticed Toby watching, "so it takes too long to write."

"But he's no slouch," whispered Chester. "This guy is great in the kitchen."

There was only just enough time to finish copying the recipe before the bell rang.

So far his day was going swimmingly. The next class, French, included every student who was in his Foods class. Mme. Bruleau was tall, thin and as black as ebony, wearing the most colourful clothes he had ever seen on a teacher.

Her head was swathed in a bright red bandana and her long legs were clad in scarlet stockings with white ducks stamped all over them. Toby couldn't help but stare and Robin, sitting next to him, leaned over and whispered, "She wears a different pair of wild stockings every day."

Madame, as she liked to be called, made them converse in their groups. Besides Robin, there was another girl, who introduced herself as Rajni, and Skull Boy in his group. They were only allowed to speak in French. When Rajni asked him in halting French where he was from, he replied fluently about recently moving from another part of the city and described his new neighbourhood. The others stared.

The lesson of the day was about clothing and Toby led the conversation. His mother spoke excellent French and on the two occasions they had visited France, she insisted that Toby speak in French too. He couldn't believe how soon the class was over.

"I heard you showing off," said Chester on their way to the cafeteria. "I think Alyssa did too," he added, ducking away from Toby's elbow.

"What d'you think about that lasagna recipe Sk—Robert?" Toby asked. Note to self—*remember to call him Robert*.

"Um—okay I guess."

"Oh man, it's nice not to have another quinoa recipe," said Chester, rolling his eyes.

"Yeah, but I made the quinoa salad one and my parents loved it," said Robin, plopping her tray down beside Toby.

"What did you guys do over spring break?" asked Robert slowly.

Toby listened as they spoke about their holidays. When it came to his turn, he told about visiting his grandmother on Truewind Island.

"Isn't that where we're going for our Odd S field trip?" asked Robert.

"Hey man, I thought that was hush-hush," replied Chester.

"Well, I overheard a couple of teachers talking about it," said Robert defensively.

Alyssa and Raven walked up just then, balancing their trays.

"They can't keep secrets from us," Alyssa threw out as she continued on towards Seymour's table. Glen, Harsten and several girls including Rajni, were there already.

"My auntie lives there," Raven stated, setting her tray down and budging Chester over. "She said our class was going to pay a visit to the reserve up there—Oyster Narrows."

"That'll be awesome," said Robert, whose grey eyes lost their far-away look for a moment.

They talked some more about spring break and when the bell rang, hurriedly packed up their things to go to Science.

"Too complicated to explain," said Chester in answer to Toby's question about how to find the science class. "You better just come with me. It's easiest to go through the courtyard."

"Courtyard?"

"Oh, I guess I didn't show you that yet."

This seemed distinctly odd, since Chester was usually pretty thorough. He led them into the counseling area, which Toby had not yet seen. A spacious main area had three offices to one side and a nondescript, barely noticeable door at the far end. Mr. McFru waved at them as they headed towards it. Other Odd S students were now trooping towards the same door. Behind it was a short hallway ending at an outside door. Chester flung it open, and they walked through.

Toby stopped short.

A lush scene of trees, shrubs and trails lay before him. He turned to Chester who grinned and shrugged. "Sort of a well kept secret," he said. "Only those who are ready to, actually come out here anyway. I'm glad they put you in Odd S."

Rhododendrons were in bloom and everything seemed ahead of schedule. There were mostly deciduous trees and bushes. Several fruit trees were starting to bud and two Japanese cherry trees were ablaze with dark pink blossoms. Beds of spring flowers lined the pathways. And was that a giant grape vine?

A flock of swallows joyfully greeted several of the students and then twittered around Toby, welcoming him to the courtyard. The Steller's jay that had been following him flapped over to say hello. A squirrel chittered excitedly until Robert calmed it down.

Toby's head was spinning. He stopped, trying to take it all in.

"Gotta get to class, man. We'll have a chance to come out here after the lesson," said Chester towing him along.

"Why didn't you tell me about this place?" Toby asked dazedly. They were approaching an open door, which he realized must be the science room.

Chester shrugged. "People find out about it when they're ready. Here's our classroom."

A pretty, young teacher with shoulder-length, dark hair stood just inside the door welcoming the students, most of whom towered over her.

"You're Toby? I'm Ms. Tanaka. Welcome to Odd S science."

The classroom was not spacious, as their class of 24 students was smaller than most at Willow Heights. There were the usual lab tables, stools, sinks and lab equipment found in any science class, but it was also filled with plants of all kinds, including a giant and deadly-looking cactus. A realistic human skeleton had one arm raised and two mice rolled around madly in little plastic balls. A well-behaved little dog called Mr. Chips sat calmly observing their antics.

Chester pulled Toby over to a stool at his lab table, just as the teacher began. Dark-haired and petite, she looked familiar and he resolved to google her later. He had planned to do that with all his teachers—to find out about their expectations—but with so much math homework, he hadn't gotten around to it the previous night.

"Good afternoon, class, and welcome back from spring break," she began. "Hopefully it was relaxing, as we have a very busy term ahead of us. As you are no doubt aware, we have a new student, so join me in welcoming Toby to Odd S."

She smiled. "It is good that you are here, Toby—we're up to a full 24 again. There is much work to be done. As you know, students are chosen carefully for the Odd S program, for their dedication to science and nature."

Actually, Toby didn't know—why hadn't he been told?

"After our lessons each day, we strive to maintain Willow Heights courtyard as the special place that it is. So remember, you're expected to work diligently on your lessons. Only then can we spend time in the courtyard to carry on our important endeavours there. Your first priority is to fulfill all the regular science requirements and maintain your good standings. Is everyone with me?"

She waited until everyone agreed. Toby, sitting at the edge of his seat, was one of the first. They were starting a unit on astronomy and had to read about types of stars then answer questions. Toby finished early.

With a start, he noticed a riddle on the top left hand side of the board.

"Like a tune stuck in your brain."

G.G. Neilson

"She likes her bird riddles," whispered Chester, when he noticed Toby chuckling.

"Okay class, let's list vegetables and herbs we want to plant," suggested Ms. Tanaka. "Think about flowers and shrubs that will attract bees and butterflies." She wrote their ideas on the board.

Then the class charged out to the courtyard. Everyone had a responsibility and Toby noticed that both Alyssa and Chester had leadership roles. Toby signed up for leafy greens, so Robert was his partner.

"It's over here," said Robert, leading him to a quiet corner of the courtyard. "I've planted one part, but the rest has to be weeded and turned over."

The Steller's jay flew onto a nearby bench and watched with head cocked. Toby took a chance to speak to the bird. He felt certain that these Odd S students wouldn't find it strange.

"Hey guy, you've been following me," Toby said quietly, in bird language. "What's your name?"

"Sami. I'm a friend of Beogall's."

Toby hooted. "I should have known!"

The bird hopped from foot to foot. "He asked me to keep an eye out for you. He can't come over—too conspicuous," cackled the creature with a hop and flap of his wings. "Besides, it's a long way from Stanley Park."

Robert inquired about their conversation, appearing not the slightest bit surprised by the exchange. "My area is animals," he said. "Especially the smaller ones—like Gulu over there." He pointed to the squirrel bustling around making a pest of himself.

Hearing his name, Gulu sped over and chattered to Robert, keeping a wary eye on Sami. Other birds approached, chirping their interest in Toby. Soon several students had gathered, impressed with his ability to communicate with a variety of birds. Suddenly a shout went up as a hummingbird buzzed into the courtyard, the first of the season. "Hey, that's the answer to the riddle," remarked Robert. "Hummingbird."

I knew it, thought Toby. Then he asked, "Do you ever put up a feeder for them?"

"Naturally. I'll go get Raven to prepare it," Ms. Tanaka pronounced and then was gone as quickly as she had appeared.

"I can't communicate with hummingbirds," Toby admitted.

"Not like Chester?" asked Michael from his nearby plot.

"Chester can communicate with hummingbirds!" Toby gaped.

Michael's partner gave him a poke. "Well, he's in Odd S now," Michael defended himself. "Why shouldn't he know about us?"

"What about you, Michael? Do you all talk with birds and animals? Can you communicate with plants?" Toby's mind was reeling.

"No way," replied Michael. "Most of us have an area of ability that we're developing. Mine is plants. But you're way ahead in your ability to communicate with birds, even without any training."

"Except Chester," said Robert. "He's the only one who can communicate with all creatures. Chester is special."

"Yes, Chester is special." Ms. Tanaka had returned—their teacher seemed to have an uncanny ability to turn up anywhere. "We all are, but Chester even more so. We all protect our abilities, but it's safe to share them here."

"But not with Peter," Michael blurted out. Ms. Tanaka quelled him with a look.

Who is this Peter? Toby looked around for Chester—the last he had seen of him was over in a far corner, dealing with the compost pile. And what other surprises are in store?

G.G. Neilson

A comment of Grams' came to him: "There are no coincidences, Toby. We are all given opportunities and we either take them or not. Eventually though, they'll find us again."

Ms. Tanaka put up a hummingbird feeder just before the bell sounded. Toby realized she was indeed talking to the tiny bird. It was a high-pitched and faint, very strange sound. He was determined to master the ability. As he listened, it struck him that Ms. Tanaka and Mr. Getty, his previous science teacher, were made for each other. He just knew it.

They had to pack up quickly for their next class, music, which turned out to be close by, and also accessible from the courtyard. The whole class was late and the music teacher, Mr. Harrington, waited impatiently, his foot tapping. He was a sprightly, middle-aged man, his somewhat thinning hair tied back in a scant ponytail.

"You people are always late when you have Science before my class," he grumbled and made them warm up with scales.

He had Toby play a few lines on the flute, solo, and then nodded with satisfaction. There were two others on flute, both girls, and Chester played saxophone. Mr. Harrington had them start off with some familiar pieces. Toby realized how much he had missed playing with others. They were every bit as good as the music students at St. Zallo's.

"Okay class, here's a new one I'd like you to try," said their teacher, handing out the music. It was a tricky piece and the class really bogged down. Toby, with years of music lessons, soon got the hang of it. He noticed that Seymour, on trombone, had figured it out quickly too. He probably knew the piece already, Toby thought uncharitably.

"Toby, could I talk to you?" Mr. Harrington asked as the class put away their instruments. "How long have you been playing flute?"

"For two and a half years at my other school—St. Zallo's."

"Oh, the private school. Did you take extra lessons?"

"We each got a weekly private lesson there."

"I see. Do you play any other instruments?"

"The violin."

"Would you mind playing something for me?"

Toby was surprised but agreed and Mr. Harrington handed him a rather worn violin. He listened intently as Toby played one of his favourites, the theme from Mozart's Concerto No. 21.

"Yes, excellent." Mr. Harrington had closed his eyes and now opened them. "How long have you been playing violin?"

"My mother started me off in lessons a few years ago."

"Yes, well you have a fine tone and an excellent ear. We have some other good musicians here. I'd like you to try out with a small ensemble. Would that interest you?"

It did and Toby said so. Leaving school that day, he felt buoyant—who knew there would be such an unusual class at Willow Heights and how did he end up in it?

Weird.

Chapter 14

Spring Plans

The days went flying by, alternating between the even days, which Toby didn't much enjoy, and the odd days, which he lived for. It was hard to get used to such a big and bustling school and the packed classes. On the plus side, his math skills were improving steadily. And after the initial buzz about the shower episode died down, ironically enough, some of the braver ones occasionally stepped into the showers after a particularly good work out in gym class.

March turned into April and the courtyard was alive with bees and birds. Chester and Alyssa, who were in charge of growing herbs, bickered endlessly about when they would be ready to offer to the cafeteria. Toby and Robert's plot flourished and they high-fived the day their baby greens made it onto the lunch menu.

"These are great!" said Chester between mouthfuls. "It's because of that excellent compost I gave you last fall, Robert."

Toby began to feel like he had been at Willow Heights the whole year. As he hung out more and more with the Odd S students, Glen became cool toward him, but still lunched with Seymour—probably because of all the girls hanging around the charming Australian. As if his good looks weren't enough, he was also a star on the track and field team—the best shot-putter in their school.

Irritatingly likable! Toby almost said it out loud as he walked down the back hall on his way to English class that day.

"Odd S-ers—they're freaks!"

Toby stopped short. His keen hearing picked up a conversation going on around the corner.

"They're not that bad, Harsten."

"You've heard the stories, Glen. Open your eyes. They talk to, like, birds and stuff. In that courtyard we've heard about. They walk around thinking they're so smart."

"Well, I can't say I understand it. But they do grow some nice food for the cafeteria—"

"Ha! I hate all that vegetable stuff. How can you defend them? And that new idiot, Toby—shower boy. He's just as bad as the one who left…"

That's when Toby rounded the corner, having had enough of this insulting conversation.

Glen had the grace to look embarrassed, but Harsten glowered at him and Toby heard him snigger "fresh towels" as he walked past, heading resolutely to English.

Mr. Draper was crabby as usual. But most of the teachers were friendly enough. The principal and vice-principal left the Odd S students to their own devices. Ms. Shepherd still filled in for Socials—Toby didn't know who the regular teacher was but noticed that lots of students went to hang out in her classroom after school. She was easy to talk to.

Mr. Harrington now had their small ensemble practising twice a week. Chester played saxophone the way he did everything—well. Robin shone on the clarinet, and Robert was an excellent percussionist. Rajni played the trumpet and Toby had to admit that Seymour's trombone playing was a huge asset. Both Rajni and Chester played guitar on some pieces. One day Mr. Harrington had Toby take out the violin for a piece.

"Hey, you're a natural," said Robin.

"Wow, you'll have to play that more often," added Chester.

So far they had just been jamming. Chester preferred jazz, the others liked pop and Rajni introduced them to Bollywood fusion.

That day, Mr. Harrington had them try out some Celtic tunes.

"Excellent. Toby, you must have played Celtic music on the fiddle before."

"Yeah, my other music teacher introduced us to it."

"I like it," said Seymour. "I've heard Ashley MacIsaac—what a fiddler that guy is."

"There's another guy from back east—Richard Wood. He's a great fiddler too," replied Toby not wanting to be outdone by an Australian.

"Well, I like the Rankin family and the Barra MacNeils…" continued Robin but Mr. Harrington cut it off abruptly with, "I'd like this group to play for the school. There's a talent show at the end of May. You'll have to get serious about preparing some pieces."

That got the butterflies going.

"But that's only a month away," wailed Rajni. "We won't be ready!"

"It's a *month and a half*," stated Mr. Harrington. "You're never really ready—in playing for others you just have to get up and do it." Then he added, "But you're good. They'll love you—you'll see."

Spring was in the air, Easter was just around the corner and third term report cards were due.

Toby arrived at science class early—it was their first block that day. He had been pondering a way to bring up the subject of Mr. Getty with Ms. Tanaka. When he walked into the classroom, she looked up and smiled. "Toby, can you go down to the resource room and fetch Robert and Michael? They like to walk here with someone else."

She gave him directions and Toby found himself exploring a section of the school he had not yet seen. The resource room turned out to be a classroom unlike any he had seen before—complete with kitchen, computer area, small sitting room and a large handicap washroom.

Toby looked around—an older girl in a wheelchair who seemed completely paralyzed, was making unintelligible noises. A boy rocked himself in a study carrel, apparently in his own world. A pleasant, plump woman with long greying hair looked up from tying the laces of a small girl who Toby was pretty sure had Down's Syndrome. He had read up on it once.

"Can I help you?"

"Um… I'm here for Robert and Michael."

"Oh yes, it's Odd S today—well come on in. They should be here soon. What's your name?"

When he told her, she seemed to have heard of him and introduced herself. Another woman arrived, a helper, and the two discussed the day's schedule, giving Toby a few minutes to look around some more.

The walls had large posters of positive sayings like "Believe in Yourself" and interesting student art. Everyone had their own individual schedule printed prominently on the board. Some students were sitting around a table in the kitchen playing a game of Go Fish.

"What's your name? I'm Norman." A slender boy with a slightly lopsided face and a nasally voice came up and stood within inches of Toby, giving him a high-five.

Toby introduced himself and was quickly peppered with, "I'm in grade 11. I'm in work experience, you know. Why haven't I seen you around? Are you new? Do you like it here?

G.G. Neilson

I came in grade 9, you know, and I like it way better than my first high school. Are you here for Robert and Michael?"

Toby didn't know where to begin, but just then, Robert arrived. "I'll be ready soon," he said, staring slightly over Toby's shoulder as usual.

Norman tried to get his attention too, but Robert ignored him and quickly stowed his jacket and lunch. The teacher went over his schedule for the day, but Robert cut her off, saying, "I know, I know." He was impatient to leave but the teacher reminded him to wait for Michael.

"Do you have classes in here?" asked Toby.

"Some. It's okay. I might do all regular classes next year though."

Toby realized that he hadn't seen Robert much in the cafeteria, or Michael at all. Maybe they ate in here.

Michael arrived, dropped off by his dad. He didn't mind Robert helping him stow his stuff, even though Toby knew that in Odd S classes, he never let anyone help him. They headed out with Norman trailing behind. "Are you going to Odd S now? Isn't that a class for strange kids?"

"Go back to the Resource Room, Norman," Robert ordered. "Right now."

"He sure is enthusiastic," said Toby when Norman turned around and headed back. "What did he mean about Odd S?"

"Norman parrots everything he hears," said Michael. "He can be a real pain."

"He's like a puppy dog," added Robert and Toby laughed. Then he felt funny laughing about the unusual boy. As they continued in silence, he wondered if the others did too.

They got to Science just as the bell rang. The courtyard beckoned, so the class worked extra hard on their lessons and flew out into the sunshine like moths to light.

But Toby hung back. "Umm, Ms Tanaka, are you married?"

That got her attention. She turned startled eyes on him, "Why, Toby—it's my policy to keep my relationship with my students on a strictly professional level."

"No, oh, no..." stammered Toby, reddening. "Why I asked is, you see, there's this great science teacher at my old school. Mr. Getty. He's not married and... and, you see. Well, maybe you don't see, but I do. I just know you guys are made for each other."

Miss Tanaka gave him an inscrutable look. "Well Toby, this is a surprise. I do appreciate you thinking of me. I'm not married, but with teaching and other activities, I honestly don't have much time for anything else."

"I just know that Mr. Getty and you would hit it off," Toby pressed on despite growing misgivings. "I sense things, and this is something that's meant to be."

She looked at him sharply. "Well Toby, I'm sure you are a sensitive person. But as an adult, I get to decide these things for myself, don't I?"

Suddenly he felt very foolish. "Yeah, of course. Look, I'm really sorry if I offended you. And... I've got work to do." He fled from the room, thinking—*stupid, stupid.* As he escaped, Toby could feel Ms. Tanaka's eyes on him. She didn't join her students in the courtyard for a long time.

At home that night, his dad had some news for him. "Well Toby, we have a court date in two weeks' time. I've hired a lawyer—a Mr. Feldman. I'll pick you up after school tomorrow and we'll go together to meet him. I was told that both charges will be heard together—the trespassing one against you and our charge of assault against Duffin Wint."

Toby hurried off to do some research on the computer. Then he remembered Mr. Getty's card and decided to call him. He dug out the small card with the varied thrush embossed on one corner and tapped in the number.

"Hello?"

"Mr. Getty? This is Toby calling."

"Toby! I was hoping to hear from you. Beogall has been keeping me informed." Mr. Getty chuckled. "He's assigned his best friend to keep an eye on you."

"That'll be Sami. Yeah, well he does keep good track of me. And I'm going to a great school." Toby told Mr. Getty all about Odd S and when he finished, there was silence on the other end.

"Whew," Mr. Getty finally said. "That's amazing, Toby! I had heard some things about Willow Heights. Through the birds. Or is it 'for the birds'?" He laughed at his own little joke. "Have you heard how things are going at your old mansion? Beogall told me there is no more chain-sawing going on there. You did a tremendous thing, Toby. All the birds think so."

"Thanks. I heard that it's pretty quiet there now," said Toby and then told him about the court case. "What do you think about the protection legislation, Mr. Getty? Could it help my case for why I trespassed?"

"Maybe," said the teacher thoughtfully. "Look, I know an environmental lawyer. I'll check with her and get back to you."

"Great! Thanks. Um… Mr. Getty, have you ever heard of Meagan Tanaka?"

"Of course. Her father is the famous scientist, Dr. Lawrence Tanaka. He has that great show about nature. Some say she's set to follow in his footsteps. I heard her speak at a science conference once about biodiversity. Brilliant talk—very impressive. Why do you ask?"

"She's my science teacher at Willow Heights."

Mr. Getty whistled. "That certainly helps explain what's going on there. And you say she communicates with birds?"

"Yep—she can even speak to hummingbirds."

Mr. Getty whistled again and Toby took a deep breath. "I, um, I told her about you. What a great science teacher you were and everything..."

"Well, I'm flattered, Toby. Maybe I'll go up and talk to her if I see her again at a conference."

"You really should. I think you two would hit it off."

"Hmmm. You wouldn't by any chance be trying to play matchmaker, would you?"

"Well, I uh, sense things you know." Toby was again feeling foolish. "It's been great talking to you again, Mr. Getty. Let me know what you find out."

After their goodbyes, Toby was left thinking that this first foray into matchmaking was going poorly. Yet the conviction remained that Meagan Tanaka and Gerald Getty were made for each other.

The next day, his father was there to pick him up after school as planned. He had asked if Chester could tag along.

"Toby, that's not a good idea. I'd like to keep him out of this, if possible."

The lawyer, Mr. Feldman, was a younger man, and greeted them briefly before quickly getting down to business. "We have a good case. Number one—Toby is young and we can argue, impulsive. Number two—the mansion had been his home most of his life and he knows all the trees and bird life there, and number three—he was there merely to take pictures of the damage. The response was excessive, even if they argue that Duffin Wint was under duress."

"Have you ever done any environmental law?" Toby asked.

The man paused before he replied, "I'm familiar with it, but it's not my area of expertise. I'll do some research before the trial."

"This science teacher that I know... well, he has a friend who's an environmental lawyer. Maybe they can help."

Mr. Feldman was taken aback, but after a slight hesitation responded with, "Okay, I guess it wouldn't hurt to hear from an—"

"And what about Walter?" interrupted Toby and despite his father's warning look, ploughed on, "He was the one that filed the information about the trees and the species-at-risk."

Mr. Feldman sounded irritated, but agreed to contact Walter, and they arranged a follow-up meeting before the trial.

On the way home Lars grumbled, "Toby, I wish you had mentioned something to me about this environmental lawyer. This case is already costing a lot—I'm not sure I can afford to get another lawyer involved."

"It's, okay Dad. They might do it for free."

"*Pro bono*," his dad muttered to himself. "That's what I've come to."

"I just thought if there was anything else that could help. I've been on the Internet… " His father rolled his eyes but didn't say anything.

Chester was waiting to hear about how the meeting went. They both agreed to do some Internet research and the following week Mr. Getty got back to him with word about the lawyer—it was a go.

Chapter 15

What Happened on Pro-D Day

Toby was feeling nervous as the court date approached, but now there was some new excitement. Ms. Tanaka was finally talking about the trip to Truewind Island. The Outdoor Ed. teacher was helping them plan the camping part of their trip.

Ms. Tanaka had already talked to Raven about visiting the nearby Oyster Narrows First Nations reserve. Now she asked Toby, "Is there anyone we should approach about visiting the bird sanctuary? I'd like to take the class there."

"Well, I guess my grandmother would know, and maybe the chief of Oyster Narrows. His name is Wesley Martin."

"I've heard the name. Raven could ask her aunt about him and you could ask your grandmother. Toby, could you prepare a short talk for the class? We should know about the place before we visit."

Toby agreed since she was his teacher, but he had misgivings about that many people visiting Westwind. The Odd S class was definitely cool, but still… Grams would know what to do.

The next day, a Friday, was a Professional Development day. Their report cards had been handed out and Toby was happy with his. His father had studied it and said, "Most of your marks are about the same as at St. Zallo's."

"But my math mark is way up."

"Yep, if ten marks is considered way up." Toby at least thought so.

Then his dad added, "I'm glad those trigonometry lessons we did together paid off. Good work."

When Chester knocked on his door early the next morning, Lars had already left for work. "No school today and you need a break, man. No practicing violin or your tennis game," he declared. "Let's go hang at the skate park."

It was sunny and warm, so the skaters working the bowl were hoodie-less. JB was doing his usual death-defying stunts, baggy pants barely clinging to his hips. Freddie, ball cap on backwards, was waiting her turn.

Loads of people were there and even Alyssa wandered over with her two little dogs. "Nice day," she said and began chatting with them. Toby was happily engrossed in their conversation when it happened.

A large German shepherd charged toward them, leash dragging behind. Bibbi and Shasta both yapped noisily and the big dog lunged toward them. Its sharp teeth sank into Bibbi's front leg. Alyssa screamed just as JB went into a high flip.

Toby saw it all in slow motion. The flip, the missed landing into the concrete bowl. JB's head smacked the edge with a crack and his crumpled body slid down into the bowl.

Chester was there in a flash and took charge. He told one of the skateboarders to call 9-1-1 and assigned two more to crowd control. JB was unconscious but breathing as Chester knelt by his head. He carefully held it stable between his forearms. Toby had never seen Chester look so worried.

A homeless man had been lingering near the edge of the park and he shuffled through the onlookers. When Chester saw him, relief flooded into his face and the man knelt down beside Chester, gently checking for other injuries. Then the man took over from Chester in a fluid motion. Toby heard him murmur a few words, which he couldn't quite make out.

It suddenly struck Toby that this man was Chester's father—the hurrying past the homeless shelter—never any straight answers about his dad. The resemblance was there and the man seemed to have a certain, confident aura about him, the same as Chester. He was a lot darker-skinned than Chester, and his tightly curled black hair, streaked with grey, was cut short. He looked up to see Toby staring and nodded briefly before continuing to tend to the injured boy.

When the ambulance arrived and the paramedics took over, the man quietly disappeared into the crowd of onlookers. JB was groaning now and the paramedics got him onto a stretcher with a quick word of thanks to Chester. Someone in the crowd patted him on the back.

One bystander asked who the homeless man was. Chester shrugged.

"I've seen him around," Toby cut in. "He seems okay—I think he hangs out here sometimes. Homeless people have skills too, you know," he added, as if the onlooker had said otherwise.

"Hey, just wondering, that's all," the boy defended himself. No-one else asked any more about the man.

The crowd had cleared when Chester and Toby went over to see Alyssa, who was crouched down, calming her dogs. The German shepherd had been quickly claimed by its owner, who had left without a word. Bibbi sported a nasty gash.

"It was my fault, wasn't it?" she asked tearfully. "I screamed just as JB was doing that flip." Toby fought the urge to put his arm around her. "I just reacted without thinking. I should never have come over here. What's going to happen? Is he going to be alright?"

Chester tried to assure her that JB was tough and would be okay as they walked her back to her building.

"I think I better take Bibbi to the vet. Will you let me know about JB?"

"Of course. Do you need any help with Bibbi?" Toby asked.

"I'll be okay, thanks."

They left her to go to Chester's apartment.

"Was that your dad back there, Chester?" Toby finally asked.

"Yeah, I figured you knew. Hey, thanks for blowing off that kid's question."

"Least I could do. What was your dad saying when he was holding JB's head?"

"Probably a prayer. He's a minister."

"No kidding! How did he end up homeless?"

"Well, he chooses to carry out his ministry that way. He says you have to walk in someone's shoes to understand what they're going through. He works for *Serving Light Ministries*, but he donates a lot of his earnings back to the homeless shelter he works at. The one near the community centre."

"You're full of surprises, Chester. What else haven't you told me?"

"That's friendship, man. You find out a little here, a little there. Hopefully you like what you see. Gotta have some surprises. I had a good feeling about you right off."

"JB's the one who razzed me the day we met and here I am, all worried about him. Life is strange. Hey Chester, can your parents uh, like, talk with, well you know…?"

"All the creatures? It's kinda complicated. My mom can communicate with plants— "

"Hey, remember Holly—the one I told you about?" asked Toby. "Her mother has that ability and Holly is developing it too." Toby paused, puzzled. "It seems like a really weird sort of communication."

"My mom says it's more like, like understanding their needs. She says you get sort of refreshed by them in return. My dad can communicate with birds and some animals. They were surprised when I started, well y'know, at such a young age."

"How old were you?"

"I'm not sure. I could always communicate with our cat—she's gone now. Some other creatures too, but not in any major way. That came later."

"Wow! I only just started, like, understanding birds. Have you ever spoken with Beogall?"

"I know about him. He's pretty young and usually birds don't communicate until they're older. There was some noise going around the bird community that he had chosen you. Birds are strange that way—the first person they communicate with, they develop a bond. It's not like that with other creatures. It's kinda strange that birds who have a human bond live longer. That first happened with…" Chester broke off.

"So do you have a bond with some bird?" Toby asked and his friend nodded. "Can you tell me who?"

"I suppose so. My parents taught me not to tell people about my abilities—gifts they call them. So I got used to not revealing things. Just to listen, observe, learn. Anyway you already know him."

"Sami?"

Chester nodded and Toby hooted. "That's why nothing that happened surprised you! Hey, I guess it was only natural that we would become friends, since our birds are."

They discussed what it was like having a bond-bird. Toby wanted to ask Chester to call Sami right then, but Marion Oldwin arrived back from her morning shift. "Chester, I just heard about JB – how awful!" she said. "I'm proud of you for helping out. Tell me what happened."

G.G. Neilson

She wasn't surprised to learn about how Chester's dad had helped.

"Hey, next weekend is Easter—the long weekend," Toby finally said. "I know my grandmother would love to meet you, Chester. Do you want to come to Truewind Island with us?" He hadn't checked with his dad but was sure it would be okay.

"Well, Easter is important to Chester's dad, but I'll tell you what," said Mrs. Oldwin, "if Chester is back here by Sunday afternoon, then it's okay with me. Now you two had better go and check on your friend in the hospital."

JB was still in the recovery room following surgery, so they went to the waiting area. Freddie was there and her usually inscrutable face bore a worried look.

"How long have you been here?" asked Chester.

"Since he was taken here. I don't know how he's doing, but I heard them on the phone to his mom. I think she'll be here soon." She told them of a few skaters who had been there but had already left.

"My mom always told me I should wear a helmet when I'm skateboarding," said Freddie, fighting back tears. "I'm going to from now on."

The waiting seemed interminable—hospital employees came and went, some regarding them curiously. Finally a man in blue hospital garb came out and asked them if they were there for JB.

"Yes! How is he?" asked Freddie, jumping up.

"I'd prefer to speak to his mother. Do you know where she is?"

"She's hoping to be here soon. I'm his girlfriend," said Freddie, "and these are his best friends. They're the ones who helped him when the accident happened."

Toby and Chester nodded solemnly. Toby was pretty sure he wasn't JB's best friend or that Freddie was his girl-friend, but wasn't about to argue the point.

"Your friend is lucky we were able to get him into surgery right away. He's had a bad brain injury and I'm not sure when he'll be back on his feet…" The surgeon stopped, looking like he had said too much.

Then, seeing their crestfallen faces, he added, "We think he's going to be okay though. He's awake now, so you can see him for a few minutes. Don't expect him to talk and don't tire him."

They entered the room on tip-toe. JB's head was bandaged and he had a lot of tubes attached all over, including one in his mouth. They stood next to his bed and Freddie stifled a sob. No-one spoke. JB's eyes fluttered open, closed and then opened and stared out at them. He moaned.

"Hey man, don't talk or anything," said Chester. "We just wanted to see you. You've had an accident but you're going to be okay."

Suddenly JB's eyes took on a scared look and he tried to say something, but it just came out as "--- see".

"If you can see me, blink your eyes, okay?" said Chester. To their relief JB slowly blinked. Then he tried to speak again and it sounded like "blurry".

"You've just had brain surgery—" Chester began. As soon as he said it, they all looked at each other. Then he hastily added. "But you're going to be fine. The surgeon said so."

"Blink your eyes if you remember the accident," said Freddie. JB just stared at her and then she said, "JB, blink your eyes if you know who I am." JB blinked and she sighed with relief. She reached out and patted his shoulder. "Good old JB. We'll get you out of here soon…"

Just then, his mother rushed in. "Oh Jerry, you're awake! No, don't try to say anything. I'm here, darling." His mother wiped tears off her cheeks and the three friends filled her in about what they knew.

"Thank you, thank you for being such good friends," she said and turned back to her son.

"Uh… we'll come see you soon, JB," said Freddie.

"Take care, eh," said Toby.

"Hang in, man," said Chester.

When they got off the Skytrain half an hour later, it was starting to get dark. Toby and Chester walked Freddie back to her building, which was quite near to the skateboard bowl. She shivered as they passed by the scene of the accident.

"I know that JB isn't one of the Odd S-ers, but you've been a good friend to him, Chester. He's actually okay, once you get to know him."

"You're a good friend too, Freddie," Chester replied and then Toby saw him wink, "but I didn't know you were his girlfriend."

She punched him arm playfully and said, "If you want the info, you have to use a little imagination."

They left her with the agreement to keep in touch about JB.

Chapter 16
Toby's Day in Court

Mr. Getty called Toby that weekend to say that his lawyer friend could meet with them after school on Monday. The hearing was to be on Thursday. Toby didn't mind missing the day of school since it was an even day. What a tough week— but he'd have a long weekend after. They were heading to Truewind Island for Easter. Maybe Alyssa would be there too.

At school on Monday, all the talk was about JB. Students clustered in little groups discussing the accident and the counselors made an announcement that they were available for anyone who needed to talk.

"I psyched myself up and went to see him," Alyssa told Toby. "Freddie was there. She wasn't real happy to see me."

"How is he?"

"He seemed okay. Freddie said he has blurred vision. He was in a wheelchair and has to be pushed around. His co-ordination is like, pretty bad."

"He'll get better, Alyssa. Chester told me they're trying to get him into G.F. Strong for some rehabilitation."

"I apologized for screaming," she sighed, "but JB didn't remember anything about the accident. Do you think they have him sedated?"

"Probably. Look, it's good you went to see him, Alyssa. I can't visit him right now, but Chester is keeping me posted." Toby paused and then added, "I've got this court case coming up—it's on Thursday. You remember the incident at the mansion I told you about?"

Her eyes widened, "Oh, I had forgotten about that. Good luck, eh. Hey, we better head to science class."

There was a light rain that day, but the students were eager to finish their lessons and get out into the verdant courtyard.

"April showers bring May flowers. Let's make hay out there," sang out Ms. Tanaka. As the students rushed out, she asked Toby to stay behind.

"I met your friend, Mr. Getty, on the Pro-D day. He said you had spoken to him about me." She paused and Toby fidgeted nervously. "It's always great to find a fellow communicator, so maybe your intuition was right. I understand that he was the one who told Beogall about you. You may not know this, but the bird community has high hopes for Beogall. He's a very talented young bird and dedicated to better relations with humans. Even if he is rather impetuous." Her eyes twinkled. "Like you."

"Who chose you, Ms. T?" Toby blurted out, realizing the second it came out of his mouth that he had just fulfilled her description.

"It's a personal matter, Toby. I'm sure you'll find out eventually, but right now, I think you have more important things on your mind. Gerald, I mean Mr. Getty, told me about your court case. Toby, I'm very impressed with what you did."

Toby turned a pale shade of crimson as she continued, "I discussed it with my father and he is willing to help fund the environmental lawyer that Mr. Getty knows. Would you mind if my father and I attend the meeting that's planned for after school?"

Toby thought his jaw would hit the floor. "That would be awesome!" he finally squeaked out. "I'd totally love to meet your father!"

Imagine getting help from the great Dr. Lawrence Tanaka! His sense of dread about the court case lifted from his shoulders. "I've been doing some research about protection legislation. I found out that they've been trying to water it down, but that hasn't gotten too far and …"

Ms. Tanaka interrupted him gently. "That's great Toby, but we really have to get out to the courtyard now, and I'm sure we'll have a chance to talk about this at the lawyer's office."

As they went to join the others, Toby could see that some were curious about why he had stayed behind, but he didn't care. Lawrence Tanaka was going to help him! And if some students were wondering why his eyes were shining after speaking to their science teacher, Chester was there to put in a quiet suggestion that it was probably about their plans for Truewind Island.

Ms. Sharma's office was downtown, and she welcomed Toby and his dad warmly. She was on the younger side for a lawyer, Toby thought, and very pretty, with jet black hair tied back stylishly and intelligent, dark eyes. She was busy squeezing more chairs into her tiny office, helped by Mr. Feldman, who had been prevailed upon to attend the meeting.

Mr. Getty and the Tanakas arrived soon after and introductions were made all around.

"I've heard good things about you, Toby," said Dr. Tanaka. He looked just like he did on television, an older, medium-built man with an unruly mop of salt and pepper hair. The same thoughtful mannerisms and that famous, friendly voice. "And you were very brave in attempting to save that ecosystem at the mansion property. It's truly a treasure."

Toby's chest swelled a little as he took a seat next to the famous scientist.

"This case is attracting a lot of interest in the environmental community," began Ms. Sharma. "I think there is enough left of the protection legislation to counter-act the trespassing charge."

"Ms. Sharma and I have discussed the matter, Toby," said Mr. Feldman, seated next to her with a pleased smile. "We will argue that you were justified in going to the property to check on the protected species there."

"Yes, and there's that one corner of the property that had never been logged or anything," Toby said with relish, "where the two old yellow cedars were. There's super old Douglas fir and hemlock there too. The old stumps and snags are where the pileated woodpeckers like to hang out. There are lots of bird species, like—"

"Toby, I think we should stick to the two protected species in our argument," Ms. Sharma said gently as his father gave him a sharp look.

"If I put you on the stand, you might be asked to elaborate," added Mr. Feldman. "But I think it best to keep it as simple as possible. Not everyone knows as much about these things as you do."

"Or even needs to know," Ms. Sharma added kindly and turned to Lars. "Have you and Toby spoken about putting him on the stand?"

"Yes, he'd very much like to since he has spent a lot of time researching this," replied Lars a bit warily.

They talked about how Ms. Sharma could assist Mr. Feldman and she thanked Dr. Tanaka for his support. "Some of my hours will be pro bono, as it's such an important case. But I think you are all too aware of how many worthy ones there are and how hard it is to fund them. And we're faced with deep pockets on the other side."

"My foundation is quite interested in this case," Dr. Tanaka remarked. "You probably know that we are working to restore and expand protection legislation on endangered species.

We've applied for a permit to view the site and we will be going there in two days. Would you like to accompany us?"

"I'd love to!" responded Ms. Sharma immediately.

Toby practically leapt out of his seat but his dad reached out a restraining hand. Mr. Feldman said sternly, "It would *not* be a good idea for you to go there at this point, Toby. It could muddy the proceedings, especially until your trespassing charge has been dealt with."

Well, that was that. He wondered if he would ever get another chance to see the place he had called home for as long as he could remember.

On the day of the hearing, Toby and his father arrived early at the imposing courthouse. They wore new, inexpensive jackets, having left all their suits at the mansion. During a quick meeting with the lawyers, they found out there was a lot of media presence. It hadn't taken long for word to get out that Dr. Tanaka was supporting their case.

Mr. Feldman looked happy and confident as he gathered their team in the cavernous courthouse foyer to review last minute details. Toby wondered if their lawyer was more pleased about the media coverage or working with the slim and lovely Ms. Sharma. After their meeting a few days earlier, Toby had overheard him saying to her, "I've been reading about your work. This case is so interesting that I am considering taking on another environmental case that has come to my attention. Perhaps I could speak to you about it over lunch sometime, Ms. Sharma?"

This wasn't match-making that Toby had intended, but wasn't he a bit of an expert now? His musings were cut short by the arrival of Suchno Whenge wearing an expensive three-piece suit. Toby heard some people use the term "Lord" as he blustered in followed by a team of lawyers and Duffin

Wint. Across the wide hall, he fixed Lars and then Toby with a steely stare and then strode off to huddle with his team.

"Well, well," said Mr. Feldman quietly, "I see Lord Whenge has employed the top three lawyers in the country. They don't come cheap." Toby gulped and the lawyer quickly added, "But we've got a good team here."

Walter arrived looking a little uncomfortable in a slightly wrinkled suit. Then Chester cut his way through the lobby towards them. Toby's eyes widened. His friend's dreadlocks were tied back in a ponytail and he wore a jacket, slacks and of all things, a tie, albeit wildly patterned. The two gave each other a high-five.

Neither of the science teachers could be there because of their teaching duties, but said they would be waiting by the phone after school to hear the news. With a sinking heart, Toby looked around for his mother, but she was nowhere in sight. Hadn't his father even told her?

The doors were opened and as they entered the courtroom, Anna Feathers rushed in. She gave Toby a quick hug before squeezing into the public gallery, among the reporters who overflowed the media area.

Mr. Feldman outlined their case and put Toby on the stand first. After swearing him in, the judge admonished the reporters not to name him, due to his age. Looking around he saw Duffin Wint's angry glare trained on him.

"I heard from our gardener that they hired someone to cut down trees," Toby replied to the first question. "I knew Walter had filed papers to get some of the trees protected, especially the yellow cedars...."

"Who is Walter?" asked the judge. "Give his full name, please."

"Walter McBean is... *was*, the gardener my parents had employed to maintain the grounds," answered Toby. "He alerted us that trees were being cut down and birds were being killed." Toby didn't think that it could hurt when a small sob got the better of him.

On cross-examination, Whenge's lawyer asked how he knew birds were killed, what proof he had and how reliable Walter was.

"Isn't it true, *Master* Myers, that you were the one who encouraged the gardener to file for the protection papers? That you were the one who took such interest in the preservation of that property?" asked one of the suits.

Toby reminded himself not to get riled. "Walter and I are both interested in the natural life on that property. It has some of the only remaining old growth trees in Vancouver. I don't think my parents knew that when they bought the place, but Walter quickly figured it out. It was his idea to file protection papers because I didn't know much about it then."

"Now Master Myers, you were the one who did the Internet research, were you not?"

"Yes, and I found out that almost one quarter of the property was eligible for protection. It was all done legally, with the signature of the owner at the time," replied Toby, glancing at his father.

This was a sore point with his dad, who had signed a paper Walter handed him at the time without understanding the implications. Such protection, once activated, impacted any and all future owners, who now was none other than Suchno Whenge. The man was fuming.

They had no further questions.

Mr. Feldman raised the assault charge and brought Chester to the stand as a witness. Chester surprised them with pictures of what Toby looked like in the hospital after the attack. Could he have really looked that bad? Toby wondered as the pictures were entered into evidence.

Listening to the events leading up to and after the attack, Toby was once again thankful that Chester was there that day.

"And tell us what happened to the weapon Mr. Wint had, on the day in question," posed Mr. Feldman.

"I was afraid that it might be used on Toby or the birds, so when Mr. Wint dropped it to punch Toby, I hid it."

Duffin had been watching resentfully and now his face reddened.

On cross-examination, Chester was so clear, concise and calm, that all they could do was get him to admit that he knew he was trespassing. They tried to dispute the contents of the video, but Chester proved to be a reliable witness. He knew the exact times all the events had occurred. They soon gave up.

Toby was back on the stand to face Duffin's lawyer about the assault charge. "Were you or were you not aware that you were trespassing?"

"I was aware, but I…"

"And did you deliberately avoid the areas of the fence which were alarmed?"

"I did, but it was because…"

"Please stick to the question. And did you or did you not invite an accomplice to accompany you?"

"I asked my friend to come along," said Toby and quickly added, "but he only came to help me take pictures of the destruction."

"So, you took the pictures and then saw Mr. Wint, who asked you to leave, *because you were trespassing*. Is that correct?"

"Yes." Toby squirmed in his seat.

"Did you leave immediately?"

"I was prepared to leave," replied Toby. He remembered his dad's trick of becoming dead calm when the pressure was on. "But Duffin had a gun pointed at me and I could see he was upset."

"Stick to the question. You didn't leave right away and the video proves it."

"I began backing away slowly. Mr. Wint was scaring me."

"Did you or did you not tell him that the world would be watching his actions?"

"At that point I was hoping to come out alive, so yes, I told him the world would be watching. It may have saved my life, because he was really mad and then he…."

"That is all for now," said the lawyer. "We would like to call Walter McBean to the stand."

Walter looked a little nervous as he made his way to the stand and got sworn in.

"What is your occupation?"

"I'm acting head gardener of Stanley Park."

This threw both teams. Toby found out later that Walter had used Lars' glowing reference to get a job with the Vancouver Parks Board. They were so impressed with his knowledge and skills that after a few weeks on the job he had been moved into the vacant position of acting head gardener.

Whenge's lawyer was clearly taken aback, but proceeded. "What was your position at the Myers', now Lord Whenge's, mansion?"

"I was gardener and groundsman there for five years."

"What are your qualifications?"

As he listed them off, Lars and Toby looked at each other. Lars leaned over and whispered, "I should have been paying him more." They later discovered that Walter had been taking courses at the local technical institute the entire time he was with them.

"Is it true, Mr. McBean, that you were let go from employment at the mansion?"

"Yes, the new owner, Mr. Whenge, did not want me there. I tried to tell him about the important natural value of the property. It is home to some rare—"

"Please just answer the question," the lawyer interrupted. "So, you were let go. And did you tell the Myers about the cut trees? Even though it was no longer their property?"

"Yes, I did. I spent a lot of time preserving that property in its natural state and—"

"Again, please just answer the question. Did you collude with the Myers in their plan to trespass—"

"Objection, your honour," Mr. Feldman jumped up.

"Go ahead and answer the question, Mr. McBean," ordered the judge. "Did you know about the plan?"

"No. I didn't suggest any plan to them. I hoped that they would do something, but I wasn't part of it."

Whenge's lawyer quickly gave up.

Ms. Sharma leaned over to whisper to Mr. Feldman, before he got up to put questions to Walter.

"Mr. McBean, can you tell the court about the rare plants and animals on the grounds of Mr. Whenge's mansion?"

Walter rattled off an extensive list of rare plants, small animals and amphibians, including their Latin names.

"And can you tell us which ones were registered?"

"I knew the value of the two yellow cypress so I registered them both. I also registered an endangered red-legged frog that can be found on the property."

"And what made you decide to do this?" asked Mr. Feldman.

"They have incredible natural heritage value. When protection legislation came in a few years ago—well, it seemed the right thing to do. The boy, Toby, was always interested in nature and I wanted to teach him about the process. He was good at Internet research and showed me his findings. So we went ahead," Walter shifted uncomfortably in his seat, "with Mr. Myers' consent, of course."

"And can you explain to the court why you went to tell the Myers what was going on at the mansion?"

"After he let me go, Mr. Whenge hired a groundsman to cut down trees. When I returned to get the last of my tools the next day, Mr. Wint over there," Walter waved in the direction of the frowning former butler, "showed me the carcasses of birds and I saw a lot of trees down. I didn't even know about the yellow cedars at the time, as they are—were, at the very back of the property."

"And what transpired between you and Mr. Wint?"

"He told me Lord Whenge didn't care about the wildlife and wasn't interested in any heritage values. He said they were in charge now and could do what they wanted."

"Thank you, Mr. McBean. Next, I'd like to call on Dr. Lawrence Tanaka."

As Lawrence Tanaka made his way forward, Toby sat on the edge of his seat. Mr. Feldman had the scientist describe what he had seen on the property two days earlier.

"So Mr. Tanaka, are you telling the court that the two yellow cedars chopped down by Mr. Whenge's new groundsman were the only yellow cedars of that age in the lower mainland?"

"Yellow cedars or yellow cypresses, their correct name, are a slow-growing tree found normally at mid to high eleva-tion," he answered in that famous voice. "These ones were unique, and we've determined they were over 700 years old. We're not sure how they got there. They weren't just unique to Vancouver, but may have been the only fully mature yellow cedars at low elevation anywhere in the province."

There was an audible gasp in the courtroom, as those present realized the enormity of what had been lost.

"And is it true that your foundation is taking steps to ensure that there will be no further losses on this property?"

"Objection!" The head lawyer for the other team leapt to his feet as Whenge growled. "That is not part of this court case."

"Since the boy is charged with trespassing and since he was there to film protected trees, let's hear what Dr. Tanaka has to say," ruled the judge.

"In our visit there," Dr. Tanaka waved toward Ms. Sharma, "we discovered that the mansion property is indeed a fabulous natural treasure-trove. We applied for an injunction to stop any further damage to wildlife there. It was granted yesterday."

There were some strangled cries from Whenge's side of the courtroom. Ms. Sharma strode over and delivered an official form to Suchno Whenge.

"Order in the court," the judge called as explosive conversation broke out.

Whenge ripped the document from her hand and flung it to one of his lawyers.

"The injunction served today to Mr. Whenge means there will be no further work on the property, pending the outcome of a court hearing. Is that correct, Dr. Tanaka?" asked Mr. Feldman. The judge looked on with a frown.

The scientist allowed a smile to creep over his face. "Yes. My foundation will be taking Mr. Whenge to court over the illegal cutting of protected trees and damage to the habitat of endangered species."

The air went out of Whenge's lawyers. They had no further questions. Whenge stared straight ahead with a stony glare.

"You will hear my verdict on both the trespassing and the assault charge by next week," said the judge.

The hearing had only lasted the morning.

Leaving the courthouse, they were beset by reporters but had agreed that only Mr. Feldman and Ms. Sharma would speak to the press.

"Way to go, Chester," Toby whispered as the media collected like wasps around the two lawyers. "Aren't you glad there's no school tomorrow? I wanna see what's in the press before we go back."

"Yeah, hey, you did real well. Congrats. We've definitely earned our long weekend off. It'll be okay at school, Toby—it's only the Odd S-ers that know about the hearing and they're cool."

Lawrence Tanaka extracted himself from a reporter and came over. "You boys can be proud for having halted the destruction of irreplaceable habitat. I'd like to write an article about this case and the mansion property. Would it be okay if I include how you young men saved it? No names, of course."

The two friends agreed, grinning at each other.

"I think I'll call you *eco-warriors*," the scientist said. "Heaven knows we'll need more young people to help our foundering environment."

Toby and Chester's grins threatened to split their faces in two.

Over a late lunch, they replayed details from the hearing.

"Wonderful news about your new position, Walter," said Lars with a tight smile. "You did a great job on the stand. But I have no recollection of giving my consent for registering those protected species."

"Well, Mr. Myers, you were always so busy," replied their ex-gardener, "but thanks for not letting on."

Lars was the only one who didn't laugh.

"You boys did a super job on the stand," said Mr. Feldman. Ms. Sharma nodded and Toby noticed she was sitting very close to him.

"We'll be trying for an early court date on the injunction," she added.

"Yes, and we have Toby to thank for his research and Walter for all his work on saving that property," said Dr. Tanaka.

"I'm glad everyone thinks we did well," said Lars looking pointedly at Toby, "but I'm not anxious to be part of any more court cases. Or to hear about anymore trespassing."

As the dishes were cleared away Toby noticed his dad's pained expression and it occurred to him that Walter was probably better off now than them. *Ironic.* He decided to be extra nice to his father.

The team split up to go their separate ways, but as Toby, Lars and Chester found their way back to the parking lot, a darkened limo crept by slowly before continuing on down the street.

Chapter 17

Easter

They were sitting at the well-used wooden kitchen table at Grams' house. Her eyes were shining. Lars had just filled her in about the court case. Toby could tell that she took an instant liking to both Chester and Anna.

"Now tell me about the camping trip that your class is planning," she said, pouring them all a second cup of green tea and pushing muffins towards Toby and Chester.

"Well, Ms. Tanaka has heard about the bird sanctuary," Toby mumbled as he took a bite of cranberry-oat muffin, "and she wants to take the class there." He had told her a little about Odd S, but wasn't sure how she would feel about a large group visiting Westwind.

"And you say there are several in the class who can communicate with birds?" she inquired.

"Yes—almost half the class. Some of them are just beginners, others are learning to communicate with other creatures... " Toby cast a quick glance at his father, whose brows were knit together.

While Grams was considering that, Chester added, "Ms. Tanaka also wants to visit the Oyster Narrows reserve and the museum. Raven, a girl in our class, has an aunt who lives there."

"Your teacher could also speak to Fern Strong's mother, Irene Cedar Root," added Grams. She paused, then seemed to make up her mind, "Yes, I think I'll take you out to the bird sanctuary this afternoon. You can meet Grandmother Eagle and ask her yourself directly. She would enjoy meeting you, Chester."

"I have some work to do on your deck, Mom," Lars quickly said. "I'll look at the upstairs faucet for you too."

"Very well, Lars. But I hope you'll come, Anna?" invited Grams.

Anna was delighted and soon they all piled into the car.

As they emerged from the trail, Chester stumbled. Toby grabbed him. "Whoa, are you okay?"

"Powerful vibes up here," said his friend, recovering. As if to accentuate what he said, a bird symphony began. The small group listened, rapt.

Grandmother Eagle circled down and stretched out her legs to land on a lower branch of the old fir. "I saw you coming," she kreed, craning her head toward them.

"Yes, and I saw you floating up in the clouds on our way here," laughed Grams.

"You have good eyesight for one so old," chortled the bird. Grams didn't seem the least offended. Then the eagle turned to scrutinize Chester. "So this is young Chester. Son of Lester Oldwin?"

Chester nodded gravely.

Grandmother Eagle turned to Anna. "And who are you?"

Anna introduced herself awkwardly—she was not at all adept at bird communication. The old eagle grew impatient and turned back to Chester. "Your father. He was a great bird communicator, but we haven't seen him of late. How is he?"

"He's been working with homeless people. He says that's his calling," replied Chester. "He doesn't get out of the city much anymore."

"You must come and meet Grandfather Gull—old Windrunner. He will want to hear about your father." With that she flew off to the arbutus tree clinging to the western-most cliff.

The four followed to where the gull sat hunched on the large rock beneath his favourite tree. He seemed to have aged even more since Toby first met him. The eagle was speaking to him in a language that Toby couldn't understand.

The old gull perked up and peered in their direction, craning his neck. "Lester Oldwin? And you say that his son is here? Show yourself, boy!"

"Grandfather, I am Chester Oldwin, son of Lester," Chester stated respectfully. "Grandson of Dewitt."

Grams gasped, eyes widening. "I didn't know," she whispered softly.

Toby's jaw dropped—he was speechless.

"Dewitt—the first one. Is Dewitt still alive?" asked the old gull after a prolonged silence.

"Yes, but he's not that well. He's living in a home for seniors and I... I don't see him much. He has problems with his vision and his hearing is going."

"Happens to us all," Windrunner cackled. "Dewitt Oldwin..." His voice trailed off. After a few seconds, he came back to the present. "Well, you go visit him boy, and give him my regards. Has he told you the old stories?"

"Yes, he says they must not be forgotten."

"Your grandfather and my great-grandfather," Windrunner mused. "They were the first ones to communicate. You know that, don't you boy?" he croaked.

"Yes, my grandfather rescued the first Windrunner in the middle of a storm. He was working on a fishing boat. He nursed the gull back from near death even though the others laughed at him," Chester recited.

Toby shivered.

"They learned that they could communicate." The gull took up the story. "They developed the first human-bird-bond.

He lived a long time, my great-grandfather. Then his son…" his voice trailed off again. "And how is your father?" he asked finally.

Grandmother Eagle said something Toby didn't understand but Chester nodded.

Grams whispered, "The ancient tongue."

"It has come full circle. I send greetings to your father." Windrunner now spoke with renewed strength and stood up tall on the rock. "You did right by coming out here to see me." Then he too spoke in the ancient tongue and Chester replied.

Who exactly is this friend of mine? Toby wondered.

Grandmother Eagle spoke but when Windrunner tried to reply, he started wheezing.

"We should go now," kreed the eagle. "Grandfather tires easily these days. Other gulls have to bring him fish." With a few flaps of her wings, she was back at her own tree.

"Good-bye, Grandfather," they said but he had nodded off.

Toby's thoughts were all jumbled. "What were you saying back there?" he asked Chester.

"Just about my family," replied Chester with a catch in his throat.

When they got back to the eagle's tree, Toby remembered to ask, "Grandmother, would it be okay if we brought our class up here? We're going to be camping on Truewind Island and the students want to see this bird sanctuary."

"Hmph. A class up here? Well, Grandfather Gull may not be up to it… When is it?"

"In three weeks."

"I've heard good things about this group and your teacher. Tell me more."

After Toby and Chester told her about how several others could communicate with birds, she said slowly, "I have been talking about the importance of bird-human communication all my life. This is an opportunity. I will be pleased to talk to the class and other birds may want to as well."

Dozens of birds flew up from the surrounding trees where they must have been waiting and listening. As birds flapped around them, Anna's eyes were glistening. A warbler landed on Toby's shoulder and its mate on Chester's. The two boys grinned at each other.

Grams gulped and said, "I, too, have been waiting a long time to see greater communication between people and birds."

Grandmother Eagle called for silence. "The serious matter we were discussing before has come to pass. We have heard that a developer is buying this sanctuary land to build a housing development. How can they do this? What do you know, Carol Myers?"

"I did hear that someone's been trying to buy Westwind. I fear that this deal is near completion. I don't know what can be done." Grams wrung her hands and the warblers on Toby and Chester's shoulders trilled angrily.

"Maybe we could help. I mean our Odd S class," said Chester.

"Yes. We can ask the Tanakas and Ms. Sharma, too," said Toby, eyes gleaming.

The bird chatter lightened at this and a few ideas were tossed around before the foursome had to make their good-byes. They drove back in silence. Anna seemed overcome with emotion, Grams and Toby were deep in thought and Chester was inscrutable as he gazed quietly out the window over the rural landscape.

The next morning, Toby said, "I'll show you around, since you have to leave tomorrow, Chester. I'll take you over to the Stronghold."

"The Stronghold—what's that?"

"It's where Alyssa's cousins live. The Strongs. You'll like them."

As they approached, the twins dashed out to see them. "Alyssa's here," one of them called out, Toby didn't know which one. "Holly and her saw you coming."

"Yes, the town mouse and the country mouse are here together," said the other and they both burst into giggles.

Toby and Chester exchanged glances, mystified.

"Oh, it's just their little joke about Alyssa and me. And we call them Giggle and Gaggle," said Holly grinning as she greeted them at the door. "Hi Chester, I'm Holly, aka the country mouse." Taz, their dog, jumped up and gave each of them an excited lick.

Soon Chester and Holly were talking like old friends. Mrs. Strong invited them for tea in a gathering that reminded Toby of his first visit there. Even little Gemmie crawled up onto his lap again.

"Black," she said touching Chester's face. He was seated next to Toby. Her eyes grew big. Then she tugged on his dreadlocks. "Where did they come from?"

"It's not polite to ask questions like that, Gemmie," said Holly, embarrassed. "There are lots of people who have hair and skin like that. You just haven't seen them yet."

"It's okay, really it is," protested Chester, laughing. "And where did you get your big, blue eyes, Gemmie?" he asked her.

"From my dada," replied the toddler seriously, and everyone laughed.

Granny Renie had been following the conversation with interest and was now studying Chester. "Are you the one?" she abruptly asked. The others stared.

Chester looked at her seriously. "I don't know," he said quietly.

Granny Renie said something in what sounded to Toby like the old language again. Chester answered her. She sighed, reached out and held his hand. "I've been waiting for you. But you're just a boy." She spoke again in the old language. This time Toby thought she said, "You need to help Toby here. With the work he has to do."

Chester nodded.

"Chester has helped me a lot already," blurted Toby. "I couldn't ask for more."

The other two stared.

"So it's true what they say about you, Toby—you pick up languages fast," said the old woman. "But you both have much to do. You must help the birds. And you girls must help too," she said, waving a gnarled hand at Alyssa and Holly.

They sat looking at each other awkwardly.

Gemmie broke the sudden hush when she crawled over to Chester's lap and played with his dreadlocks. "I want a dolly that looks just like you."

Everyone laughed, and the mood lightened.

"Weren't you talking about visiting Fairwind today, Holly and Alyssa?"

"Yes! Hey Mom," said Holly excitedly, "could you drive us? We'll show Chester and Toby around."

"We want to go too!" the twins wailed.

"You can go next time, Judy and Jeanie," said their mother. "Besides, I need you to look after Gemmie." Little Gemmie smiled up at the grumbling twins and held out her arms to be picked up.

There were lots of visitors in the town of Fairwind for the holiday weekend. As they strolled about, Holly introduced the two boys to lots of people that she knew. Chester drew some stares.

"Fairwind is kind of small," offered Holly. "Don't often see people with dreadlocks around here" Then she quickly added, "But I like them."

"It's okay. I've been stared at before," said Chester.

"Hey—there's a beach close to town," said Alyssa. "Let's go there."

Loads of kids were hanging out at Moraine Beach. Soon they were wading and splashing in the shallow water getting soaked. Toby noticed Chester and Holly clinging to each other, laughing.

"Hey, why don't you come back here tonight? We're having a party," said one of the locals as they were leaving.

"Thanks, but we've already made plans," Holly replied.

On the long walk home, she told them that she wasn't allowed to go to beach parties, which sometimes got out of hand.

"What are those plans you mentioned, anyway?" asked Chester, nudging her.

"Well, there's a pretty cool movie on tonight. Wanna go?"

"Let's!" exclaimed the others together.

When Toby crawled into bed that night, he had trouble falling asleep. The old cot had been set up for Chester.

"Are you awake?" Toby asked quietly.

"Yes."

He could see Chester's eyes open, gleaming in the faint light of the crescent moon.

"Where did you learn to communicate in the old language?"

"My father taught me and he was taught by his father. The first Windrunner taught him. I think I'll go see my grandfather. He'd be happy to know that I've seen Windrunner," Chester paused, calculating, "four."

"You're such a show-off at math," said Toby. He could hear Chester chuckle. "What did Granny Renie mean when she asked if you were the one?"

"I dunno… but," Chester sounded a little self-conscious, "my parents are protective of what they call my 'gifts'. But they also say that I'll have to use them for good."

"What do you think it is that we're supposed to do?"

"I think we're supposed to speak for those who can't speak for themselves. My parents told me that anyways, and it makes sense. They said there are others willing to help. Toby, you've already helped with what you did at the mansion property."

"I couldn't have done it without you, though."

"Eco-warriors stick together. Hey, what can we do about Westwind?"

"To start with—research," groaned Toby and they both laughed. "You know, I think Holly likes you."

"I like her too. She's pretty cute. And you know what? I think Alyssa is warming up to you."

"Really?"

"Yeah, man. A couple of times I noticed her looking at you. I think she wanted you to hold her hand at the movie tonight."

Toby leaned over and swiped his friend. "Yeah, well I didn't see you holding Holly's hand."

"Yet," said Chester, and swiped him back.

They didn't talk any more but Toby was awake for a long time and he thought Chester was too.

He woke up in the middle of the night in a cold sweat. In his dream a huge storm raged at Westwind. Wind tore at the trees until finally the old arbutus toppled over, taking Grandfather Gull with it. The bird couldn't save himself and plummeted into the frigid waves. Under the tree, jutting out of the newly exposed ground were some old bones. Beogall was there in the clearing, flapping his great wings, saying, "What does it mean, what does it mean?"

Toby had a strange feeling that he had had this dream before. He didn't want to wake Chester, but really wanted to ask him about his dreams—did everyone have dreams that seemed, like, *to mean something*? It took a long time for sleep to come.

The next morning, Chester had to catch an early ferry back to have Easter supper with his family. Toby walked over to the Stronghold but the place was a madhouse and the girls ignored him since they had to help with Easter preparations. He wandered back forlornly, stopping a few times to listen to birds.

When Anna and Grams were occupied with Easter supper preparations, he asked his dad, "Have you heard from Mom?"

"I phoned her about the court case. She was sorry she missed it but said something had come up."

"Why didn't you tell me?" Toby demanded.

His dad shifted uncomfortably. Toby slammed the door on his way outside. The sparrow, Rio, was there but he didn't feel like talking. A host of chickadees flitted busily in the shrubbery but Toby ignored them—he needed to think.

What would it be like to communicate with all the creatures like Chester? He heard a new sound and looked up to see two starlings chattering in an old alder. With his ability growing daily, Toby realized life would never be the same. The starlings stared at him briefly and then continued their conversation.

Easter dinner was a wonderful baked squash casserole, savoury roast vegetables and warm, fragrant buns. Grams insisted on a grace of what they were thankful for. "We should always count our blessings," she said for about the hundredth time.

Not my mother keeping in touch with me, Toby thought. "I'm thankful for my friends," is what he said aloud.

They got back to the condo early the following morning— his father wanted to beat the ferry rush. There was a message waiting from his mom.

"Tobias dear, hope you had a wonderful Easter. Sorry to have missed the court hearing, but I'm proud of you. Let's be in touch."

Was this her idea of meaningful communication? He sent her a quick message back. He had practicing to do and could hear that Chester must have had the same thought, even through the concrete ceiling. He pounded on the floor in a signal they had devised and sure enough a few minutes later, Chester showed up. They did some jamming together and then headed over to the basketball courts.

"I went to see him," said Chester on their way over.

"You mean JB?" Since the accident, they hadn't been back to the skatebowl. Chester nodded. "Is he still at G.F. Strong?"

"No, he's home now. Some therapist comes in. He's got a teacher that visits and gives him lessons. He's in a wheelchair but is getting a lot of movement back."

"Does Freddie visit him?"

"Yep. Regularly. Someone else does too."

"Who?"

"Flame."

"Never heard of him."

"Her. She's a robin."

"Holy crap! Seriously?"

"Yep. She saw the accident and started hanging around his apartment. When JB sat out on the balcony, she started landing there."

"JB can't communicate with her though, can he?"

"He's just beginning. All that time sitting around. He had heard the rumours about us Odd S-ers, so he decided to try listening to her. His vision is still blurry but his hearing is excellent."

"JB talking to birds. You know what this means, don't you?"

"What?"

"If JB can learn, anyone can learn." Toby started laughing so hard that Chester joined in. People walking by gave them strange looks.

That evening, his mother finally phoned him. She asked about the court case, and then he found out the reason why she couldn't be there.

"Tobias dear, I have some news for you," she announced near the end of their conversation. "I had an appointment on the morning of your court case—to see the doctor. I'm pregnant. You'll be having a little brother or a sister in six months."

Chapter 18
The Camping Trip

"You've been pretty quiet today. What's up?" asked Chester. It was Tuesday morning after the long weekend and they were at their lockers. Toby stood staring numbly into his.

"Just stuff. People've been badgering me about the court case," Toby complained. "I just don't feel like talking about it." With so much to think about, it felt like his head would explode.

"Get over it, man. You may as well learn to deal with stuff like that."

Toby looked at Chester sharply. It didn't sound like his friend.

"Like, I mean, only the Odd S-ers know that you're the one from the news reports," Chester explained. "Ms. T is cool, she'll help them handle it. You'll see."

He was right. Ms. Tanaka discussed the court case for a few minutes and then she said, "That's it for now class, and if you want more information, just read the papers or get the news on-line. No decision has been made in the case, so let's let Toby have some peace." Toby mentally noted to be eternally grateful to her. "He'll tell us when he has news. Now we need to get down to planning our camping trip to Truewind Island!"

The class mood changed in an instant. They clamoured for information.

"As you know, we'll be visiting the Westwind Bird Sanctuary. I hope you'll meet Grandmother Eagle, an old and venerable bird," said Ms. Tanaka. "The area has been used by the birds practically forever, and of course, I know you will show the utmost respect. I'm happy to report that we will also be visiting the Oyster Narrows First Nations there. Raven will tell us about that next class."

Everyone talked animatedly about Truewind as they raced out to the courtyard. Ms. Tanaka kept Toby behind for a few minutes. "Would you be willing to talk about Westwind to the class?" she asked him.

"Sure," he agreed. "Um, Ms. T, how do you know about it?"

"I know of many important bird meeting places. I visited Westwind once with my father. Besides," her eyes twinkled, "a little birdie told me about your visits there."

A few days later, Toby's father had some news. "I heard from the lawyer today. The trespassing charges against you were stayed."

It felt as if an elephant had climbed off his chest.

"But there's going to be a note in your file. You're not to be found in the vicinity of the mansion."

"That's not fair!"

"I think you're lucky. But listen to this—Duffin has been charged with assault. He has to serve a probationary sentence doing community service."

"What does that mean, Dad?" asked Toby.

"Oh, he'll have to put in some community hours, picking up garbage or working in a senior day program or something like that."

Toby hooted as that picture played out in his mind.

"Whenge was given a hefty fine for cutting down the trees but charges were dropped about killing the birds, due to lack of evidence."

Toby was outraged.

"But Toby, we carried the day," argued his father. "I know that a big fine is not much of a deterrent for a wealthy man like Suchno, but the publicity and loss of face will be awful for him, not to mention the court injunction against further cutting. In fact it worries me a little."

It worried Toby too. The man would seek some sort of revenge.

Such troubling thoughts had little time to linger—the new term was in full swing and homework was being laid on like crazy.

When Ms. T announced the verdict to the Odd S-ers, there were hoots and cheers and much slapping of Toby's back. By then, they were eagerly getting ready for their camping trip and teachers were making them do double duty since they would be missing two days of lessons.

Toby awoke to a violent rain-storm the day they were supposed to leave. His dad drove him and his gear to school saying, "I don't like the look of this weather. Call me if your plans change."

No-one was overly disappointed when Ms. Tanaka announced that the trip would be postponed until the next day. "While rain is part of camping, I don't know if everyone has the type of gear required," she added.

"What about the birds and animals?" called out Robert. Everyone stared at him since he was usually so quiet. "They have to live outside with rain all the time."

"Very true, Robert. That's what I appreciate so much about this class. You are always thinking about the natural world and have such compassion." Robert's normally dull grey eyes shone. "But we are just part of the natural world, even though we do such unnatural things to it!"

Ms. Tanaka turned and wrote on the board, *I live like a* _____.

G.G. Neilson

Her students were mystified. Then she explained, "Since we're caught up in the science curriculum and since we can't work outside today, I will share something with you that has great meaning in my life.

"Grandparents can be an anchor for us. My grandfather died a long time ago, but my grandmother only recently. When I was about your age, she said to me that she lives like a maple tree. I asked her what that meant and here's what she told me.

'I am old but strong. I put down roots into the ground and hold it in place in storms. In my branches I support wildlife as I stand rooted to the same spot. I provide strength to the community around me by living like a maple tree.'

"Then she asked me what I live like. I had never thought about it before, but I realized that I was a lot different than her. What popped into my head was that I live like a hummingbird. I am curious and I like to travel and see the world. I am small but fast and I can be fierce when I need to be.

"I'll never forget how my grandmother smiled when I said that. Then she said, 'We need all types in the world. Everyone has their special role to play'.

"When she died recently, I thought about how she had lived her life. How she stayed in one place and had deep roots in her community. But like the hummingbird, I like to migrate. Many of us teachers like to leave in the summer – maybe it's to rejuvenate. But we return every fall to do our work with a new group of students.

"Now in your camping groups, I want you to answer this." She pointed up to the board as each student pondered how to answer.

In Toby's camping group were Michael, Chester and Seymour.

"I live like a tortoise," said Michael almost right away. "I move slowly and awkwardly on land, but I'm a good swimmer. I am strong and persistent and I can carry my own load. My parents say they can depend on me."

The others nodded.

"I live like an…" Toby was just about to say owl. At first he thought to say a blue heron, but then realized that it would be silly, since he was bonded with one. "… like a dog," he said instead, surprising himself. He had never had a dog. "Or maybe a wolf. I am loyal and friendly, but I will protect what I think is right from people I consider bad. My family and friends are important to me. I have good hearing and I can sense things that others can't."

Chester stared at him quizzically.

"I live like a kangaroo," said Seymour, jumping in. The others laughed, but he said, "It's true. They are powerful and fast. And unique. They are attached to their family and their own country." Toby had never seen Seymour looking so serious, or so sad.

They turned to Chester, who was still considering. "I live like music," he said finally. "I know it's not alive, but to me it is. I get inspired by music, the beat, how it lifts your spirits. And it… it helps me to do the right thing. "

Other groups were still talking, so they listened in and found out that Robin and Raven lived like the birds they were named for. Toby wanted to hear Alyssa's, but she had already finished. He wondered if she had been listening for his answer. More likely, for Seymour's.

The bell went for lunch and they trooped out, reflecting. Ms. Tanaka reminded them that they would be heading for Truewind the next day, rain or shine, so be ready.

The next day was overcast but the worst of the rain had blown over. In the night, snug and dry in his bed, Toby felt relief that they weren't camping out. He added some extra socks and a small tarp to his bulging backpack, just in case.

There was a hubbub of excitement as Ms. Tanaka gathered them together on the ferry and reminded them that they were "ambassadors for Willow Heights Secondary."

"Wait! Where's Seymour?" asked Alyssa.

"Unfortunately, class," said Ms. Tanaka, "there was a death in the family and Seymour is flying out to Australia today. We will miss him."

"Oh," said Rajni, disappointed. "I thought he was a little down."

"Yes, his grandma has been sick for a while," their teacher said with a worried look.

The tug of happiness Toby felt, that Alyssa wouldn't be mooning over the handsome Australian, was quickly replaced by a wave of remorse—what would he feel like if Grams died? He resolved to be very kind to Seymour when he returned.

They were met by a school bus at the Truewind ferry terminal and taken to Camp Northbreeze, a scout camp near the village of Leeside. They set up their tents around a large fire pit. Soon they had unpacked their lunches on the long picnic tables. As they chattered like magpies, a few birds flitted by curiously but Toby didn't have a chance to speak to any. Chester seemed quiet.

After lunch, they were joined by a cousin of Raven's, who was there to escort them to the Oyster Narrows First Nations community. "Here's the band hall," she said as the bus pulled up to a large building. "Notice how it is built in the shape of a longhouse. Can anyone tell us what the three totem poles depict? Not you, Raven."

"That one in the middle looks like a man wearing a large hat sitting on top of a killer whale," said Robin, pointing to the largest pole. "And is it sitting on a salmon?"

"Yes. See how the arms are stretched out in a gesture of welcoming? The salmon is very important to my people, so it's the base of everything."

"The one on the right looks like an eagle sitting on the shoulders of a bear," said Toby, admiring the sculpting.

"That's right and another name my people use for eagle is Thunderbird. What do you think about the third one?"

"It looks like a raven carved on the top," said Alyssa slowly. "Is it sitting on a frog... "

At that, a real raven appeared and perched on the carved one. It peered curiously at them and did a little hopping dance on the totem pole, and finally gave them a manic stare, all the while chattering raucously.

Ms. Tanaka gasped. Raven's cousin stared. "Well, that's unusual," she said looking around at the group in wonderment. "I don't recall that ever happening before."

It was obvious she couldn't communicate with birds, since the raven was clearly welcoming their class. Then it flew off as suddenly as it had arrived.

Chief Wesley Martin was waiting inside the council chambers. "Welcome to the offices of the Oyster Narrows people, Rushweshuqs, in our tongue," he began. "We were the first self-governing tribe in Canada," he said and explained how their government worked. Then he took them into a small museum filled with carved wooden masks, finely-woven cedar blankets and a large painting of what the area must have looked like centuries earlier.

A woman who looked familiar to Toby, explained the artifacts to the students. Then she pointed to a glass enclosure holding an old basket containing bones. "These were stored in the provincial museum in Victoria," she told them. "These bones are of an ancient ancestor, taken from here decades ago. Only recently have we managed to get them back."

They were given free time to look around the gift shop and buy something if they wanted. Toby didn't have any money so he stayed in the museum

"I see you're interested in the masks," the woman said.

"I was here once before with my grandmother," said Toby. "She told me this raven mask had been given in a potlatch ceremony."

"Why yes, that's right—it's the oldest mask in our collection. Who's your grandmother?"

"Carol Myers."

"Oh, so you're Toby. Well, I'm Gloria Martin. Fern Moss, your grandmother's neighbour, is my cousin. Nice to meet you, Toby. I hear you are going to visit Westwind tomorrow. The chief will be accompanying your class. But I heard that you've been up there already."

"Are you all related?" Toby blurted out.

"Yes, Toby, we're all related. However, if you mean Chief Wesley Martin, why yes, he's my father. In the past, we had hereditary chiefs but now they are voted in. My father has been chief for a long time. People like him after problems with the previous… Well, like anywhere else, there are politics." She gave an apologetic look like she had said too much and quickly continued, "But I volunteer here. So do other band members. It just so happened it was my day."

"I read something on the Internet about those bones," said Toby staring at them. An image from a recurring dream materialized in his mind. He shivered. The dream bones were so similar to these ones, only smaller.

"Yes. It took many years to get them back. We will be interring these soon. I think I see your teacher calling you."

That night they built a campfire and Ms. T. let them stay up singing campfire songs. Chester and Rajni strummed their guitars and took requests for songs. Then people began clamouring for Toby to play his flute.

He reluctantly got it out (why else had he brought it?) but in the still night air the music he breathed into the instrument seemed to float magically around their heads. He was gratified to hear a faint sigh from Alyssa. Into the silence that reigned again, an owl hooted.

Robin asked Ms. Tanaka about her father and she told them about a trip that she had taken with him and her family to South America. "We still keep in touch with the native people there. It's a wonderful culture that is being lost."

"Why is it being lost?" asked Michael.

"Companies are cutting down the Amazon rainforest and the people are losing their land and their way of life. The wildlife there is amazing."

"Is that why they call it Amazon?" wondered Robert. "Because it's amazing?"

"Well, I never thought of that before," said their teacher and they all fell into silence. The stars were brilliant and Robin pointed out constellations she recognized.

"How about one more song before we turn in for the night," Ms. T. suggested.

"Maybe Toby could play the flute for us again," requested Alyssa, moving a little closer to him. The others listened spellbound until well after the last haunting note evaporated.

"That was simply sublime," said Ms. Tanaka finally, breaking the spell. "But now it's time to go to your tents. Try to get some sleep—we have a big day tomorrow."

As they got up to go, Alyssa squeezed his hand and said, "I could listen to you all night."

Toby had trouble sleeping, remembering the soft pressure of her hand. Later, rain moved in and he lay for a long time listening to it drumming on the tent.

"Hey Robert, do you know that you snore?" asked Toby the next morning over breakfast. Everything was still dripping, but at least the rain had stopped.

G.G. Neilson

"Yeah, sorry," he replied between mouthfuls of steaming oatmeal. "You could've woken me."

"Right. Leave our tent and get wet going over to yours," Toby said sarcastically, scooping more porridge from a big pot. He was keeping a close eye on Alyssa's tent and was rewarded with a smile when she emerged, looking tousled and lovely.

After breakfast Ms. Tanaka had them gather around and asked Toby to speak about Westwind Bird Sanctuary.

"It's a beautiful place – it takes up the whole northwest part of the island. An old eagle and an even older gull live there as well as many other birds. There is a small cormorant colony that nest on the rocks below the ridge, so we'll have to avoid that area. Flocks of all sorts of birds come and go. Sometimes you can see harlequin ducks, marbled murrelets and scoters in huge groups, out on the water. Sometimes even a kingfisher."

"Thank you, Toby. Does anyone have a question or anything to add?" their teacher asked.

"I've heard that there is a housing development being planned there and the birds are upset," said Alyssa, her beautiful voice full of concern.

"And I was talking to a few Oyster Narrows people yesterday," said Raven. "They said that land still belongs to them and they want it kept as a bird sanctuary."

"Here's our bus," said Ms. Tanaka, "Let's keep these things in mind as we gather up there."

The bus let them out a long hike from the glade. Everyone piled out and Ms. Tanaka had to restrain them. "Keep to the path," became her mantra as they jostled along. Walking through the damp forest, there were shouts whenever plants they had only read about were recognized. Alyssa was kept busy answering questions about this or that species, as she knew more about plants than even their teacher.

"Quite the girl," whispered Chester at one point. They had dropped behind since Chester was walking slowly. "I saw her cosy-ing up to you last night."

"You're just jealous." Toby gave him a quick nudge with his elbow. "Hey, what's up? Why've you been so quiet?"

"Uh, it's a little difficult for me here. All these creatures."

Toby stopped and looked at him. "Wow, I hadn't thought of that. Are you like, getting signals or something?"

Chester nodded grimly. And was it Toby's imagination or did it seem, even with his dark skin, that Chester looked a little pale?

He could hear a cacophony of birdsong up ahead and classmates shouting as they entered the clearing. When he and Chester arrived, they were paying their respects to Grandmother Eagle, who had just been introduced by Chief Martin.

Grandmother Eagle peered around and waited for silence before she launched into the story of the first bird bond. Ms. Tanaka translated for those who couldn't understand, which was more than half the class. The eagle didn't mention that the first man was Chester's grandfather, Toby noted gratefully. His friend didn't seem himself.

Then the chief stepped forward and made a blessing. "Great Spirit, open these people's hearts to your wonders. Help them to see the beauty in this place and all of nature. Welcome Odd S class to the ancient territory of the Oyster Narrows people."

He told them about his people's relationship with the place, going back thousands of years. "This has long been considered sacred ground. There are legends of my people coming here to commune with the birds and refresh their spirits. There are even legends about how these giant stones, we call them the talking rocks got here. There were, and may still be, plants that medicine people used for a variety of purposes."

Toby saw Alyssa look around, studying the nearby shrubbery.

"And now Westwind is under threat from a land developer who wants to build a high class housing development here," announced the chief somberly. "This we cannot allow."

There was a chorus of, "How can we help?"

"You could spread the word," said Chief Martin slowly. "Tell your parents to write to the politicians."

"We can occupy it," said Alyssa. Everyone stared at her. "You know, we could put up a blockade and stop them. I've seen it on television," she added.

"What if we got arrested?" asked Michael.

"What if we did? It's important to save it," she continued valiantly.

"Well, First Nations have done that in other places," Chief Martin responded thoughtfully. "We are exploring legal routes right now, but it's a good idea. Alyssa, isn't it? You are brave to suggest it."

"Yes. Listen to the girl!" intoned Grandmother Eagle. "We need everyone's help to save this place."

"Yes, any help to save this place," squawked one of the crows.

"Brave girl," echoed the other.

Seeing the determination on her face, Toby realized that he didn't know Alyssa Moss as well as he thought he did. By the time they took out picnic lunches, people surrounded Alyssa, wanting to know more about her idea.

Toby and Chester slipped away to go pay their respects to old Windrunner. He croaked out a hello and promptly fell asleep.

"If you look down there, you can see where the cormorants nest," said Toby, pointing. Chester leaned over the edge.

One of the cormorants looked up and said something to him in the old language.

"What was that all about?" asked Toby as they walked back to the group.

"Sad really. It was complaining about how there's so few areas they can nest now," Chester muttered.

When they re-joined the others, Ms. T said, "Because we are missing some school, we have some review to do," to a chorus of groans. The birds looked on quizzically.

After ten minutes of grilling her class with science questions, their teacher looked at her watch. "We have just enough time to get out to the road to meet the bus."

The students didn't want to leave. "It would be nice to stay here longer," said Robert.

"I'd love to camp up here sometime," said Alyssa.

The birds looked startled. "I don't know about that," said Grandmother Eagle, "but you are welcome to visit us."

They left reluctantly. Chester was the only one anxious to leave and headed out first.

Alyssa stayed behind with Toby for another look around. "It's so beautiful here," she breathed quietly in that voice that Toby could never get enough of.

He grabbed her hand. "I like your idea, Alyssa. An occupation. Do you think it could work?"

"Why, thank you, Toby." Her eyes were shining and she didn't make any attempt to pull her hand away. "I'm sure it could—it's been done in other places. Where were you at lunch?"

"Well Chester and I, like, wanted to pay our respects to old Windrunner. I'm, um, sort of worried about Chester," Toby confided. "I think it's hard on him that he can understand so many creatures."

"Ohhh!" she said, her eyes widening. "I hadn't thought of that. Look, I know something that may cheer him up." She gave Toby a significant look. "You know how we're going out to the Oyster Narrows reserve tonight? Holly's going to be there."

That evening, the Oyster Narrows people treated them to a fabulous feast of salmon, shellfish and other traditional food. Toby was glad that they served the bannock and vegetables separately. The campfire and roasting food aromas combined to make everyone's mouth water.

When Holly came rushing up to them, Chester broke into a huge grin. The two of them sat with their heads together over supper. They were still like that when the drumming began.

Oyster Narrows people of all ages got up to dance in a snaking circle. Some wore cedar bark robes lined with some sort of fir and broad-brimmed cedar hats with intricate designs. Others had cedar skirts and used carved wooden rattles to punctuate their dancing. Several wore headbands with raven feathers woven into them.

"This one is the friendship dance," said Holly as she got up and pulled a grinning Chester up to dance with her.

Soon others were invited into the snaking circle. Someone threw something aromatic onto the fire and Toby breathed in the fragrance as he watched the dancing.

"That's sweet grass," Alyssa said. "C'mon, let's dance!"

It looked complicated to Toby. He resisted but Alyssa persisted. She was light on her feet and teased Toby, "You have two left feet."

"I tried to warn you," he grinned.

Robert went over to watch the drummers. "Why don't you join us," invited a young woman drummer. Bashfully, he sat down, and she handed him a plain drum, skin stretched over a round frame. Some of the drums had elaborate designs etched onto the skins. It didn't take Robert long to get the hang of the rhythm.

"Hey, you're good," said the young woman who introduced herself as Pearl.

His classmates had stopped to listen.

"You'll have to drum with us again," said Pearl. A smile shone from Robert's face.

They didn't get back to their tents until late that night. Michael had returned earlier and was sound asleep when Toby and Chester crawled in.

"Hey, your dancing was something! You picked it up fast," said Toby quietly as they lay in their sleeping bags. "You sure seemed to enjoy spending time with Holly."

"You said it. I didn't even know how much I missed her. She said she would come visit me in Vancouver. Said she could, like, stay with Alyssa."

"Hey, do you think our class can actually help out?" wondered Toby aloud.

"Well, we've got to try, Beorand," said Chester.

"What does Beorar mean anyway?" he whispered back, wondering about Chester's bird-bond name.

"One who stands or understands. It can mean both." He heard Chester roll over. "I've still got a bit of a headache. 'Night, man."

Toby listened to sounds outside the tent and thought he heard an owl swoop by. His hearing was even more acute at night. Many creatures scuttled about and he wondered again how it would be to communicate with them like Chester.

He awoke early the next morning, trying to capture an unremembered dream. The plaintive words of one of Aunt Heather's poems drifted through his mind.

Tiny bones, impossibly tiny,
curled up, askew.
A small pointed beak
nestled on top.

G.G. Neilson

Grey feathers and down
still attached.
Sadness, loneliness reign.

He must have been dreaming about a dead bird—the poem stirred up such sadness. The words had stayed with him ever since he had read them in a file of his aunt's poems and came back to him whenever he discovered small remains...

Suddenly he heard something that made him leap out of his sleeping bag and crawl hurriedly out of the tent. "Beogall! You're here!" Toby ran over to his friend.

"I stayed overnight at your grandmother's—very comfortable there," creeled the young heron in that sonorous voice that Toby was getting to know so well.

Grinning like a fool, Toby introduced the heron around as people started emerging from their tents. "And this is my teacher, Ms. Tanaka."

"So nice to see you again, Beogall," she said.

"Gerald sends his best," replied the bird. Was she blushing?

"Beogall, you surprise me," Toby exclaimed. "You didn't tell me you're on a first name basis with my teacher."

"Lots about me you don't know," he added "Beorand" almost inaudibly. "Keeps it more interesting, don't you think?"

The great blue heron was a huge hit with the whole class. People begged him to tell them what it was like to live in Stanley Park. Toby translated for those who couldn't understand.

Soon Ms. Tanaka had to urge them to get on with breakfast. Toby suddenly realized that he was still in his pajamas. He fled into the tent.

"I was going to tell you man, but hey, those sure are cute jammies," Chester chuckled when he came in a few minutes later to pack up. "Alyssa told me she likes the purple penguin look," he added, ducking out of the way of Toby's jab.

Ms. T. was urging everyone to clean up as Toby emerged from the tent. "Remember, pick up all your garbage. Always leave a place as you found it, or better," she admonished. "Make sure you have all your things. We have to put on some speed if we're going to make that ferry."

"I better get going," Beogall said. "I had to wait until you got dressed." Was the bird actually grinning? Toby wondered as they said goodbye.

His friend left abruptly, as always. Leaving Toby with a longing sadness, as always.

As they waited in line for the ferry, Grams arrived in a flurry. "I just had to see you Toby. Are these your friends?" She looked around beaming. "Holly wanted to come see you off too."

Holly stepped forward, smiling coyly at Chester.

"I'm sure that if your friends would like to come up again, we can find places for them," said Grams.

"Yes, and some people can stay with us too," said Holly with a shy look at Chester. He grabbed her hand. The others pretended not to see.

The ship's horn blasted, and they hurried to the ferry.

Chester and Toby turned just before they boarded the ship. Grams and Holly were still there, waving.

Chapter 19

What Happened After the Talent Show

On Monday morning, Ms. Tanaka let them talk about the camping trip for most of the class.

"What can we do to help save Westwind, Ms. Tanaka?" Alyssa asked finally.

"For now all we can do is wait and see what develops. We have to let the birds take the lead on this one. Now class, let's carry on with our review."

"What about Seymour, Ms. T? What's going on with him?"

"Oh, yes. Thanks for asking, Rajni. Seymour won't be back for a while. Australia is so far away—you can't just go for a week. He has family to see there. He sent word that he really misses us. I've emailed him our review work."

Toby had competing twinges of happiness and remorse. However, next class was music and without Seymour and his trombone, their small ensemble floundered. They would have to revise their pieces for the upcoming talent show.

"Maybe we can add a couple of Toby's Celtic pieces."

"Excellent idea, Robin. We'll have to drop a couple of the jazz numbers though, " said Mr. Harrington, brows knit together. "I want all of you here after school to go over some new numbers. And Toby, there's a flute solo which I think is perfect for you."

Mr. Harrington worked them hard later that day and praised them on their progress.

"Excellent work on the violin, Toby. Good tone on the flute solo. Now really let the runs flow. Improvise a bit if you'd like."

Toby was determined to practise like crazy, especially violin, which he now played in most of the pieces. Mr. Harrington was positively rhapsodic about having a violinist in the group.

"But, what if I flub it in front of the whole school?" he confided to Chester on their way home.

"Hey man, compared to your shower incident, this will be a piece of cake,"

"Don't remind me. But I'd hate to let any of you down."

"Oh man, you just don't know how good you are. If there's any letting down, it'll be one of us."

The day of the talent show loomed and they practiced every day. The end of the school year was also fast approaching, so teachers were working them overtime to get ready for exams. Toby fell into bed exhausted every night and didn't remember his dreams at all.

When the day finally arrived, Toby thought he had practised enough, but still… As he waited in the wings, his nerves were so bad that even his calming techniques weren't working. Their group was on last.

First up was a band led by Glen called *Highway Closures*. They played a couple of old numbers by the Beatles and then really switched it up with a Justin Bieber song. The audience clapped and sang along. Their last number, their own original, "Met her at the bus stop", was met by wild applause.

"Man, they're good," whispered Chester. Toby nodded nervously—how would they measure up?

Next up was a group of dancers with some great numbers—both tap and jazz. The audience clapped enthusiastically. A soloist Toby hadn't seen before sang a Carly Rae Jepsen song and Mr. Harrington accompanied her on the keyboard. She was nervous and her voice was wavery and slightly off-key. Toby felt sorry for her, but also admiration – pretty brave to go out and sing in front of the school. On your own. There was very little applause after her performance until Mr. McFru stood up and clapped mightily. Soon others joined in. Chester grinned at him, mouthing a silent *See?*

The next act was a surprise. As Michael made his awkward way to the stage, Toby felt the whole Odd S class holding its collective breath. They needn't have worried.

"I just took an IQ test," their friend quipped and then waited. "The results were negative." The audience cracked up.

"I used to live in the real world, but I got evicted," he continued in the same dead-pan style. "But at least I've learned that it's better to understand a little, than to misunderstand a lot."

Michael played the audience and when his stand-up act was over, Mr. McFru didn't have to encourage the applause.

Then the assembly waited expectantly for the last act.

As their group headed onto the stage, Toby was momentarily blinded by the lights and looked around wildly. He knew that the whole school was there. He patted his shirt where the feather lay beneath and took a deep breath.

Their first number was a Celtic piece Toby had introduced to the group. Chester was on the guitar, Robin had her clarinet ready and Robert was poised on percussion. It was a lively piece that required all of Toby's fiddling skills. At the end there was silence.

But only for a second. The applause was loud and genuine. Toby and the others looked at each other with grins that split their faces in half. The next piece was a popular song and some hummed along, while most clapped. Mr. Harrington smiled broadly as it ended and then he turned to the audience, "Now for a more classical piece."

He led them from the piano, nodding them in with his head. The clapping after, while not enthusiastic, was genuine. Then Robin put down her clarinet to sing the mournful words to "Dream Angus" in a lovely high voice, while they backed her up on fiddle and guitar. The audience responded with ardent applause.

Mr. Harrington told the assembly they would finish up with a flute solo. As Toby fumbled to get out the instrument, the music teacher announced, "Toby Myers has only recently come to our school, but has made a great contribution to our ensemble. We await great things from this young man." *How to put the pressure on*, Toby thought as he felt his face warm up and his hands trembled. He hoped the flute, clutched in his twitching fingers wasn't waving around with nervousness.

He could hear muffled whispers of *shower boy*. Barely detectable, he heard a snigger and then *fresh towels*—certain it was Harsten. Principal Standing stood on the stool that he always had with him in assemblies and peered with dark displeasure into the crowd until silence reigned.

Toby thought about the birds; how they sang with heart and soul. He took a deep breath and relaxed into the music of *Morning* from the Peer Gynt Suite. He was one with the intricate flow of notes. The audience disappeared and the joy of the sound became his universe. The final note hung in the air for several seconds. Total silence lasted for an eternity.

Then the whole school rose as one and gave Toby a standing ovation. Alyssa was near the front and jumped up, her eyes glistening. She clapped long after everyone else had stopped. Their eyes met and Toby was hardly aware of the audience calling out "Encore, encore!"

Mr. Harrington sprang up to conduct the group in a final lively number that ended just as the last bell of the day sounded.

The performers all gathered to congratulate each other. "I knew they'd love you!" Mr. Harrington was beaming. Toby turned to see Harsten cast him a malignant glare before slinking out of the auditorium.

JB wheeled over. "Wow, you guys are great. Wish I could play music like that."

"Toby, I'm speechless," said Alyssa, her eyes shining. She had arrived at his side.

"Gotta stow these instruments," said Chester and led the others away.

"I've always loved music, Toby," said Alyssa, "but I didn't know how much until I heard your playing today. You can truly move people. Would you play for me sometime?"

"Anytime, Alyssa. And if you don't find me too much of a lurker, come over to my place anytime," he said, grabbing hold of her hand.

"Well, I do know where you live." She gave his hand a squeeze.

Seymour finally returned the following week. His classmates expressed their condolences. Many students had also lost a grandparent. The Australian seemed changed and struggled to catch up. Toby was genuinely kind to him.

Alyssa had started spending loads of time at their apartment. One day she asked if he knew *Over the Rainbow*.

"How does it go? Sing it for me," he urged.

"What? You don't know it?" Toby wasn't about to admit that he did.

She took a deep breath and sang:

Somewhere, over the rainbow,
Way up high,
There's a land that I heard of
Once in a lullaby.

"Alyssa Moss, you have a beautiful voice. You should have been in that talent show. Sing me the rest."

She knew all the verses. When she finished Toby murmured, "I could listen to you till the cows come home."

"What a dreamy expression, Mr. Myers," Alyssa laughed. "Sounds like one of your Grams'."

"It is. But seriously, Alyssa. Has Mr. Harrington heard you sing?"

"He asked me to for the talent show, but I… I just couldn't."

"Chicken!"

"Yeah, I guess I am. But Toby, you are teaching me that I have to get over stuff. I have to learn to put myself out there." She said this so earnestly, with her lovely eyes trained on his, that he leaned over and kissed her. She looked startled but didn't stop him. Her lips were as soft and sweet as he had dreamed about.

They started spending all their spare time together and even the fast-approaching exams couldn't dampen Toby's ardent happiness. People at school called them an item.

"I'll have to start charging her rent," his dad joked one day after she left. They had been studying together—exams were just around the corner.

"Then you can give Anna a share of it, after all the nights you spend over at her place," Toby grumbled.

"Touché. Anyway, Alyssa seems like a nice girl. But Toby, you're too young to get too serious."

He fought down the urge to say something nasty and realized his dad must wonder at the hours they spent in his room. "It's not really that serious." Hand-holding, hardly any kissing… But he wasn't about to tell his dad that. "We just like to hang out."

"Toby, how come Chester hasn't been around lately? What's going on with him? Are you still friends?"

"Of course." But he realized that he had been completely ignoring his friend. He thought about his study sessions with Alyssa—he should have included Chester.

The next day at school, he sought out Chester and realized with a shock that his friend was not looking himself. "Hey Chester. How's it going?" They were on their way to their last French class of the year.

"Okay. You?" Chester responded quietly and slouched into class. Toby watched him move to the back of the class and noted that he didn't participate much. Maybe he was stressed about the upcoming exams.

The entire period was spent on review. Mme. Bruleau, wearing bold yellow, orange and red tartan stockings, worked them hard all class, even extending it into the break.

Exhausted and finally on their way to music, Toby asked, "Hey Chester, can you come over to my place after school today?" He realized that his friend hadn't been much into music lately either.

"Sure, man," Chester mumbled.

"What's with him?" asked Alyssa after Chester bolted his lunch and left, ignoring a question from Robert.

"I'm not sure," Toby replied. "Hey Robert, I don't think he heard you."

"Well, I hope he's not turning out like… " Robert began, but stopped after a look from Alyssa. "Hey, are you two, like, FBO?" he quickly asked, changing the subject and they laughed. It sounded strange coming from Robert.

After school, Chester knocked on the door and shuffled in. Toby poured glasses of juice and they sat out on the balcony. The terrace was ringing with birds and the dogwood tree below the balcony was in full bloom.

"Hey man, are we still buddies?" asked Toby.

"What do you mean? Of course."

"Then, as your friend, you need to tell me what's going on with you. Are you worried about the exams or something? You're a good student Chester—you'll be okay."

"It's not that. I went to see Peter."

"Peter who? Oh—do you mean the kid that left the Odd S class?"

"Yep, him. Did you ever hear why he left?"

"No—everyone's been, like, hush-hush about it. But I heard that he went around telling people about our gifts."

"He did not *go around telling*!" Chester barked. "He told a couple of people, but he has pressures of his own. He suffered what they call a nervous breakdown. He's in some sort of facility."

"Oh. Sorry to hear that. Why did you go see him?"

"Why not? Look Toby, it's not easy being, well, special. I mean... Peter is a bit like me."

Toby's eyes widened, "You mean he understands all the creatures?"

"Yeah, pretty much. His dad called him a freak."

"Man, that's rough. I guess I'm lucky that Grams is so supportive. My dad is a bit weird about the whole thing though." He wondered how his mother would take it if she knew.

"Peter's dad wanted him out of the Odd S class, but his mom insisted that he stay in. He told me that his mom has some sort of affinity for plants, but would never let on to his dad."

Toby didn't know what to say.

After a bit Chester continued, "My parents moved to this condo in the city to protect me. Peter lives in a house with a big yard. It's near Turtle Lake Park. I suggested that he move somewhere else with less wildlife around. He blew up at me—called me a freak like him."

"That's downright... Look Chester, you're no freak. You're about the sanest, coolest person I know. You just have to get used to the whole communication thing," Toby reasoned.

"What do you know about it?" Chester got up and paced around the balcony. "You don't understand. They're all in crisis—all the creatures. They can't understand why we're doing all this shit to them. They're crying out for help. And I can't do anything."

His voice rose and he was becoming more and more agitated. "The only one who understood was Peter. And now he's gone mental."

"Hey man, I think we can do something to help. Look at our class. At Ms. Tanaka. We're gonna help the birds at Westwind." Toby tried to reassure his friend but was growing steadily more alarmed. Chester had a feverish look on his face.

"It's gone too far! See, there's this new housing development being built out near the mental hospital. There used to be woods there; birds, animals and all. Now it's gone. Nothing. It felt dead when I walked by. I felt dead too. I felt like, like I had been shot."

He stopped pacing and stared wildly at Toby. "Peter's not the only one going mental," he cried out in a tone that made Toby's blood freeze. With outstretched arms Chester shouted to the sky, "It's not fair! It can't go on!"

Toby leapt up and grabbed Chester's arm. "C'mon Chester. Pull yourself together."

"Leave me alone!" Chester yelled and shoved Toby away violently.

Toby was still reeling when Chester climbed onto the railing. He was too late as he tried to grab his friend. He was left clutching a piece of Chester's shirt as his friend disappeared over the balcony.

Part 4 – Westwind Bird Sanctuary

The Bird of Time has but a little way
to flutter — and the Bird is on the Wing.
Omar Khayyám

Chapter 20

The Flocking

"I have a bad feeling about this," said Grandmother Eagle. She had flown over to the old arbutus overhanging Grandfather Gull's rock.

"You're just old. I'm older and I feel like that a lot."

"Windrunner, you heard what those young gulls were saying. And what about that song sparrow—what's her name? She really gets around, that one." Grandmother Eagle shook her elegant head and the whole tree trembled. "If it's true, our beloved Westwind will be destroyed for a housing development. Humans have taken over more and more—we have so few areas left. What will become of us?"

Other birds listened from their perches in nearby branches or from the talking rocks and twittered unhappily. Berook, a barred owl, swooped silently to a nearby grove of trees, unnoticed.

"Well… then…" The ancient gull was having a harder and harder time thinking straight. As he mulled over the current situation, scenes from his earlier years always intruded. "Long ago, when I was young, I remember a 'Flocking' that took place here to discuss an important matter," he recalled ponderously.

As soon as he said it, there was a hue and cry among the assembled birds.

"A Flocking!" was twittered and trilled around the glade.

"There hasn't been one in my lifetime," said one of the crows.

"No, not in our lifetime," agreed the other.

Suddenly the barred owl swept into their midst and landed at the top of a small hemlock. The branch bent low with her weight. She hooted for silence. The effect was instant, since so few birds had ever heard her speak.

"A Flocking used to be called in times of great urgency," she hooted. "Danger is imminent. You must call for a Flocking but you must also call in the humans who can help us."

"A Flocking with humans?" Grandfather Gull muttered. "I need time to think about this."

"There is no time. Berook is right!" exclaimed the old eagle. "We need all the help we can get. We cannot lose Westwind and there are many humans who feel as we do."

"Well, maybe it's the right thing to do..." said old Windrunner, nodding slowly.

"It must be organized carefully," intoned the owl. "We need to include representatives of all the affected bird communities."

And so the plan for a Flocking at Westwind Bird Sanctuary was set in motion.

They discussed what needed to be done, then Grandmother Eagle and Berook assigned jobs. At once birds flew off in every direction. Berook disappeared as silently as she had arrived. Nesting mothers and younger birds were left to enjoy the peaceful sunshine, the lazy buzzing of insects, and gentle breezes flowing from a sleepy ocean, playing over the grasses and tree branches of Westwind.

After the others left, Grandmother Eagle returned to her Douglas fir and surveyed the beautiful terrain jutting out into the ocean, encompassing the north-western shore of Truewind island. She cut a solitary figure on her tall tree.

G.G. Neilson

The sanctuary wasn't her original home, but how she loved it. Carpeted with ferns and wildflowers, it was furrowed with gullies where the birds could always find water. Tangles of smooth-barked arbutus clutched the steep-sided slope. It wasn't clear whether they held up the bank or the bank held them. Groves of Douglas fir, cedar and hemlock spread over the rolling landscape. But here was an open meadow dotted with shrubs and the unusual talking rocks, so-called since they were used by the birds to sit on when they collected together to talk. Humans called it the glade.

Westwind provided for the needs of many species of birds—both resident and migratory. It had been their sanctuary and meeting place since long before humans ever showed up. "Since time beyond remembering," the old eagle muttered sadly. "What would we do without it? Not even the Oyster Narrows people have an older claim on this land than we birds."

Carol Myers dozed in the sunshine on her deck where she had eaten lunch after a morning in the garden. She woke when the sparrow began its beautiful song right next to her old wooden lawn chair.

"Heavens! I must have nodded off. Rio, is that you? What is it?"

The sparrow quickly sang out her message and flew off. Grams got up stiffly from her chair and went inside to make a few phone calls.

A delegation of two crows and three swallows arrived at the Oyster Narrows Reserve and told of the plan to three generations of Martins—old George Rocky Ground, Chief Wesley and his son Brian. They quickly began making plans about who to include in the Flocking. Brian went to consult his bird-bond, a raven named Woodley who liked to hang out at the band offices.

At Cypress Gardens, the scene was quite different.

Toby was quaking in shock on the balcony. Taking a deep breath, he forced himself to look over, dreading what he might see. There was Chester. Miraculously, he had landed in the big, old, dogwood tree. He saw his friend thrashing about—he seemed to be tangled in the branches.

"Chester!" he shouted with enormous relief. "Are you okay?"

"Yeah, I'm good." Chester's voice was muffled.

Toby raced down the stairs and out onto the terrace. Chester, barely visible in the foliage, was high up in the tree, subdued. His arms and legs were entwined in the branches. Toby peered up, wondering what to say to the several people now gathered around.

"I'll call 9-1-1," someone offered.

"It's okay, I'm fine," Chester called down, sounding embarrassed.

Toby turned to the small group and said, "My friend was doing a stunt and just, like, fell. You don't need to call emergency, but could someone get a ladder?"

"I'll get one," said a man, whom Toby recognized as the building superintendent. He left with another onlooker to fetch it.

When they returned with the ladder, Toby climbed up. He determined that Chester only had a few scratches. As he started to un-pry his friend, the branches untangled immediately from his limbs. Toby helped him down. When the onlookers saw that he was okay, they drifted away. Toby thanked the building superintendent.

"He should go to the medical clinic—get checked out."

"Thanks, but I'm good," said Chester. "Just a stupid stunt."

"Give me your name young fella. If it happens again…" said the superintendent. Chester reluctantly gave his name and Toby said, "I'll take him back to his apartment now."

G.G. Neilson

A few minutes later Chester fumbled for his keys as Toby numbly studied the door. What should he say to his friend? He was startled to see that a great blue heron had been painted into the scene on the door. He touched it and shivered as a tingling ran up his spine.

Chester finally got the key into the lock and pushed the door open.

"Can I get you anything? Water? A bandage?" asked Toby. "One of those scratches looks more like a cut," he said, pointing to some blood on Chester's arm.

"No. Really, I'm good. Don't tell my mom, okay? She already worries enough about me."

"That totally freaked me out! What were you thinking?"

"I was just feeling riled. That's all. I knew that tree would catch me."

"How did you know that?" Toby gripped Chester's shoulders, their faces inches apart.

"It happened before."

"You pulled that stunt before?" Toby shouted.

"Calm down." Chester struggled out of Toby's grip. "It was a long time ago. I was a kid."

"What the...?" Toby was flabbergasted. He could talk to birds, his friend could talk to all the creatures. But none of it prepared him for this.

"I was upset then too. I couldn't calm down. I jumped out of my window and a tree caught me."

"What! That's crazy." As soon as he said it, Toby hoped Chester hadn't heard—maybe he shouldn't bring up the crazy card.

"We were living in a house out in the suburbs," Chester was saying almost to himself. "It was only a second storey window. But they decided it would be better to move into the city—easier to cope."

"Chester, what exactly happened just now?" Toby was feeling calmer.

"I thought that tree would catch me and it did. It wouldn't let go until you climbed up the ladder to get me."

"Chester, are you listening to me?" Toby had raised his voice again and Chester nodded. "You're meant to be here. You're meant to help out. I totally believe in you, in what we're supposed to do. You've got to promise me you'll never do that again."

"I won't. It just came over me. The hopelessness of the situation."

"There's always hope. Your painted door tells me that. The beautiful plants in here tell me that. The love your family has for you. All of our bird friends. Sami."

Just then the Steller's jay landed on the Oldwin's balcony and pecked on the glass.

"I heard something bad about you, Chester," squawked the jay as they opened the door. "Did you really jump from the balcony?"

"Sorry, Sami. I don't know what came over me. The dogwood tree caught me."

"So I heard. They're all talking about it. You #~%*!" It must have been a bad word in bird language since Chester reddened, even through his dark skin.

Sami continued, "Well, something's come up. The birds need your help. Pull yourself together." The jay did a little hop, and bent his head to peer intently at Chester.

"What's come up?" the two asked together.

The jay told them about the Flocking. They were to tell the others.

Chester put on a clean t-shirt and they headed out. They reached the skate bowl before they found anyone they could tell. Freddie was there chatting with JB. He was often at the bowl again now, coaching some of the younger skaters from his wheelchair.

"Hey JB, Freddie," said Toby. "Have you seen Alyssa?"

"Nope." They both frowned. Jeez, they didn't still blame Alyssa for the accident, did they? He scanned the area and saw her leaving her building with her two dogs and a small boy in tow.

"Thanks anyway. I think I see her. You doing good?" JB nodded.

Chester hung with JB and Freddie, while Toby jogged over to Alyssa. Her young charge was totally engrossed with the two dogs as Toby told her about the plans in a low voice.

Her eyes widened into saucers. "This weekend? I'm supposed to mind Ben here, but I'll see if I can get out of it. Hey, you look a little pale. Why did you hurry away so fast after school?"

"I had to talk to Chester," said Toby, "but I think he and I are good to go. I'd like to head up to Truewind after school tomorrow."

"Well, I'll try to make it there on Saturday. But don't forget we have exams next week."

Toby reached out and squeezed her hand, "How can I forget?"

"Toby, do you think JB and Freddie will hate me forever? They don't seem to want me around and Ben would like to go over to the skate bowl."

Toby still held her hand, "Just a matter of time, you'll see. Here's Chester."

As Chester joined them, Sami was nearby, flapping from bush to bush. Ben waved excitedly at the bird. "What dat bird, Lyssa?"

Toby and Chester left Alyssa to her young charge and her dogs.

A varied thrush showed up at the open office window of Anna Feathers. She phoned Lars out on the 11th hole where he was working on the sand trap, so when he returned from the golf course later that evening, he was not surprised to find his son packing for a trip over to Truewind Island.

"Communicating with birds and now a Flocking, whatever that is," Lars muttered. "Just promise me you'll be careful," he said, watching Toby throw a load of laundry into their apartment-sized washing machine.

"Dad, I have my phone. Grams and I talked and she'll be at the Flocking too."

Lars sighed. He mumbled to himself, "I worry about my mother's influence on that boy."

Two days later a strong breeze was blowing in from the ocean at Westwind. An excited assembly of birds and about a dozen humans had gathered there. The babble was overwhelming and even Grandmother Eagle could not seem to quiet them. Beogall had flown in along with several other herons and he and Toby were busy catching up. The elusive cormorant, Sevo, had left his ocean lookout, pledging to let the others know what was decided. Old Windrunner struggled over to a closer rock to join the throng.

A shadow passed over the sun and everyone looked up, startled, as the barred owl swooped onto a nearby tree and hooted for silence. You could have heard a fir cone drop.

"Time is now short," began Berook. "The two men, humans call them surveyors, were here again yesterday. Humans, tell us what you know about this development."

Grams began, "The news is bad. Westwind is part of a large tract of crown land—"

"What does that mean, crown land?" asked a young gull despite the shushing efforts of older gulls.

"It means land owned by the state, in this case, the province," replied Grams undeterred as she continued. "However, this piece of land has now been sold and is slated for a housing development."

There were screeches of indignation at that. Some birds flapped around and a few feathers floated to the ground. Into the racket Sevo squawked, "Can't it be stopped?

"Well," now it was Toby's turn, "LSW Holdings arranged to buy the parcel. But I think there's like, a grace period in effect because the announcement was only just made in the trade papers."

"Who is LSW Holdings anyway?" asked Grandmother Eagle, bristling. "Why should they be allowed to buy what belongs to you all? Actually it belongs to us, the birds."

"LSW stands for Lord Suchno Whenge," Toby replied, "and it's his company that has applied to buy it."

"The same man who took over the Myers' mansion and cut the trees," Beogall chimed in.

A raucous ruckus broke out among the birds. A warbler shrilled, "And killed birds!"

At this, the chirping and trilling grew deafening. Berook finally hooted for silence.

"Mr. Whenge has been seen here on Truewind Island—at the government offices in Fairwind," added Grams.

"What can be done?" asked one of the crows.

"Yes, what can be done?" echoed the other.

The birds each had their own opinion on the matter.

"One at a time," called out Grandmother Eagle.

"I know of a development that was stopped over on Vancouver Island," said Chief Wesley.

"It wasn't that long ago..." added Brian.

"What did they do?" asked Rio excitedly. "Maybe they could help us."

"Well, they—"

"Wait! I hear something," said Toby, straining to hear.

The raven, Woodley, shot up immediately to check it out. He returned shortly. "It's one of those strange aircraft. The ones that can hover."

Soon, everyone could hear the distant hum of a helicopter.

"We birds must disperse at once!" hooted Berook. "Humans—find out who is coming and see what you can do. We'll wait to hear from you."

"We'll gather back at the Stronghold," said the chief.

The barred owl disappeared silently into the firs and most of the other birds melted away.

Chief Wesley Martin and his son Brian, Grams, Toby and Chester were quickly delegated to speak to whomever might be in the helicopter. The others quietly slipped into the woods as the helicopter approached. Like a huge angry bird, it alit in the clearing where the Flocking had been just minutes before.

Toby was hardly surprised when Duffin Wint emerged before the beaters had stopped turning and opened the door for Suchno Whenge. Another man descended carefully behind him. He was very tall, with a curly fringe of hair around his balding head, clutching a briefcase, which looked out of place in the meadow of wildflowers. Some robins had remained pecking unobtrusively in the grass. Other songbirds flitted in and out of the shrubbery. Just a normal afternoon at Westwind.

Grandmother Eagle sat silent as a statue watching from her tree and Grandfather Gull had retreated to the cover of the arbutus at the far edge of the glade.

The men noted the delegation waiting there and Whenge said a few words to the man with the briefcase, then turned to Toby.

"I might have known you would be involved here, boy Myers. Just as bad as your father," he snorted.

Toby ignored that and said, "What brings you and Duffin to our island today? And to this spot in particular?"

"You're the smart one, you tell me. And did I happen to see a flock of birds here earlier with you? What is it about you and birds?"

"I'll have you know that this place has been a bird sanctuary for as long as I've lived here, which is a long time," Grams spoke up. "The people of Truewind Island will never let you take it for a housing development."

"So young Myers has told you. He does his research, I'll grant you that," said Whenge, peering at her closely. "And if I'm not mistaken, I'd say that you are his grandmother and mother of that idiot, Lars."

Grams gave him a look that might have turned his heart to stone if he had one. Duffin for some reason had the grace to look embarrassed.

"My people have lived on this island since time immemorial," Chief Wesley pronounced, stepping forward. "We have never given up our rights to the land. It is not the province's to sell, or any government. You should leave right now."

Whenge looked at the chief with some interest. "Well, I appreciate what you're saying, but the province is negotiating with the band right now as you know, to add a nice chunk of land to the reserve in exchange for this piece. We made a very fair offer which the government is kindly disposed to." Suchno spoke in an oily voice. "My developer here, Mr. Calliston, will plan a beautiful development," he went on, waving to the man with the briefcase, who smiled and nodded. "In fact, we'll even keep the name, Westwind Sanctuary—it has a nice ring."

At this, there were loud squawks of defiance and Suchno looked around the glade. "Have you trained those birds to understand speech, Myers?" He glared at Toby. "You got that heron to do its thing on me that day, I'm sure of it. Is it here now?"

"With respect, Mr. Whenge," Chester, who had been silent up to now spoke, "the birds do not have many places left. Their numbers are in decline and it is up to us to help them out. They need this sanctuary. Surely you can see that."

"That's *Lord* Whenge to you, young man," said Suchno, glaring at Chester. "Yes, I recognize you now—you were in court that day and you were illegally on my property along with boy Myers. For your information, this is now my property and I order you all off of it," he announced, making a threatening gesture with his large arm.

"Mr. Whenge," said Chief Wesley, "my people have not given up the rights to this land. And the loss of this habitat would be no small matter. Besides, it does not yet belong to you officially."

A shadow of anger passed over Whenge's face before he resumed his oily tone. "It is close to being finalized, I assure you. It will be an astounding development and it could mean jobs for your people. We'll keep some natural areas that birds can use."

"Just like Wattasaga?" Toby burst out, "wall-to-wall development? I've been there—it's been destroyed! The place used to be thick with birds... " Brian Martin put a restraining hand on his shoulder.

Whenge looked at him as if he'd like to strangle him on the spot, but resumed calmly, "Chief Martin, we invite you to a planning meeting—we welcome your input. I can assure you, it will be worth your while. In the meantime, Mr. Calliston and I have some looking around to do—he wants to plan the most sought-after development possible. I assure you, he's the best."

At that, the three men started walking around the area while the pilot stood by his chopper, surveying the glade. The others looked at each other and left.

Chapter 21

Decision at the Stronghold

As he became airborne, the ecstasy of flight overtook Beogall as it often did. While most herons like to stand and wade, Beogall loved the air. He had taken off from a hidden section of Westwind where the bad men, as he thought of Whenge and Duffin, wouldn't see him. Although he and Toby communicated well, he couldn't understand the complexity of human speech. It was so very different from bird communication—not as intuitive. So much bird talk is conveyed by tone, undertone, even empty space. Humans had to spell out all the details.

But Beogall understood the gist of what he had overheard and knew it wasn't good.

Birds were making their way surreptitiously to the Stronghold, a place he had been to only once. But once is all it takes for a bird. His elder explained that birds had three-dimensional maps in their brains, while humans had a flatter perspective. Even when they flew in planes, humans didn't view things the way birds did. They couldn't feel the air and its messages. He often felt sorry for them.

The humans hiding in the trees were quiet—he didn't think the bad men had spotted them. But all the birds knew they were there. He saw them begin to leave quietly, in ones and twos, after the confrontation with that awful man who broke up their flocking. Any crackling of twigs sounded natural.

Beogall was certain that the man at the chopper wasn't even aware of them.

Why did people have to fly anyway? The glorious air is where birds and flying insects belong. It was well-known in the bird community that many died in the engines of those flying machines, sucked in when they least expected it. But then again, birds were killed daily by fast-moving cars. Why couldn't things be simpler—just let others live and be.

Now he was looking down on Westwind—a real jewel from above. What would the birds do if it was taken over by humans? But he had faith in Toby—he would do the right thing. The heron knew he had chosen well. There was something about that spine-tingling feeling that he had, that first time he met Toby face to face. And those friends of his would help him.

Beogall headed higher. Some said it wouldn't work out with Toby, that he was just a spoiled rich kid. But the heron had heard that Toby loved birds so he had set out to find more about him. And sure enough, the boy and Walter had preserved the beautiful forest at the mansion.

Then he had heard of troubling things about to happen. He was a very curious heron and got around. Yes, he had even seen that bad man prowling about the place with that butler when the Myers weren't there. Maybe he shouldn't have done that thing, but he couldn't stand that gloating face or the fact that Toby would be moving. But what destruction ensued—could his impulsive action have brought that on?

Then, just when he thought all was lost, Toby and his amazing friend stopped the devastation. What a day that was! That small area was the last of a vast ancient forest, which included Beogall's own home in Stanley Park. Toby had put himself at great risk—yes, he was proud of Beorand, his human bond.

The heron could just make out the three men walking around Westwind far below. He had avoided flying overhead so they wouldn't see him, even though humans seldom look up or notice birds. The whole southern end of Truewind Island was on his right wing and on his left wing, to the north, a small mountain range. Such a lovely place with more wooded areas, too high up for humans. Too high even for blue herons. He knew there were marbled murrelets who nested up there in the oldest trees. Oh yes, he had heard about their habits—now that was one amazing bird.

The ocean was a calm expanse today and in the distance gulls coasted on the air currents. Far away a tug-boat towed a line of barges and a giant ferry was headed to Vancouver Island. Beogall was adventurous enough to have gone over there once.

In the opposite direction he could see a smaller ferry chugging toward Truewind Island. On a whim, he decided to ride the air currents over the town of Fairwind for a quick look before turning to the Stronghold. They would be expecting him soon.

"Well, what do we do now?" The question was posed by Fern Strong. The birds and people from the Flocking gathered around the wide deck at the Stronghold.

"We cannot allow this to happen," stated Granny Renie simply. "You must go and take over Westwind Sanctuary."

"Yes!" Alyssa nodded vigorously. She had arrived from the ferry less than 20 minutes before, just as everyone poured into the Stronghold.

"They won't be able to ignore us," agreed Toby, seated close to her.

"An occupation," the chief spoke slowly. "It is our responsibility to prevent the loss of the Westwind sanctuary. Yes, this is the right course to take."

G.G. Neilson

As one, the birds all voiced their approval for this plan. Maybe these humans could save their sanctuary yet!

Everyone was assigned a job: whether it was telling others, organizing the occupation, talking to the media, or writing to politicians.

"You're to talk to the birds of Stanley Park," Toby excitedly told Beogall, who arrived late. "We have to arrange for as many people and birds as possible to occupy Westwind!"

Beogall was quizzical. "Aren't they going to know we can communicate?"

"We think some suspect already," Chester interjected. "No-one really knows how it'll play out."

"Besides, they need to understand how many birds are affected by this," added Toby.

"What're you two supposed to do?" the bird asked.

"The usual. Internet research," Toby replied. "It'll be easier to do that back at the condo. We have to head back tomorrow." He grimaced, "Exams."

"Also, we have to talk to Ms. Sharma," added Chester. Beogall gave him a puzzled look. "You know, the environmental lawyer."

"Well, school is now officially over for me." Holly grinned as Alyssa stuck out her tongue at her. "So I can help up at Westwind."

"No such luck for us," said Alyssa. "But we can be back here by the end of the week."

While Toby, Chester and Alyssa were finishing their exams at Willow Heights Secondary, Holly helped to organize the protest on Truewind Island.

When the same two surveyors arrived at Westwind early the following week, they were turned back by a small group, which included Grams, Holly and Fern Strong.

"We'll need more people up here," said Grams. "It was hard to get those surveyors to leave. What do you think, Brian?"

Grams was glad Brian Martin, the chief's son, was there. She had watched him grow up and always liked him. Too bad that he and Heather…

"We're just getting organized, but look at the people here already," Brian reassured her, waving a hand to indicate the small but determined group of Truewinders. "It will be easier when news spreads. We'll get more people out—you'll see."

Whenge was furious when he heard about his surveyors being denied access. He contacted the government official he had been dealing with. "You should arrest the whole lot of them!" he ordered the man.

"I'm sorry, but I have no authority to order police to arrest the protesters," the man replied warily. "The property doesn't belong to you officially. It is technically still crown land so it would be against their civil rights to arrest them."

"I will contact your superiors!" Whenge shouted, as the man held the phone away from his ear. "Those… those radicals are preventing me from surveying for my development. It will be the best housing development that's ever happened on that island. It'll be legendary!"

"I appreciate your situation," the official said politely, "but we must wait for due process."

"You'll be sorry," said Whenge, slamming the phone down.

"Who'll ever be able to afford those places?" muttered the civil servant, still holding the phone away from his ear. "Certainly not me."

Suchno quickly made another call. "Get Dakon Turf on the line. Now! Lord Whenge calling." The call was transferred right away.

"Dakon, those idiots on Truewind Island are blocking my surveyors."

"What? At Westwind?"

"Yes, of course at Westwind. Who do they think they are, blocking the best thing that's ever happened to that snivelly backwater?"

"Get the police to break it up."

"Of course I'll try that. That boy Myers is involved in this."

"He's already given you too much trouble. Why not use your political connections? You've given a lot of money to certain campaigns…"

"Of course, of course, I'll use my influence. Your job, Dakon, is to call in those two people we used before. You know the ones."

"You mean, Mack Butcher and Toulie Palmston?"

"Who else? Let me know if they're available. We might be needing them again."

With that Whenge again slammed down his office phone. He composed himself and ordered his secretary to fetch him some phone numbers.

Chapter 22
What Berook Did

The occupation started as a small rag-tag group. "Don't worry," Holly had said to Toby, Chester and Alyssa before they left for Cypress Gardens. "It's not really rolling yet. And you'll be back here in a few days."

Soon the Odd S class knew all about what was happening on Truewind Island. Some said they would come up and support the occupation, but others had summer plans.

"Our protest hasn't had much news coverage," Grams complained to Toby on the phone the night before they were to return, "except in the local paper."

"I saw something on the Internet about it," he replied.

"Oh good—I'm not much for checking on the computer. Fern and Holly put out a press release. We've been taking turns going there. Maybe it's a good thing there's not much publicity, at least until it's better organized."

"I'll see you tomorrow, Grams. Chester and Alyssa will be coming too. Some others from my class might come up later."

"Lovely. You know your friends are always welcome here. But I imagine Alyssa will stay at the Stronghold."

"I guess. Bye." Toby enjoyed a momentary daydream about Alyssa staying with them but quickly shoved the thought from his mind to get packed.

His dad was not happy about him leaving. "How long will you be there?"

"As long as it takes, Dad. You're so busy, you won't even know I've gone," said Toby. "Are you still going on that golf tour?"

"Yep." Lars perked up. "It'll be good to do some serious golfing again. Mr. Frobisher thinks I'm in the running to be the next Golf Pro at Trout Creek Links. I'll email you all about it."

The next day, Grams drove them up to Westwind Bird Sanctuary. The atmosphere was festive, even though the group was small. Truewinders who hadn't seen each other recently, chatted and caught up as they held their signs aloft: hand-painted banners with slogans like "Protect our Birds", "Save Westwind for Posterity" and "Crown Land is Not for Sale." There were also creative ones in the shape of birds and trees. One sign boldly stated, "Go back to Wattasaga".

Toby and his friends grinned as they joined the throng. The occupation had now been going on for almost a week but had yet to make it to the six o'clock news, a sore point especially with Alyssa. She was talking about it again when Toby recognized two familiar faces. "Dalton! Thompson!" he shouted, rushing toward them. They high-fived.

"We knew you would be involved with this," laughed Dalton.

"Thought you might need help with the unruly crowds," joked Thompson.

After Toby introduced his friends from St. Zallo's, Dalton begged them for details about how the protest was going. Toby gave a short run-down, then Thompson asked, "How long are you here for?"

"Might be a while, so we'll need all the recruits we can get."

"There's been interest from all over the province," Holly chimed in. She pointed to where tents were going up. "The off-islanders are camping there."

"Then they go play tourist during the day," said Chester with a grin.

There was a grinning round of high-fives when Alyssa piped up, "Now that exams are over, we're here for the duration."

They compared notes about their exams then Toby asked, "Hey, how's my old buddy, Milton Turf?"

"Milton barely passed science," Dalton clucked. "Mainly due to his failing mark on that ecology project. He couldn't prove to Mr. Getty that no life forms had been injured in his study."

"Yeah, Milton didn't think insects should count as life forms," said Thompson rolling his eyes.

"The death of a sparrow in his study made Getty suspicious too," Dalton added.

"Still a jerk!" Toby angrily uttered.

"Yeah. He calls me *Injun* and *Warpaint*," said Thompson.

There was dead silence as everyone's jaws dropped. Finally Dalton managed a strangled, "I would have said something if I had known, Thompson."

"Why, that guy is a bully!" exclaimed Alyssa. "You should tell the counselor."

"They would put a stop to it!" declared Holly. "He sounds like a nutbar."

Jeanie and Judy arrived just then with their mom, so there was another round of introductions. Fern left with little Gemmie in tow, to visit her Oyster Narrows friends. The twins rapturously trailed the older teens as they toured the glade.

"Impressive," murmured Dalton.

"Holly helped organize it all," Chester announced proudly.

"You sign up for shifts over there," Toby pointed in the direction of a large colourful tent. "Plus they give out information about the sanctuary and the birds that use the place."

"It's supposed to be a media centre too, but..." Alyssa muttered.

"Do you really think you can stop the housing development?" asked Thompson. "I heard that the guy is rich. He'll know how to get his own way."

"Hey, did you know that Milton's dad works for him?" Dalton interjected.

"Suchno Whenge? No kidding?" Toby choked. Birds of a feather flock together, popped into his head—but that was being unkind to birds.

"We're getting word out over the Net, but the main-stream media is just not covering this," Alyssa complained bitterly. Boy, was she ever upset about that, Toby thought, eying her.

"We've been helping, too," the twins chimed in sync, then looked at each other and giggled.

By now they were close to the cliff and a view of the ocean, which was calm today. Toby could see Grandfather Gull looking grumpy indeed, hunched on his rock under the old arbutus. He didn't point out the old bird, who obviously wanted to be left in peace.

They drank in the view, somewhat marred by an enormous tanker nosing past a distant island.

"What about the birds?" Dalton lowered his voice, "Are they helping out?"

Toby looked sharply at his friend. He had told Dalton about the problems at the mansion and the court case but had left the birds out of it.

"I hear things you know," said Dalton with a wink. "A little birdie told me—that sort of thing." Toby's eyes widened. "You were the one that made me pay more attention to birds. Mr. Getty introduced me to a feathered friend…"

Before Dalton could say anything further, the Ranting Grannies started singing. Grams, wearing a hat patterned with purple hydrangeas, led a group of older women, while one played guitar. To the tune, "Oh When the Saints," they sang loudly:

Oh when the trees, are all cut down
Oh when the trees are all cut down
We will all mourn and be torn asunder
Oh when the trees are all cut down.

Oh then the birds, will all have flown
Oh then the birds will all have flown
They'll all be gone and we'll be left to wonder
When the birds will all have flown.

So join with us, stop this destruction
Join with us to halt construction.
Then all will be well, and birds without number
Will have Westwind for all of time.

They sang like raucous crows. Then Grams called out, "Everyone join in for the second time through!" The crowd got into the spirit and those who couldn't remember the words cheered and clapped.

Using a megaphone, Brian Martin thanked everyone for coming out to stand with the people of Oyster Narrows and the Truewind Islanders. "People are starting to come from off-island. Thanks to you, we have about 200 strong here now and I'm convinced there'll be more. Please pick up your garbage. We want to keep the place in its pristine state."

The woman from the information tent handed him a note and he continued, "Mel here wants to remind you to sign up at the information tent for shifts. Tell your friends and neighbours to come as well. We need coverage 24-7."

A bright sun shone down on the carnival of protesters. Soon a line-up of people formed at the information tent. An enterprising businesswoman from Fairwind was selling wraps and fruit drinks and there was even a face-painting

G.G. Neilson

booth where shining cheeks were being adorned with colourful images of birds. A couple of local constables arrived to
patrol the site, but left when they determined everything
was peaceful.

Beogall and a few other herons had flown in for a few
days earlier to bolster the birds but had already returned to
Stanley Park. The many birds flitting about that day stayed
out of the way, keeping a wary eye on the protesters from the
safety of shrubs and tree branches.

Berook, with her keen eyesight, spotted the trouble first.
A large truck was bumping over the rough trail toward
the protesters.

The owl did not like to be seen, especially during the day,
but decided to take a risk. She swept low over the protesters
and then veered sharply, flying swiftly toward the oncoming truck.

That got everyone's attention. The horn blared deafen-
ingly as the owl hurtled toward the truck. A collective gasp
went up as the owl banked up and away from the oncoming
vehicle at the last moment. The truck screeched to a halt.
Then resumed a slow lumber toward the protesters who
quickly got into a blockade formation.

Chief Wesley Martin stepped forward with both hands
held out, palms raised in a *stop* gesture. Behind him stood the
young friends and Brian, backed by the rest of the protesters.

The truck halted and Duffin Wint unfolded himself from
the cab. He approached the chief stiffly, holding out a warrant.

"This states that you and all of these people must vacate
this area," he said tersely. "Lord Suchno Whenge is taking
over the site to begin preparation for his development. His
legal development," he added, looking pointedly at Toby.

"The people here are protecting the rights of the birds of
this sanctuary," the chief stated. "We speak for them. We recognize only the ancient rights of the birds, the first occupants

of this land. My people and the people of Truewind Island have decreed it is theirs to be held in perpetuity."

"This land has been officially sold to Lord Whenge by the province," Duffin objected.

"With all due respect, Mr. Wint," said Toby stepping forward, "the order has been challenged and is now before the Supreme Court. People all over the province and the country are objecting to this order as we speak." Toby held up his phone. "Ten thousand people have signed onto our site 'Save Westwind for the Birds'." Actually it was a little shy of that amount, but Duffin wouldn't know.

"We will stay until the province overturns it!" shouted Alyssa.

Several protesters started a chant, "LSW, go home, LSW, leave the birds alone." The whole crowd took it up as one.

Duffin Wint stared long and hard, first at Toby and then at the chanting crowd. His fists were clenched into tight balls. He looked back at the two other men who were still in the truck.

"There's the CBC!" Alyssa shouted. Sure enough, a CBC van had lumbered into the clearing and squeezed in beside the truck. A crew quickly leapt out and began setting up.

Finally! thought Toby.

Duffin turned to head back to the truck when a reporter rushed up to ask his opinion of the occupation.

"This is an illegal protest," he barked. "We'll be back."

"What will you do about it?" the reporter asked, swinging a microphone towards him. "Who will you bring with you?"

But Duffin waved her aside and climbed into the truck, scowling. They sped off, kicking up stones, as the camera crew and protesters watched.

Chapter 23

Going Viral

It had been an exhausting day at work for Heather Myers. She curled up with her cat, Ginger, on the couch and turned on the evening news. Unlike her older brother Lars, Heather was born on Truewind Island. When Toby was only a small boy, his aunt had followed a boyfriend to Toronto, but had always vowed it was a temporary move. The relationship was over, but an excellent job kept her in the big city. When she returned once a year to visit the island and her mother, she usually saw Lars and Toby, but Barbara Myers had not encouraged visits. Still, she adored Toby and once flew him out for a week-long visit with her.

Her eyes grew as big as saucers when she recognized Westwind Bird Sanctuary, and she immediately turned up the sound.

"The occupation has been going on for a week," said the newscaster. "The group has been peaceful but determined. Marcie, what have you found out about this story?"

A young woman with shoulder-length dark hair began talking. Heather could see Grandmother Eagle's tree in the background and she was struck by a pang of homesickness.

"Thanks Linda. I'm here on Truewind Island, British Columbia, where the residents are protesting the development on a scenic parcel of land that was crown land, but has now been sold to a developer. We have noticed a lot of birds around, which is probably not remarkable, given that the locals call this a bird sanctuary."

As the camera panned the open glade that Heather knew so well, the reporter continued, "Behind me, there are close to a hundred protesters and organizers expect more to come."

Heather gasped at the size of the crowd—surely there were more than one hundred? She looked for people she knew.

"I have with me, Chief Wesley Martin of the Oyster Narrows band, here on Truewind Island." The reporter turned to him and asked, "Chief Martin, can you tell us what is bringing all these people here?"

"This land is the traditional territory of the Rushweshuqs or Oyster Narrows First Nation. We have never given up our rights to this land. More importantly, it also belongs to the birds."

"But Chief Martin, the province has made a deal to trade this land for another piece of land on Truewind Island," said the reporter. "Our sources tell us that Westwind Sanctuary has now been sold."

"That so-called deal is being challenged. My son is helping organize this occupation so I will let him speak," said the chief, turning to a younger, thinner version of himself.

Brian! The years have been good to him, Heather thought. So he was now a band spokesman. Why hadn't she kept in touch with him?

"LSW Holdings want to put a fancy housing development here," said Brian. "They will sell the homes for astronomical prices and this sacred territory will be lost for all time. We will not let that happen."

With a start, Heather remembered that LSW Holdings was the same company responsible for the worst of the developments in Wattasaga where her ex-boyfriend's parents lived. She had taken Toby out there to see them that time he had visited. He seemed very interested in what the old couple had to say about the disappearing farmlands, wetlands and birds.

"Other First Nations groups will join this protest from around the province," Brian continued. "We are prepared to stay here until LSW holdings withdraw their plans and the province declares this a protected area."

While the cameras panned over the sea of protesters, Heather wondered absently if Brian was married. They zoomed in on Grandmother Eagle sitting in her tree looking very stern. Heather wondered why she hadn't heard anything about this. The gulf between Toronto and Truewind Island suddenly seemed like a vast chasm. She felt it like a kick in the stomach.

"OMG! Is that Toby?" she yelled and the cat scampered from her lap with a *miaow* of complaint. Sure enough, it was—and the reporter called him forward. One of the young people standing with him looked familiar. Could that be Fern's girl, Holly? What a beauty she was. Heather eyes were glued to the screen as they interviewed her nephew.

"Toby Myers, aren't you one of the people organizing this protest?" asked the reporter.

"I'm just one of many," Toby replied. "We all feel that Westwind must be preserved. The birds have too few places left. Such a development would spell the end of this place as a sanctuary for them."

"Our sources tell us that you are quite concerned about birds. You seem very young to be involved with something like this."

"I've always been interested in…" Toby was about to say 'ornithology' but figured he would sound like a nerd and quickly added, "I don't think there's an age limit on being interested in nature. Lots of people want a healthy environment. Look at the crowd here."

"Whoa there, Toby," said the reporter. "I understand that you've done a lot of research about this issue and that you've been running a Facebook page and a Twitter feed. Is that true?"

"I've been doing some research and friends are helping with the Internet campaign." Toby waved his hand in the direction of the others. "There is legal precedent in reversing the decision to sell the land."

"You have Alison Sharma, a well-known environmental lawyer, on your side. Isn't she the same one who helped you at your recent court case?"

Far away in Toronto, Heather snorted. Her mother had told her about the court case. How could a reporter bring it up if Toby wasn't supposed to be identified? She held her breath as Toby responded.

"You said earlier that I am young and it's true that I'm a *minor*," Toby emphasized the point. "However, as a young person, I have to ask how much of the natural world will be left to us if development is allowed everywhere. That's why I'm here and if you'll excuse me, I have to get back to helping out."

Toby turned away and if the reporter knew she had been out of line, she didn't show it. "Well, there you have it, Linda," she beamed at the camera. "We'll keep you posted about developments here at Westwind Sanctuary on Truewind Island."

"Thanks, Marcie. Looks like a beautiful spot. In other news…"

Heather stood up quickly and turned off the television. Ginger leapt from the couch to go hide under the table while Heather went to call her mother.

But of course, she wasn't in. Carol Myers was at the occupation.

Back at Westwind, Toby's friends were congratulating him for a good interview and for keeping his cool.

"She shouldn't have mentioned that court case," said Chester and the others agreed.

"But it's great that we're getting national coverage now," said Dalton. "That can only help our cause."

Toby grinned at Dalton's use of *our*.

Jeanie and Judy came dashing over, having heard about the interview. "Our friends are texting us like crazy!" Judy exclaimed.

Grams came up and gave Toby a hug. Word had spread like wildfire around the encampment about the television interviews. The CBC crew had taken a few more shots, and was now packing up. Jeanie said she had overheard them talking about trying to get an interview with Lord Whenge.

Some local reporters and another news team from Vancouver showed up and also wanted to interview the organizers. Brian Martin, designated as spokesman, came over to the group crowded around Toby.

"This is starting to get big," he began, smiling. "I'll speak to the press on behalf of the band, but I think it's good to have your younger voices, too. You did well Toby—you kept focused on the message and didn't let them sidetrack you." He looked around the faces. "I recognize some of you from the camping trip a few weeks back."

Toby introduced his friends and Brian turned to Alyssa. "Yes, you're the gutsy girl who first suggested an occupation." Her cheeks took on a rosy hue. "I've seen you with your Aunt Fern. Welcome all of you," he said expansively. "Could you help by reminding people to pick up their garbage? We sure don't want the media side-tracked by photographing a mess here. This is a sacred place after all. And whenever I'm being interviewed, I'd like one of you young people to appear with me."

They agreed enthusiastically and Brian took Holly with him to be interviewed by the local media. The twins raced after them excitedly.

"I'm tired, Toby," said Grams. "I'm going home now, but I'll have supper holding for you and your friends whenever you're ready. Don't be too late. Dalton and Thompson, you're welcome to stay at our place."

They thanked her and winked at Toby as she left, since he had already invited them to stay.

"See, I said you'd be welcome."

"Your grandmother is cool," said Dalton. "How come I never heard about her before?"

"We really didn't visit her much. My mom preferred to go to other places than Truewind."

"I would just as soon come here as to any of the resorts my parents take me," Dalton replied. "This is one beautiful place. And a bird sanctuary too. It's heaven!"

"Hey, tell me about you and the birds, Dalton," said Toby, remembering their earlier conversation.

Before replying, Dalton glanced toward Alyssa and Chester. Toby nodded that it was okay to go on.

"Well, that day Beogall landed on the path at St. Zallo's had a big impact on me. Then when I heard about your old mansion and your help with that… Well, I ended up talking to Mr. Getty about it. You texted me, Toby, but he gave me information as well."

"Go on," Toby urged.

"One day a Steller's jay appeared in our yard when I was out doing my pond research for science. It took a while, but this jay finally made me, like, understand it was trying to communicate."

"Totally awesome, Dalton," said Toby.

"I can't say that we have much communication going on or that I can understand other birds, but Myrtle is really patient with me. She insisted that I come here."

"Hey, speaking of birds," Toby clapped his forehead, "they'll be waiting for some news. Anyone want to walk into the forest? I should tell them what's going on."

They all did and watched in amazement as about a dozen birds descended, chattering like crazy to Toby while a pair of warblers landed on his shoulders. Toby gave them news and they flew off excitedly. Both Dalton and Alyssa said they had picked up on some of the conversation but it was way too fast for them.

"I really have no knack for communicating with birds," said Thompson. "Dalton knows, but I can communicate with some animals, especially the canine and feline families. One time I ran into a bear in the woods and I caught a glimmer of something there too." Toby stared at him in surprise. "But I guess Chester speaks to animals better than I can."

They turned to Chester who tried to brush it off.

"Chester, you're among friends here," said Alyssa. "Granny Renie says you're 'the one'—that you can communicate with almost anything in the natural world."

"I don't know about that," Chester shrugged. "But there is always communication going on. Living in the city makes things easier."

"Wow!" said Dalton, eyes wide with astonishment. "How about these trees? Are you getting, like, vibes from them?"

"Vibes is a good word. Plants aren't like animals. You sense stuff from them, especially if they're in distress. I pick up more from trees if I'm standing over their roots. These trees are old and they don't bother with us much. With the smaller plants, you just get wisps of things…"

Alyssa nodded slowly. "That's how I would describe it too. You can definitely sense something from the trees if they're threatened. Right now, while I wouldn't say they're feeling happy, at least they're not super unset about all the people here. They're happiest when there are birds around—" She stopped as they all turned toward the noise of people rustling along the trail.

A man and a woman trudged toward them. They were both casually dressed in jeans and jackets. He was tall with medium length blondish hair and had not shaved in a few days. The woman had short, spiky hair and sported a piercing through one of her eyebrows.

"Can you tell us if we're headed the right way to Westwind Bird Sanctuary?" asked the man.

"Sure, you're almost there," replied Toby.

"We've come to join the protest," the young woman said, her voice silky.

"I'm Matt," said the man, "and this is Sarah. We're members of 'Birds Everywhere' and we wanted to come and help out."

"We're on our way there now," said Chester. "You can come with us."

"Thanks. How are things going anyway?" asked Matt as they hiked up the trail.

As they talked, it was obvious the couple had done their homework. At the information tent, the pair signed in.

Holly, Jeanie and Judy were there too, trying to arrange for a ride back to the Stronghold.

"We've been looking for you, Alyssa," Judy complained. "We're supposed to go home soon."

"Mom and Gemmie left already," added Jeanie.

"I signed us up for shifts over the next few days," said Holly. Then she gave Chester's hand a squeeze. "We'll have to spend some time together after all this is over—just the four of us." She turned to the twins. "C'mon, I've arranged a ride with one of Mom's friends."

As the girls left, Toby grinned at Chester, "I bet you're looking forward to spending time with Holly. Hey, what do you think about that couple who've come to help?"

"The group they represent is legit. Why?"

"I just have a weird feeling about them," said Toby. "Let's find out their last names—maybe I'll do some checking."

Toby chatted to the young woman stationed at the tent, who gushed about his great interview, as Chester looked down the list of names. He nudged Toby when he had the information and they moved away.

"They're Matt Murphy and Sarah Parker," Chester informed him.

"Okay, I'll look them up on Birds Everywhere when I have a chance. Why don't we go see what they're up to?"

They found Matt and Sarah talking to some of the local residents, telling them what an important cause it was and how they were so keen to come and help out.

"We've really got to stop this development, no matter what!" declared Sarah emphatically. "Hey, Toby, how long do you think it's gonna take?"

"Who knows?" He shrugged his shoulders.

"Surely you can't stay here forever. What if there's no action?" she asked.

"We're taking it day by day. Our numbers speak for themselves."

"Is it true that Alison Sharma is looking into it on your… our behalf?"

"It's true. How long are you here for?" Toby asked.

"We can stay for a few days. Well, we're going to look around some more." With that she and Matt headed off to speak with another group of people.

It was starting to get dark when the friends got a ride home with Brian.

"It's been so hot and dry," Toby said to Brian. "I'm worried about campfires. The birds are feeling nervous too with all those people around."

"I made an announcement about no campfires the first night," said Brian, keeping his eyes on the road. "But a reminder is good. A fire is not the kind of attention we want."

Chapter 24

The Occupation Spreads its Wings

Grams wasn't feeling well as she left Westwind. *Too much excitement*, she thought as she drove home carefully. She had a little sit down and then went to splash water on her face.

I'm not used to being around so many people anymore she told her reflection in the mirror. *Carol Myers, you are looking really old.*

You still look beautiful to me.

Thanks, dear. I love you too, said Carol to Carl's picture. They often spoke together like this. It was comforting—she often asked what he would do in a given situation and was thankful for his advice. Forty good years together… but still not long enough.

Grams started making dinner. Preparing food was relaxing—like second nature to her. And so nice to have people to cook for. The baked pasta with vegetables, once in the oven, could be kept warm for an hour or two.

As she got out the spare bedding, worry pangs struck. What if something bad happened up there? Who were they to think they could stop this thing?

Then she got two phone calls in a row that helped put her mind at ease.

"Mom—I've been trying to get a hold of you! I saw the Westwind protest on the news. And Toby!"

"Heather! Where are you? Your voice is so clear."

"In Toronto, Mom. Why didn't you tell me about it?"

"Why, I intended to, dear. It's just been so busy around here. Toby and his friend Chester are here and two more are staying tonight...," her voice petered out.

"No worries, Mom, you must be swamped. Are you feeling okay?"

"I... I'm just a bit tired. We've revived the Ranting Grannies, and most of the song-writing has been left to me. Some of them just can't remember the words."

Heather laughed. "They never did bother about staying in tune. I saw Brian Martin being interviewed on television. Then they talked to Toby—he was super. He's looking so grown-up. God, how I want to come out and see you."

Carol's heart leapt. "Would you? That would be wonderful. Could you get time off work?" She knew how Heather loved her job—would she ever leave Toronto?

"I have holiday time banked. I'll look into it tomorrow." Heather paused and then asked, "So is Brian some sort of a spokesman for the group?"

"The Chief has him organizing this protest for the band. Maybe Wesley wants to keep him occupied. His latest girl-friend left a few months ago." Carol wondered whether she had remembered to tell Heather earlier. She added, "I think he still carries a torch for you... Heather?" It sounded like snuffling on the other end. Could the girl be crying? "How long can you come for?"

"Umm..." There was a catch in her throat, "I'd have to wrap up a few things at work and then I might be able to come out for a couple of weeks. Mom, take care of yourself. We'll talk soon."

Suddenly Carol felt a lot better. She hadn't spoken to Heather for a while—too busy with the protest. Was Heather was still carrying the torch for Brian too? They had a stormy on-again off-again relationship in high-school. Then Heather met someone in university and moved out to Toronto with him. It had only lasted a few years. She was still thinking about Heather when her phone rang again.

It was Lars. "Mom! I saw the protest at Westwind on the news! Toby did a great interview."

"Lars, he was just amazing. He loves birds so he's in his element—and all those people supporting this protest. It's marvelous."

"That boy is full of surprises—I don't admit to understanding him. But I'm proud of him."

"Toby is special—he's turning into a real... Lars, your sister just called and she wants to come out here."

"Wonderful! Oh—I saw that Brian Martin is some sort of a spokesman for the cause. Did she ask about him?"

"Of course she did. I think I forgot to tell her that his latest girlfriend is now out of the picture. All this business—Toby's friend Chester is here too, and two others... "

"Don't wear yourself out, Mom."

His mother gave a slightly giddy laugh, then asked, "How's the golf tour going, Lars?"

"Just great! I played my best round today." He gave her a few details and then said, "Well, give my love to Toby—if he still remembers me."

After they made their goodbyes, she turned on the television—the six o'clock news was just airing. It must be the same news that was live back east three hours earlier. Grams was impressed with Brian and wasn't that a shot of Grandmother Eagle? When Toby's interview was over, she let out her breath.

After checking on supper, she went outside. Sure enough, Rio was there waiting and they exchanged news. The birds were happy, if somewhat apprehensive about all the support. Rio would fly back to tell the others about the news coverage. As she turned to go back in, Brian drove up and the four boys piled out.

They were hopping with excitement about the day and attacked their meal with gusto as Grams looked on with pleasure. "You made the six o'clock news," she remembered to tell them.

"Cool, we'll watch it on the computer later," said Toby between mouthfuls.

"Aunt Heather phoned." Toby looked up to see his grandmother's face shining. "She's going to try to come out here."

"That would be awesome!" said Toby with a grin.

"Your dad phoned too—he's proud of you."

Toby paused in the middle of a bite of roast carrot, to look at her.

"For your great interview."

"Oh. How's his golf tour?"

They discussed that over the remains of supper. Then Toby set up the cot in the family room and pulled out the couch. Grams heard the boys talking long into the night.

The next morning, she was up early as usual. After laying out breakfast for when the boys got up, she made a trip into Fairwind to replenish supplies. Talk in town was all about Westwind. People were pouring in from all over. The town's two motels were turning away guests and B & Bs were filling up. She ran into Fern Strong.

"My house is full," her neighbour laughed. "Well, fuller than usual with my own four. Plus Alyssa. Did you ever meet my sister, Sharman?"

"No, I don't think so," said Grams. But her memory was a bit fuzzy.

"You know, Alyssa's mother?" Fern gave her a puzzled look and then added, "She's here too, and Mom of course. The reserve is hopping—loads of our people making their way here."

The boys were just crawling sleepily out of their beds when Grams returned. "I heard in town that droves of people are arriving for the protest," she told them.

Toby and Chester whooped. Over breakfast they chatted happily about the day ahead. It was late morning when Grams dropped them off at the trail to the glade.

The crowd was growing but something seemed different about the mood.

They found Alyssa, Holly and the twins with a group of young people listening to Matt and Sarah.

"We've got to show we mean it," Matt was speaking, pounding a fist forcefully into his hand. "Get our message out—make a splash."

"Let them know we won't be pushed around," added Sarah.

"Actually, our organization is doing just fine," said Toby, stepping in. "How was it up here last night?"

"Awesome to be sleeping under the stars again," Matt enthused.

"You have a little piece of paradise here," added Sarah.

"We aim to keep it that way. Were many people here? Any reporters?"

"Not many stayed—it was pretty low key," Sarah replied. "No reporters—were you expecting some?"

"Hey, interest is building." Toby's arm encompassed the growing crowd. "I'm going to check in. See you later."

Thompson, Dalton and Holly and the twins stayed with the group, while Alyssa accompanied Chester and Toby. After checking in, they went to see how Grandmother Eagle was faring.

She was upset. "Some people lit a fire last night!"

"I thought Brian Martin warned people not to make fires," fumed Toby.

"Yes, he did, but then he left. You all left—there was no-one here who could talk to us," she complained. "We set up our own watch, we were so worried."

"Maybe we should stay up here tonight," Chester suggested.

"I would feel better if you did. Grandfather Gull is unhappy about this crowd. I'm not sure it's doing any good."

"Windrunner is just used to being here alone," said Alyssa haltingly. Toby stared at her. It was the first time he had heard her speak to birds. "It just takes time, Grandmother. You'll see," she continued awkwardly.

"Hmff!" the eagle chuffled.

They turned to leave, but the bird called out, "There's a couple that came yesterday. I don't like them. They left garbage around. Young Windrunner went over and picked it up. Could you find one of those garbage bins for it?"

They followed her to the base of a hemlock tree, where sure enough, was a neat pile of torn papers, an empty chip bag, a candy wrapper and two empty beer cans. Toby and Chester put the garbage into their packs.

"Hey, look at this!" said Alyssa, studying a small scrap of paper. "This could be your name." She handed the slip over to Toby.

Sure enough, the letters "Tob" were on a small piece of ripped paper. He stared at the slip of paper, trying to recall something. Then it struck him. He had never told Matt and Sarah his name but she had used it when they were talking with the young people. Maybe someone else had told her his name…

"Here's something." Chester had been hunting through the garbage and showed them a shred of paper with the words "watch out --". It looked like it was from the same paper. "Ominous," he commented.

"Yeah, and this looks like an application for membership for Birds Everywhere," said Toby, showing them another shred of paper.

"It doesn't seem like those two have been members for very long," Alyssa pointed out.

"Let's hang on to these," Toby suggested and stuffed them into his pocket.

They hiked over to a far corner of the clearing where the eagle had directed them and they found evidence of a recent fire. Chester fished through the ashes and found a cigarette stub. "Look at this," he showed the others.

"Disgusting," Alyssa pronounced.

"Morning. What are you folks up to?" Matt was sauntering toward them.

"Hey Matt –did you build a fire here last night?" Toby demanded.

He hesitated and then said, "Yeah man, it's dark up here and it gets cold at night. Is there a problem?"

"The place is tinder dry. There was an announcement about no fires."

"I didn't hear any announcement."

"Do you smoke?" asked Chester, holding up the cigarette butt.

"Hey, you caught me there. I'm seriously trying to quit." He offered a grin.

None of them grinned back. "You better quit right now," said Toby. "No smoking allowed here."

They left to find Brian. Matt just stared after them, the grin replaced by a grimace.

Brian Martin was just getting ready for another interview as they approached and he waved them over. "Chester, want to say something after I speak?" he asked.

Chester agreed and asked Toby with a grin, "How does my hair look?"

"You don't want to know. Good luck."

While they were waiting for the cameras to set up, Toby was startled to see people pouring in. Matt had joined Sarah in the middle of a large group of young people and was talking intently. Sarah looked over and saw Toby watching. She poked Matt when the interview with Brian started.

Brian talked about their cause and then declared, "This is a peaceful protest. We have a democratic right to be here to make our views known." He paused then introduced Chester. "As one of the young people here, Chester is helping to make sure that Westwind Sanctuary will still be here for his generation."

"Why did you get involved with this?" asked the reporter, turning the mic toward Chester.

"My friends and I are really concerned about the natural world. We've been taught that we're all interconnected. That it's, like, important to preserve areas like this… for their bio-diversity. Lots of birds use this place."

"It sounds like you've been well educated. What school do you go to Chester?"

"Willow Heights Secondary."

"Isn't that where Megan Tanaka teaches?"

"Yes, she's my science teacher—she's super."

"I understand that she and her father, Dr. Lawrence Tanaka are on their way to Truewind Island. Do you think they will join the protest?"

"That would be awes—" Chester's words were cut off as a huge roar went up behind him.

"DO WE WANT WESTWIND SAVED?" It was Matt shouting.

"YES!" screamed the crowd.

"WHEN DO WE WANT IT?"

"NOW!"

"DEVELOPERS GO HOME!" led Matt.

G.G. Neilson

"DEVELOPERS GO HOME! DEVELOPERS GO HOME!" the crowd responded and the chant carried around the clearing.

The cameraman turned away from the interview and panned the crowd. Matt and Sarah, with their backs to the cameras, raised their fists and so did some in the crowd. Matt screamed out, "Down with developers!" Others took up the chant and soon "Down with developers" echoed around the glade as television cameras recorded the commotion.

Toby was aware of how disturbed the birds were by the shouting. *This is getting out of hand*! He approached the screaming crowd, wondering what to do. He saw Matt's jacket discarded on the ground. In the mayhem, Toby slipped over and took something from the pocket. Yelling and leading the crowd, Matt didn't notice.

Toby found Chester and they went to round up their friends.

"We have to get these protesters calmed down," Toby told the others. "The birds are really upset."

As they spread out, Brian Martin had the same idea, since he called out over the megaphone, "I'd like to remind people that this a peaceful protest. Our strength is in our numbers. And in our message."

As he spoke, two people emerged from the trail and into the clearing.

Meagan and Lawrence Tanaka strode over to Brian, who welcomed them with relief. "Dr. Lawrence Tanaka! It's an honour to meet you. Would you mind saying something to the crowd?" he asked.

The popular scientist took the megaphone. "I'm Lawrence Tanaka and it's a pleasure to be here," he began, over the noise of the crowd.

A sudden hush came over the protesters.

"This is a truly important cause you have come to champion. Westwind is a special place—a sacred place and you are doing a noble thing, fighting for it to be spared from the machinery of development. You are speaking for those who cannot speak for themselves. The birds."

The crowd clapped and cheered. The mood had changed in an instant.

That evening over supper, Toby and his friends were ebullient about Dr. Tanaka's visit.

"It was great that he came," enthused Dalton. "I got to talk to him."

"Me too," said Thompson. "And didn't he change the mood of that crowd!"

"It was great that Ms. Tanaka came too," said Chester. "Too bad they had to leave so soon."

"I still think we should spend the night up there," advised Toby. "Who's in?"

They all were.

Chapter 25

Trouble

Grams was frowning.

They were packing some things and Chester mentioned the campfire, even though Toby nudged him. He didn't want to worry his grandmother further.

She was indeed alarmed. "Oh, dear! That place is as dry as tinder this time of year. Who built the fire?"

"There's two people who arrived yesterday. They say they're from Birds Everywhere. Matt Murphy is the guy, and he said it was cold which is why he built it."

"Said he hadn't heard an announcement about not making camp fires," added Chester.

Grams wrung her hands, muttering, "Back in the day when Gramps and I attended protests for peace, we heard about professional agitators. Gramps had a name for them," she puzzled then continued, "They could turn a peaceful dem-onstration into something awful and bring on all kinds of bad publicity."

Toby and Chester looked at each other.

Earlier, in his room, Toby had quietly shown Chester what he had 'found'. "Matt was pretty busy riling up the crowd so it was easy to liberate his wallet," he remarked.

"You stole it?" Chester was incredulous.

"Keep it down, man—just borrowed. I'm not taking any-thing from it. Could you return it to him tomorrow? You could say that you found it."

"Oh man, you need my help again and that usually means trouble," Chester rolled his eyes.

"It's obvious that *you* couldn't have taken it, since you were far away *and* being interviewed when it went missing," reasoned Toby. "Since you didn't run into Matt again, it makes sense that you didn't have a chance to return it."

"I worry about you sometimes, Toby. You're willing to do anything for the cause, aren't you?" asked Chester.

"To save birds. Pretty much anything," agreed Toby.

"A real bird warrior."

Toby laughed. "Yep. You are too. Remember what Dr. Tanaka called us—we're eco-warriors."

"That totally describes Alyssa and Holly, too," said Chester. "I guess it describes us all. Okay, I'll do it. We're in this together. Now that we have it, we may as well look through the thing," he said, grabbing the wallet from Toby with a grin. "To make sure I return it to the rightful owner."

But when the two looked through Matt's wallet, they quickly changed their minds about how to return it. A busi-ness card caught their attention. They stared at each other speechless. Then they returned everything to the wallet just as they had found it. Toby thought about phoning his dad, but then he would have to admit to taking the wallet. No, he couldn't risk it.

There was still some light in the sky when Grams dropped them at the trail. Dalton was enlisted to return the wallet to the Lost and Found. Toby didn't give him the particulars and he was savvy enough not to ask. The girl on duty thanked him saying that Matt had already come by to see if it had been turned in.

Some Oyster Narrows people had started a drumming circle in the middle of the glade. The haunting chants drew people in. Soon the circle grew into a mass of people swaying and listening. Someone whispered, "It's Rushweshuqs language—a bird dance."

A sliver of moon appeared as the four headed to their spot to settle in for the night. Birds had finished up their evening songs and the spooky swoop of an owl overhead had some people shivering. Toby shivered too, but with delight. He wished he could have been up there sweeping through the twilight, senses alert to any sound or movement, wing feathers outspread in the cool evening breeze.

"What planet are you on, Toby?" Thompson had been trying to get his attention. "I asked you what the girls are up to tonight."

"Oh, sorry. They had to baby-sit. Mr. and Mrs. Strong went into Vancouver, so they are all spending the evening together with Gemmie."

"They're pretty cool. Are you and Alyssa serious?"

"Well, I like her a lot, if that's what you mean. She seems to like me too. Sort of a turn-around from when we first met. She called me a lurker then. How about you, Thompson— anyone special?"

"Kind of hard when you go to a private boy's school. But one of the Rushweshuqs girls had her eye on me I think. Do you know Raven Charlie?'

Toby slapped his shoulder. "Way to go—Raven is cool. She doesn't live up here but she has family here. She goes to my school."

"Why haven't I seen her around?"

"She doesn't live at Cypress Gardens is probably why. She lives in the next development over."

"If you two can get your minds off girls for a minute, could we talk about the occupation?" Dalton spoke impatiently.

"How long do you think it'll take? I have to get back home soon."

"Sorry to inconvenience you, but there's something important going on here." Toby realized this wasn't fair and dropped his sarcastic tone, "I heard from the lawyer and she filed an appeal. She said all the public support we're getting is helping."

"And if more well-known people like the Tanakas lend their support," Chester added, "it'll help too. But probably we'll be here a while yet. Some kids from Willow Heights said they would come."

"Brian says we still need more media," Toby ruminated. "We've put a lot of stuff on UsLive. But…" He lowered his voice and told the others what he and Chester had found out about Matt. They couldn't decide if they should tell someone about it and then lapsed into silence.

Stars were pricking through the darkening sky and the night air was cool as they settled into their sleeping bags on top of a groundsheet. They had all opted to sleep in their clothes.

A breeze off the ocean was tinged with salt and Toby lay half-asleep listening to the quiet conversations going on around them. A faint smell of smoke filtered through the air—reminding him of their earlier camping trip—how Alyssa had really warmed up to him when he played the flute by the campfire…

Suddenly he shot out of his sleeping bag with a yell and raced toward the smoke, the others following.

"What are you doing!" he howled as he came upon Matt and Sarah, sitting with a few others around the blaze.

"Hey, cool it," said Matt. "The fire wasn't my idea, but like, these people have taken all the necessary precautions. Besides, a campfire is just the ticket to bring people together."

"Has it occurred to you that this is precious habitat we're trying to save? Has it occurred to you that a fire would be just what the developer would want?"

Toby almost added something else, but stopped himself. He began to stamp out the campfire.

One of the campers jumped up and pushed him away, shouting, "Hey, we'll put it out when we're ready to!"

Toby pushed him back. "You were told there are to be *NO* fires!"

The young man shoved Toby again and Chester grabbed him. "It doesn't matter how careful you are," he said to the boy. "Do you see any water around here?"

Some of the others had leapt to their feet, trying to prevent the fire from being put out. Dalton and Thompson stepped into the fray.

"Out of my way, fatty," hissed the boy Dalton was restraining.

Matt stepped forward from behind Toby and Chester. "Hey guys, it's time to put it out anyway," he said in a conciliatory tone.

"Yeah, we should hit the hay soon," added Sarah who materialized from behind Dalton and Thompson.

The others huffed a bit, but let Toby and Chester stamp out the fire, carefully making sure there were no embers left. Toby noticed Mel from the information booth was with them and wondered whether she had returned Matt's wallet to him.

They trudged back to their sleeping bags and decided to set up a watch. Chester volunteered to go first. "I'll set the alarm on my phone," he said, reaching into his pocket. "Hey! It's not here!" He checked all his pockets.

"You can borrow mine," said Dalton, but his was missing too. In fact all four of their phones were missing.

"I bet it was Matt and Sarah!" gritted Toby.

"Yeah, they were behind us during that shoving match," said Thompson. "I bet that's when they took them. What are we going to do?"

They were divided on whether to march over and demand them back from Matt and Sarah or wait and tell Brian about it in the morning. In the end, they decided to wait.

"It so happens that I have a watch," said Dalton. "Bit of an old-fashioned idea, I know, but it was my grandma's gift to me, so I like to wear it." He handed the timepiece over to Chester for the first shift. "Wake me up in two hours."

Toby lay awake for a long time. He heard some unrest from the nearby birds who twittered anxiously about the fire. How did Matt get the phone from my pocket? he wondered. Too weird.

The sliver of moon had disappeared and Toby was thankful for the warm sleeping bag Grams provided. "Sometimes Gramps and I slept under the stars on the deck," she had reminisced. He looked deep into the sky now, wonderingly. He couldn't remember Gramps very well—he was quite sick and frail when Toby was small. But he had built the cabin while commuting a job in Vancouver. He must have been quite a guy. As amazing as Grams. An owl hooted nearby and Toby fell asleep thinking about Alyssa.

She and Holly arrived at Westwind very early with some bad news.

"Toby!" she shouted. "There're news reports about fights going on. Personal information from your cell-phone has been shared. They're calling you a trouble-maker, that you go around making things bad for Lord Whenge. And worst of all, he's won the court case to keep Westwind for his development." She started sobbing and Toby put his arms around her. But she turned into an azalea bush and shook when he stroked her.

Holly looked lovingly at Chester as she said, "It's too late for Westwind, but it's not too late for us." She lay her head on his shoulder and Chester turned to him. "It's okay, Toby, there'll be other battles to fight." His friend handed him a badge that said *Eco-Warrior.*

Just then large machines showed up to start ripping out the trees.

"NOOOOO!" screamed Toby.

Thompson shook him awake. "Well, that's gratitude," he carped. "We let you sleep through your shift and you have a nightmare instead."

Toby looked groggily around at his three grinning chums. "Oh, sorry. I get these intense dreams." *Did everyone get dreams that seemed so real?* "How did it go overnight anyway?"

The sun was creeping over the horizon, casting rosy fingers around the glade. The first birds were busily warbling, gathering breakfast, some even building nests.

"All's calm on the western front," declared Chester.

Over a breakfast of Grams' muffins they discussed how they were going to get their phones back.

"They stole them!" declared Dalton. "Maybe we can charge them."

"Or maybe we could just go and take them back," said Thompson pointing. "Looks like everyone is still sleeping over there."

"I don't know if that's such a good plan..." Toby clapped his head, "I should have thought of it before! The birds can get messages out for us."

Grandmother Eagle agreed with the plan, when Toby and Chester went to see her, "We have our messengers. I'll send out Rio, your grandmother's friend. She can bring news back and forth."

"Grandmother," Toby said respectfully, "you know when we talked about that other way the birds could help?" The eagle nodded solemnly. "Well, I have a feeling we might be needing that kind of help soon."

"I see." Her reply was a quiet rumble. "I've been expecting it."

"We'll try to be careful so that no birds are filmed communicating with us. But if it's safe—could we use the signal for the birds to help us?"

"The signal. Yes, I remember it. The birds will help. In fact, they are eager to." Then the old eagle confided, "I was excited at first about this protest. We all were. Now we're not so sure about this human crowd. The campfires, the mess, the shouting… " The big bird hopped briskly from one foot to the other. "Some of the humans aren't nice. The couple that arrived two days ago—they're the worst."

Toby and Chester exchanged glances. "We don't like them either. We need to be vigilant. Could the birds keep an eye on those two?"

"Certainly," intoned the eagle.

"As soon as we get some reinforcements here, we'd like to go into Fairwind and talk to some people we know," said Toby.

"We'll get this thing back on track, Grandmother," Chester tried to reassure her.

"You're good boys and I know you'll do your best." She bent her head low to peer at them. "I'm worried about Grandfather Gull. He hasn't been talking to anyone. He just sits on his rock and stares off into the distance."

Toby and Chester looked over to the arbutus. The outline of old Windrunner could be seen beneath it, still as a statue. Suddenly Grandmother Eagle made disapproving noises.

Crows and eagles are not the best of friends, so when several flapped over, she was less than pleased. Her attitude changed as soon as the first crow squawked, "Three trucks are headed up here. They're filled with workmen. Doesn't look good."

"Doesn't look good," echoed the others.

"One is towing a machine," said the first. From her tone, Toby saw a mental image of an excavator and said the word.

"An excavator," the crows repeated as they flew off.

Toby and Chester hurried off to rally a line of defense. It was so early in the morning that only a small group of bedraggled overnight campers stood together as two pickup trucks and a larger truck towing the excavator on a trailer approached. A man in the lead truck climbed out; Toby recognized him as a local man.

He cleared his throat. "I have orders here to begin clearing the first section for our new development," he said, and he shoved a legal-looking paper at Toby who had been pushed forward by the others.

Toby let it fall to the ground without looking at it. "With all due respect," he said gravely, "we are legally occupying this land. We cannot allow any clearing to go ahead."

"Guess you hadn't heard that there's been an injunction filed and if you don't let us start work, you can each be fined or thrown in jail."

They all gasped and Toby looked confused. "We haven't heard anything about it," he stalled for time. "I'm sorry, but we can't let you pass."

The man bent to retrieve the paper. "I would have thought you people would be up on all the news, but I advise you to look at this because we're going ahead." He motioned to the others who piled out of the trucks, including two men who looked like security police.

Toby turned to the rag-tag group behind him and said, "We've come too far to give up now. Are you with me?"

Some didn't look at all confident, but then Chester shouted, "Yes!" with Dalton and Thompson quickly joining in. Soon everyone called out their support. They joined hands and stretched across the clearing as best they could.

"Sure hope we get reinforcements soon," Chester murmured.

The workmen started pushing into the line, moving whomever they perceived to be weak. The line had been pushed back by about ten feet when finally a group of newcomers arrived. "Hurry! Come join us! We need help!" people shouted to them.

The newcomers rushed in and soon there was a pulsating crowd pushing back against the workmen.

"Peaceful resistance!" Toby shouted, but without Brian and his megaphone it was no use. Punches were thrown and the line broke up in several places. One workman started up a chainsaw and attacked a small tree. Toby ran to give the signal to Grandmother Eagle.

No sooner he had done so, the workmen were immediately beset with dozens of birds attacking and pecking at them. One of the security men drew a weapon and pointed at the birds.

"If you shoot a bird, I will have you charged!" Toby bellowed. The man hesitated and Toby looked around wildly to see where the other guard was. That was when he discovered that a television crew had just arrived on the scene and was filming the bird protesters.

He groaned but quickly realized it might help their cause. "You'll be shown on national television shooting birds," he shouted at the guard, pointing toward the cameras. "Call the other security guy and tell him that."

The man glared resentfully at Toby but put away his weapon and took out his phone. Toby scanned the area with a growing sense of panic, looking for the other guard. Someone should tell Grandmother Eagle to call off the birds—then he saw Chester heading over to her tree. *Damn, we forgot a call-off signal*, he thought.

A shot rang out. Grandmother Eagle dropped from her tree where she had been rallying the birds moments before. "NOOOO!" Toby screamed.

As she fell, Chester sprinted the last few meters and caught her in his arms.

Toby looked around wildly for the other guard. He finally saw the man and raced toward him shouting, "Don't shoot!"

Another shot rang out and Toby felt a *phsst*. A bullet had grazed his outstretched arm. But it found its mark in Grandfather Gull who was in flight headed in his direction. The elder Windrunner flapped his wings valiantly and then went limp.

Brian Martin arrived on the scene just in time to see the old gull topple slowly through the air. Running behind him were Alyssa, Holly and the twins.

"AIEEEE!" Brian screamed, "Grandfather!"

They all watched in horror as the old gull turned over in the air, fluttered his wings weakly a few more times and went tumbling towards the far trees. The old bird disappeared from sight over the edge of the cliff.

Chapter 26
Battle for Westwind

Brian ran and stumbled over to where the old gull was last seen. He didn't notice his arms and legs getting scratched and gouged by brambles and bushes as he scrambled down the cliff.

Toby's head spun in both directions before he sprinted over to Chester who was cradling Grandmother Eagle.

"Toby, you're hurt!" cried Alyssa, rushing to him followed by Holly and the twins. He looked down to see a bloodstain growing on his sleeve.

"Just a graze. It'll heal," he said grimly, gripping his arm. He stared at Grandmother Eagle.

Chester lay the old eagle down carefully and probed her chest gently. "She's still alive," he said to their questioning eyes. "But she's losing blood and will need help."

Alyssa whipped out a first aid kit and gave him a cloth bandage, which he applied to the bird. Then she turned to Toby, "Let's get that arm bandaged."

As he removed his shirt, he saw her eyeing his muscles. The gym workouts are finally paying off, he thought, as she expertly tended to him. "Are you always this well-prepared?" he asked.

"Girl Scout training," she answered. "There, that should do for now."

"I'm going to see if Grandfather Gull survived." Toby choked a little over the words.

"We're good here," said Holly as she and Alyssa bent over the old eagle.

Toby laid a hand on the bird's head briefly before he and Chester returned to the glade.

The scene was a nightmare. A second film crew had arrived and was filming what had now turned very ugly. Some of the protesters wore masks—were those two Matt and Sarah? The birds, already riled, were going crazy—now pecking at everyone, friend or foe.

The friends stood numbly, watching.

"What do we do now?" Chester muttered.

"This is totally out of hand," replied Toby. "And without Grandmother Eagle, the birds are going ballistic."

"Toby, we need to call in our bird-bonds!" cried Chester. "If anyone can help, it's Beogall and Sami."

"Of course!" Why hadn't he thought of it? Right now, he needed Beogall. "Let's go!"

The two raced towards the far edge of the clearing, near where Grandfather Gull had plummeted down.

"You first, Toby. Hurry."

Toby racked his memory as he took out the feather. He drew in a deep, calming breath and then formed the call. Since it didn't sound human, he didn't worry about drawing attention to himself. But down below, from the rocky beach, Brian looked up. He knew what Toby was doing.

Chester had his feather out and performed his call next. To Toby's ears, it sounded more practiced and quite different from his own call. Then they waited.

"Do you need any help, Brian?" Toby shouted down. He could see Brian wading into the water. He signaled *no* and made his way toward the lifeless, grey form barely visible, floating a ways out. They could see Windrunner the younger, watching from the shore.

Brian gently plucked the crumpled body from the next wave. He brought it back to shore in his arms. They could see him speaking and then he waved a feather over the emaciated, limp form.

In the distance, flapping towards them were two familiar forms. Toby's heart swelled with relief, then pride as Beogall and Sami landed beside them, exhausted.

"Need some rest," gasped Sami.

While their feathered friends gathered strength, Toby and Chester filled them in on what had happened.

"You should have called us earlier," Beogall finally managed.

"We should have," agreed Chester.

"Thanks for coming so fast," said Toby gratefully.

"Once again, I anticipated your call," Beogall explained. "We flew to Deadman's Island yesterday."

"You are an incredibly clever bird," Toby said fondly. "We really need your help in calming down those other birds." He pointed over to where hundreds of birds were flapping and buzzing around the workmen who swatted and swore in vain. With two film crews recording them, the security police had put away their weapons.

Beogall and Sami took off without another word. The sight of a great blue heron and a brilliant blue Steller's jay winging over them, seemed to quiet both the crowd and the birds.

Toby and Chester followed them and could hear the two calling off the other birds and Toby wondered, not for the first time, what it sounded like to people who could not understand.

"Maybe the worst is over," he voiced.

How wrong he was.

"Hey, man, is that smoke I smell?" wondered Chester.

"FIRE!!" someone screamed.

They whirled around to see several tongues of flame coming from the bush near Grandmother Eagle's tree. Toby's first thought was for Alyssa and Holly's safety. They charged in that direction and found the girls a little way into the bushy area.

They had the eagle bandaged up and cradled on a bed of boughs laced together.

"Are you okay? You have to get out of here," said Toby urgently.

They both looked alarmed and Holly said, "Is that fire?"

The boys nodded grimly.

Alyssa looked startled. "We didn't know. Too engrossed with taking care…"

"I'll take Grandmother to the path," said Holly taking over the bundle. "I'll try to get a ride out—if she gets help in time, she might make it." With that she headed resolutely to the path.

"We have to call for help!" Alyssa said, reaching for her phone. She frowned. "There's no reception!"

"I was afraid of that," said Toby. "I asked Grams to be on standby so I'll get word to her. Young Windrunner was on the beach and he's the fastest bird around."

With a pounding heart, Toby raced back over to the cliff. The swift young gull left his post and flew up immediately at Toby's call. Then he took off like a shot, winging towards Grams' cabin with news of the fire.

When Toby returned to the clearing, the workmen, many protesters and some birds had already left in panic as well as one of the camera crews. Only the young people and some locals remained. A brisk wind was whipping the flames with frightening speed. Beogall and Sami were busy trying to prevent panic among the remaining birds.

Alyssa was in high gear and had organized those who remained into brigades. A group headed by Dalton was gathering sleeping bags and blankets to put out small fires as they sprang up around the clearing. Another group was in charge of safety—acting as fire lookouts and watching the backs of everyone else.

"Thank heavens, you're back!" she cried as Toby came up. "I've rounded up buckets and rope. There's no water left in the gullies—too dry. We'll have to use the ocean."

Her plan dawned on Toby as she ordered, "You four," pointing to Thompson and three other local boys, "come with us to the cliff."

Toby, Judy and Jeanie followed with the buckets. "We'll head down now," Alyssa told the four. "Stay here. You'll be pulling up these buckets when they're filled with water. Only douse flames where you can do so safely."

They looked at each other questioningly as she, Toby and the twins navigated down an old path to the beach below.

"Call in four big birds now, Toby," she commanded. "Quickly!"

He called and Beogall, Berook, Woodley and a young eagle joined them on the beach. Translating her orders, Toby instructed the birds to each carry the end of one of the ropes up and over the large branch of the big arbutus tree. The birds immediately zoomed up and dropped the ropes over the branch and into the waiting hands of the four surprised boys.

Down below, they quickly tied the other end of the ropes to the buckets and filled them with water. On Alyssa's signal the boys began hauling the filled buckets up, using the arbutus branch as leverage. They helped each other, grabbing buckets, undoing the ropes and quickly emptying them onto the hotspots. Then they lowered the buckets down again to be refilled.

"Keep track of your own end!" shouted Thompson. "Put it under a rock." One of the buckets came off the branch, but Beogall fetched the end of the rope and tossed it back over the branch. "That's a smart bird!" said one of the bucket brigade boys.

It was hard work for Toby and the twins. Alyssa supervised, yelling out when a bucket sailed down to be reloaded. Brian was almost hit when he returned from his mission with Grandfather Gull, grim-faced. She outlined the plan to him.

"Oh God!" was all he said and scaled the cliff like a mountain goat.

By throwing the seawater onto areas directed by the safety crew, the bucket boys were keeping the smaller blazes at bay.

A rising wind played havoc with the volunteer efforts, sending sparks across the clearing to start more small blazes. Brian grabbed his megaphone to help direct Dalton's crew, who were putting out any new fires with the commandeered sleeping bags, now tattered and burnt. Brian found them more blankets and they raced around the clearing, putting out flare-ups wherever they could.

Suddenly a shout went up from the bucket brigade, "Thompson!"

His shadowy form could be seen surrounded by flames. They redoubled their efforts with the buckets, trying to put out the fire wall surrounding him.

Thompson knew he was in trouble. He realized he hadn't been aware enough of the movement of the fire—he was surrounded on all sides, with only a small circle of safety. It was getting hotter. Sweat poured off his body. As he looked around for an exit, a tongue of flame lashed out and an arm of his shirt caught fire. He thought he was done for and offered up a prayer to the Great Spirit. He mentally prepared himself.

"Look!" someone cried out. Overhead the sight of a great blue heron swooping into the flames with an old jacket in its beak was met with gasps of amazement.

Inside the circle of flames, Thompson whooped as a jacket dropped from the sky onto his head. He used it to put out the fire on his shirt and pat down the area around him. It would only buy him a bit of time—the smoke was making him woozy.

He vaguely heard whoops of joy but didn't know they heralded the arrival of the fire truck. There was not a second to spare. The fire crew pulled out the hose with Brian shouting to them, pointing to where Thompson was last seen. Within seconds, water gushed over the whole area.

A dripping form crawled out of the stream of water, his shirt partly burned from his body.

"Thompson!" cried Raven rushing toward him. She had arrived behind the fire truck, hitching a ride with Fern Strong and now knelt beside the trembling boy. "Fern, can you help with his burns?" she pleaded.

Fern was frantically looking around, but stopped momentarily to examine him. "He looks okay for now, Raven. I've got to find the twins! After that, I'll look for a plant we can use." She rushed over to Brian. "Have you seen Jeanie and Judy?" she sobbed.

The CBC television crew, struggling to film the scene, seemed to have gotten their second wind.

Back in Toronto, Heather had just tuned in and watched in horror as she saw Westwind Bird Sanctuary burning. A fire truck spewed long lines of water onto the fire. Wait, were those kids with buckets in the background? Surely they weren't trying to put out the flames with buckets? Where were they getting the water?

G.G. Neilson

The camera then panned to the familiar faces of Brian and Fern. Heart in her throat, Heather was riveted to the screen.

"It's okay, Fernie. The twins are down on the beach, below Grandfather's rock. They've been refilling the buckets with water," said Brian, pointing to the bucket boys.

Fern collapsed onto him as she said, "Thank you, thank you, thank God."

This conversation was captured on air, to be replayed many times in the next few days. The cameras followed Fern as she rushed off to assist a young man. They panned in on his burns and showed an attractive girl with him.

Heather let out her breath. She knew that Fern had learned about healing plants from Irene Cedar Root, her mother, and so wasn't surprised to see her disappear into the forest.

Heather looked for Toby. "Dear God, I wish I was there to help," she moaned. She had finally gotten time off work and would be flying out the next day. "It won't be soon enough!"

She wanted to phone her mother, hoping she wasn't there at Westwind, but couldn't take her eyes off the live coverage.

"For those tuning in, I'm Marcie Lu reporting live from Westwind Bird Sanctuary, scene of a citizen occupation. A fire has broken out! We don't know the cause, but it's been hot and dry for the last few days," the journalist explained.

Cameras returned to the smoky scene of blazes being gradually squelched by streams of water. "The fire-truck arrived just in time to save a young man trapped by flames," her voice-over continued. "Brisk winds have added to the danger. A crew of teenagers is drawing up buckets of seawater from below the cliff here to fight the blaze. Let's go over there now."

Suddenly a shout went up. "We're out of water!"

"I'll radio for the other pumper-truck," yelled one of the volunteer firefighters. She fiddled with her radio and then gave it a shake.

The journalist could be seen approaching the cliff so familiar to Heather. Her heart did an extra flip as she saw Brian charging towards it. He shouted to those waiting below, "There's no more water in the fire truck! You'll have to carry on!"

With a whoop of delight she could see Toby, an attractive girl and the twins as the camera panned down the cliff to the beach. Like a well-oiled machine, they filled the empty buckets that were flung to them.

"Those crazy kids!" shouted Heather to the consternation of her cat.

Just before the cameras pulled back again, she saw Toby wave like a windmill. A gull flew over to him and she knew he was speaking with it. She wondered what other viewers would think. But communicating with birds is not like anything a casual observer might imagine. The gull took off like a bullet and was out of sight in an instant.

Then the camera was on Brian as he enlisted new recruits for the bucket brigade. "You three—replace these others," he said, pulling three very tired-looking young people away and gesturing to new recruits. "Come on guys," he encouraged, "there's still blazes to fight—and the fire-truck is out of water."

"Looks like the bucket brigade still has their work cut out for them," said Marcie Lu with a worried frown. "For people just tuning in, we're here at Westwind on Truewind Island, scene of a protest but now scene of a dangerous fire." The camera zoomed to several blazes still burning and then past to a group of people just arriving. "Several brave protesters have been fighting the blazes and a fire-truck arrived to help but it is now out of water."

The fire fighters were calling to each other that they couldn't get a message through to send out the second truck.

The camera was on the move again. "Some people have been fighting the smaller blazes with sleeping bags. You can see firefighters getting out fire blankets. Wait, what's this?"

A note was handed to the reporter as the camera zoomed in on a far section of the clearing. At first Heather didn't know why, but then it became apparent. A tall black youth could be seen constraining a large blond-haired man, probably in his late twenties.

Dozens of birds flew around the man menacingly including a Steller's jay that seemed particularly angry. The man's feet were tangled in something. Roots? Heather wondered.

She watched, astonished, as the young man communicated with the birds. He hadn't yet realized that he was being filmed but when it dawned on him, he looked toward the camera and stated loudly, "Mack Butcher, aka Matt Murphy, you are under arrest for causing this fire. I am conducting a citizen's arrest."

"You punk. You have no idea who you're dealing with. I'll have *you* arrested," the man snarled, struggling to stay upright. He didn't know he was on air, being too busy swiping at birds as they buzz-bombed him.

"Here's the evidence." At this, the young man held out a small can of fire starter which he held up to the camera. "I found this on you. You've been caught in the act of a crime. Mack Butcher, you set fire to Westwind Bird Sanctuary. Are you working for Suchno Whenge?"

"Why you little…" the man stopped, suddenly aware that there were cameras trained on him. "This… this minor," he said in a wheedling voice, "has it all wrong. I didn't start the fire. I'm here to help the cause."

"No, you aren't. You lit a campfire the first night you were here. You were seen and heard inciting this peaceful protest to violence. You and your partner Sarah Parker aka Toulie

Palmston, were seen wearing masks and encouraging others to do the same."

"You're hallucinating. What drug are you on?" The accused was now waving an arm, trying to get the youth to stop.

But he carried on resolutely. "Your mission was to undermine and discredit this peaceful occupation. You work for Suchno Whenge, who wants to take over this sacred land and turn it into a housing development for the wealthy."

Heather whistled. Wow! Who was this kid with the dreadlocks? Wait! Dreadlocks! He must be the one her mother had mentioned. And didn't her mother intimate that he was *the one*.

She was glued to the screen, hoping he would say more. But Mack Butcher complained loudly that he had rights. "I have nothing more to say without my lawyer," he growled sullenly and turned his back to the cameras.

"Well, that was most interesting," stated the reporter, eyebrows raised. "We're sure to hear more about this." The cameras returned to the fire, still being fought with buckets of water. "Sources here say that the long-haired girl on the beach below is directing operations. We overheard someone say that the birds helped out too. Well, viewers at home, this place is known as Westwind Bird Sanctuary, so why not?" she chuckled. "Let's go over there now. You're watching live coverage here on CBC."

Back on the cliff edge, the camera first zeroed in on the girl, who Heather thought must be the one her mother had told her about, then Toby and the twins. All four doggedly filled buckets being hurled to them, non-stop.

Heather screamed aloud as one practically hit Jeanie on the head, grabbed out of the way in the nick of time by Toby. The cat jumped off her lap in disgust.

"We can fill the buckets, Alyssa!" Toby shouted. "You call out."

The girl nodded and stood guard as Toby and the twins toiled on. They looked beat, especially the twins. Alyssa looked straight up at the camera then and Heather could see that she was very pretty indeed and understood why her mother said that Toby was smitten with the girl.

For the first time since watching the newscast Heather smiled.

Then Alyssa screamed. "Watch out!"

As Heather watched in horror, a large tree, she thought it was an arbutus, came tumbling down the cliff straight toward Judy and Jeanie. They stood rooted to the spot. A great blue heron appeared out of nowhere and head-butted the missile just enough that its path altered a couple of inches. A barred owl appeared in the air behind the heron and pushed it another couple of inches.

The tree crashed beside the twins, its branches scraping their arms and legs. But it looked like they were safe.

The reporter gasped. "That was close! How did those birds know to do that?"

The bucket brigade had stopped to peer down as Toby and Alyssa abandoned their post and sprinted over to the girls. "Are you alright?" they asked, and the twins nodded, hugging each other tearfully.

Then they went to check on the birds who had collapsed on the beach.

"Brave birds," said Marcie Lu. "Let's hope they're okay."

Just then a huge commotion on the other side of the glade got her attention. The camera whizzed away from the beach scene and zoomed in there. The second fire truck had arrived.

Chapter 27

Aunt Heather

The following day, Heather's flight touched down at the Vancouver International Airport in the late afternoon. She was going to take the Skytrain to downtown and make her way out to Horseshoe Bay, but Lars insisted on meeting her. She took an instant liking to Anna Feathers who was warm and friendly and seemed a good fit for her brother.

Lars filled her in about Westwind Bird Sanctuary as they drove her to the ferry. The last of the fires had been extinguished by the second firepumper truck. The young people were being hailed as heroes and the man charged with starting the fire had been released on a substantial bail, which, it was rumoured, was paid by Lord Suchno Whenge.

"How are the two birds injured when they head-butted that falling tree out of the way?" Heather asked anxiously.

"You mean Beogall and the owl?" asked Anna. "Toby and Alyssa stayed with them for a long time. They were both taken to the Stronghold. Fern's mother and Holly are looking after them. And the eagle is there too. A real wild-life recovery centre."

"I think the owl was Berook," said Heather worriedly.

"Berook? Are you into the bird thing too?" Lars frowned.

"Lars, you know I can speak to birds. Berook was to be my... my bird bond, but something came up."

Lars let out an exasperated sigh.

"I'm sorry that you can't speak with them, Lars, but did you ever really try?"

Her brother didn't say anything. Heather turned to his companion, "Anna, can you speak with birds?"

"A bit." She glanced at Lars. "But I'm not at all adept."

At the ferry terminal they made their goodbyes, "Thanks for the lift. Look, we'll get together soon. I know you've both got work commitments."

"It's good that you're here." Lars surprised her with a peck on the cheek.

On the ferry, Heather could hardly sit still. Her mother would be picking her up. But it was to Brian that her thoughts turned—she kept re-playing in her mind how she would greet him when the time came.

Once she had written a poem about seeing someone from the past on the ferry. How did it go?

The mountains stood shoulder to shoulder
huddled together around the rim
of the ocean,
as once again we crossed over.
It was then with a start
that I saw him.

She could only remember snatches of the rest—*that face from the past, the years slipped away.* She would look up the poem—was that file still at home? Heather stared enraptured, at the oh-so-familiar scene until the ferry jostled against the pilings.

"Brian!" her heart fluttered like a schoolgirl's. "I was expecting my mother."

He gave her a long hug. Was it more than just an old friend's embrace?

"Your mother is busy with all those kids to feed, so she asked if I would come get you. You're looking great, Heather."

"You're a sight for sore eyes yourself." *Why was she using one of her mother's expressions?* But he grinned when she said it.

"I watched as much news coverage as I could. This was the soonest I could get away from work. I feel so out of touch..."

He guided her toward his car—an electric Leaf. "We'll talk on the way."

"Hey, I love how quiet this car is!" she said as they crawled into line behind the other ferry traffic. "Brian, you were a great spokesman."

"Well, my dad kind of pushed me into it. And I couldn't let the young 'uns down. They're the real heroes. We're talking about some sort of event to recognize them, but don't tell them. When things turned nasty—was it only yesterday?—I was real worried about how it would end. Then the fire..." His voice trailed off.

"And how is Grandmother Eagle?" Heather brought him back to reality.

"Holly is being hailed with saving her life. She's got Granny Renie's touch when it comes to healing. I'm happy to report that Grandmother Eagle is back to her grumpy old self. She's taken to upsetting the Strong's dog."

Heather laughed.

"And here's something strange." Excitement filled Brian's eyes. "The fire didn't do all that much damage. Lots of underbrush was burnt, and some smaller trees, but only a few big old trees. The old arbutus, the one Grandfather Gull used to sit under on that big rock..."

"Yes?" Heather prompted, impatient with Brian's long pause. She had forgotten how this used to drive her crazy.

He reached over and patted her knee. It was like a pulse of electricity.

"You always were the impatient one, Heather," Brian grinned at her slightly sheepish expression. "Well, here's the thing. That tree came down—probably because of all the buckets being hauled over the main branch."

"Yes, I saw it on the news. It almost crashed into Judy and Jeanie!"

"Right—and that's when Berook and Beogall got hurt. Pushing it out of their way. Well, when the arbutus came down, underneath were some ancient human bones. And," he paused. This time Heather didn't interrupt. "There were bird bones too."

Heather gasped.

"They're being analyzed..." He continued in a far-away voice, "My father sensed old Windrunner was hiding something. He thinks Grandfather Gull knew about that burial ground. He says the fire was destined to happen."

"Maybe it was all destined," Heather voiced.

"Like us?" Brian asked. She looked at him with wide eyes. His long hair pulled back into a ponytail. His brooding, dark eyes. Yes, she could get used to him again.

"I was sorry to hear about Windrunner, Brian," she said softly. It was her turn to pat his knee.

"My father knew his time was soon... He said that maybe Windrunner wanted it this way. He was ready to give up the secrets of that tree."

"It's hard though to lose a bird bond, even if he was expecting it—not that I have one, myself. I know how the loss affected my mother though."

Brian took an audible breath. "Heather, you could still carry out that bird bond. Woodley and I think you should. Berook always seems a bit lost to me and you know, she's getting on."

"I saw her on television. She does look a lot older."

"Do it, Heather. Do it this trip."

They were now at the driveway and they hadn't yet shared much about their recent lives. Her mother was at the door with tears in her eyes and they shared a long embrace. "I hope you'll stay for supper, Brian," Carol Myers finally said.

Toby enthusiastically introduced his aunt to his friends. The supper table was awash in happy conversation about the occupation.

Heather exclaimed how she had watched all the drama unfold in far-off Toronto. "It was amazing how you fought that fire! Such bravery. And Chester, how did you know that man had set the fire?"

"We were suspicious of him and his partner. They seemed intent on disrupting everything, so I asked Sami to keep an eye on him."

"Who's Sami?"

"My bird-bond. He's a Steller's jay." Chester grinned widely as he said this and Heather swallowed hard. "He told me that Matt or Mack, his real name, was doing something in the forest. Unfortunately, the fire was already started and he was about to leave. I grabbed the empty can of fire-starter and got the trees to hold him."

Heather gave him a startled look.

Grams said quietly, "Chester communicates with all the creatures – I've been waiting all my life for such a one." She beamed broadly at him.

Under the table, Toby kicked his friend.

Chester looked supremely embarrassed and tried to shrug it off. "With a lot of them, you can't really call it communicating… Anyway, the trees held Mack with their roots. Sami got the birds to attack him. I gotta admit that I didn't insist that he call them off."

They all shared a laugh.

"And how's the boy who got burned?"

"You mean, Thompson," said Toby. "He's in the local hospital. Raven has spent lots of time there."

"I went to see him and they said he'll make a complete recovery," Dalton added happily. "He's gonna be released in a couple of days."

"That's great! Well, I'm looking forward to finally going up there and helping out!" Heather exclaimed. "How's it going now?"

"Awesome!" Toby grinned. "Some kids from our Odd-S class came up today. There's loads of people now and great media coverage."

"It's real peaceful, even with the super-large crowds," Dalton remarked.

"I'll take you up there tomorrow, first thing," Brian said, squeezing her hand.

Dalton had to leave the next morning, but not before confiding to Toby, "This experience has changed my life. I want to be an eco-warrior, too! I don't care what my parents think."

Grams took Dalton to catch the ferry, while Brian arrived to take the rest out to the occupation. The mood there was celebratory as they showed Heather around. She greeted two local constables on their walk-about, whom she remembered from her school days. Soon Heather found other old friends, while Toby and Chester hung out with several Odd S-ers who had arrived that day.

Later, when they all gathered back at the cabin, Grams called out excitedly, "Will you look at that!" Supper was over and she had her old television set turned on.

They crowded around to see a large group of people demonstrating outside the provincial legislature in Victoria. The camera panned to a crowd carrying banners that said "For the Birds" and "Shame on LSW!" Toby and Chester whooped when they saw their classmates.

"There's Robin! And isn't that Robert?" Chester exclaimed.

"We demand that Westwind be kept as crown land and a bird sanctuary forever," one of the protesters told the reporter.

"Hey, that's Mr. Getty!" Toby laughed out loud.

"We have a petition here, signed by 38,000 people," announced the Science teacher, looking at the camera.

Grams gasped. "That was the one we all signed. Who knew it was going to get so many signatures so quickly?"

"There's the letter-writing campaign too," said Heather. "They've been working on it over at the Stronghold. Who's this Mr. Getty?"

"He's my science teacher from St. Zallo's," replied Toby. "He was the first one who knew I could communicate with birds."

The next day, Toby and Chester were allowed to make the trip to Victoria to join the growing protests outside the legislature. They were staying with a friend of the Oldwins.

"It's great what you're doing here," said Chester when they caught up with the Odd S-ers.

"The least we could do," said Robin, "after all you guys have done."

"Michael wanted to come too, but couldn't," said Robert. "Robin's aunt is letting me stay with her."

Ms. Tanaka beamed at them all. "I'm so proud of you young people. You are a real voice for the birds."

"Yes, and we're having an affect!" Mr. Getty was standing close to her. He lowered his voice. "We think the province is close to overturning the sale of Westwind!"

They talked some more and Ms. Tanaka asked, "I saw that agent provocateur was arrested, but what happened to his partner, the woman?"

They looked at her quizzically.

"Agent Provocateur—someone hired to stir up the crowd."

"Oh. He was caught red-handed by Chester," said Toby grinning at his friend. "But they didn't have anything on Toulie Palmston. I think she was the brains of the operation."

"Sensing things again, Toby?" Mr. Getty grinned and then glanced at Ms. T. with a wink.

"As a matter of fact, I found Suchno Whenge's card in Matt's, I mean Mack's wallet—" said Toby defensively and then stopped.

They all stared at him and Chester interjected, "Yeah, we came across it in all the commotion." He shrugged. "We had to look in it before we could turn it in."

Toby could have hugged him, but just said, "We kept a close eye on them after that."

Two days later, after Toby and Chester returned to Truewind Island, the province announced the reversal of the sale of Westwind Sanctuary. Watching the news item at the Stronghold, a group of a dozen humans and three convalescing birds, whooped and high-fived. Grams dabbed at her eyes.

On the news item, Marcie Lu managed to catch up to Suchno Whenge and asked on camera what he planned to do.

"I will sue for damages!" His tone was arrogant.

"What do you think about Westwind becoming a permanent bird sanctuary, Mr. Whenge?"

"That's Lor.." began Suchno, before he changed his mind. "No comment," he snapped, turning his back on the reporter.

"We'll update you on the situation when we can," said Marcie Lu. "There are rumours that the birds have been helping the cause." She laughed, "But we can't get anyone to talk about it—so it's unconfirmed at this point."

The shot of Chester communicating with the birds was replayed. Strange sounds could be heard. "An informant told us that the young man has been under a lot of stress and was prone to speaking in his native Kenyan," she added as a voice-over.

At the Stronghold, there were hoots of laughter.

The loudest was from Chester. "My roots as a Canadian go back three generations!"

Granny Renie patted his knee. "Yes, your roots go deep." Then she peered around the room, "I knew you young people would help—you are true eco-warriors! The birds finally have been granted their sanctuary." She sighed contentedly.

"This calls for a celebration!" Fern's eyes were shining.

"Yes, we are very grateful," said Grandmother Eagle. "But we're also happy that humans can now leave us in peace. I need to get back to Westwind." She was perched on the back of a tall, old chair in the Strong's living room, which she had commandeered.

"Are you sure you're well enough to leave?" Holly asked tentatively. She and Granny Renie had tended to the old eagle for nearly two weeks, and she was slowly getting the hang of communicating with the bird.

"Yes, dear," the eagle said, and her large eyes blinked a couple of times. "If not for you, I would have died. I'll be fine now and Westwind is where I belong. I hope the crows haven't taken over."

"I'm feeling well enough to leave, too," croaked Beogall.

"Maybe a few more days. That smart head of yours got quite a knock." Toby looked at his friend with concern, then changed his tactic. "Aren't they feeding you well?"

Beogall squawked in protest. Berook had the good sense not to say anything.

The next day, six of them plus three birds piled into the Strong's van and Brian drove them to Westwind. A new sign at the entrance to the glade loudly proclaimed, "Westwind Bird Sanctuary - *We remember the friends who helped to preserve this land for all time. Rest in peace, Windrunner, who gave his life for the cause.*" A rock with a gull sitting on it was painted on a corner of the sign with an arbutus tree beside it.

Grandmother Eagle nodded regally when Toby read what the sign said.

Then she flapped her giant wings and took off in the direction of Windrunner's rock. They heard her stark cry and then she shot into the sky emitting a plaintive keen. They watched the old eagle soar in a few wide circles before she swooped down to return to her fir tree with its singed lower branches.

A bird chorus began first as an aria then as a symphony of sound welcoming her back. Toby wondered if everyone's spine was tingling.

In spite of the hubbub, Toby overheard Berook and Heather make plans to do a bonding ceremony before she left. Beogall nudged Toby with his beak—he had heard too.

As they turned to leave, Grandmother Eagle said, "You are welcome to come here anytime. But please leave the rest of the crowd at home."

Chapter 28
Toby Has a Birthday

Before he left Truewind Island, Grams baked a cake for Toby. "You must all promise to return before school starts," she had said to Toby and his friends. "And bring the other young people who helped out."

"For sure, Grams!" Toby assured her. "I'll phone you soon."

Heather had planned her vacation so she would be there for Toby's birthday. Her goodbyes to Brian the day before were sad—theirs was to be a long-distance relationship, "For the time being," she told her mother. It had been hard too, leaving Berook, now her bird-bond. "I'll come again soon, I promise," she told the owl, who hooted mournfully before disappearing into the trees.

Now they were shoe-horned around the small table in the condo, jostling and joking. Chester and his mom, Alyssa and Anna, joined Lars and Heather to celebrate Toby's birthday. "It's only the second time I've been with you on your birthday, Toby," said his aunt. He could only vaguely remember the first time, but was grateful that she had arranged her flights for his benefit. He was sure that fifteen would be an auspicious year.

Chester's father could not be there, which was just as well, as the group of seven were squished as it was. Lars had made a fabulous baked pasta dish, which he served with salad and garlic bread. Anna had baked a chocolate zucchini cake with some of the many zucchinis Grams had pressed on her. Marion Oldwin was enlisted to bring a large container of homemade lemonade.

Toby was especially enjoying his close proximity to Alyssa. He felt a little sorry for Chester, but they would be going to Truewind Island for a few days in late August. Toby thought Grams had something up her sleeve, but she wasn't giving any hints.

The meal was almost finished when there was a knock on the door. They all looked at each other. No one had rung up on the intercom. Anna was closest, so she went to answer it.

"Have I got the apartment of Lars and Toby Myers?" a beautiful and elegantly dressed woman poised there, inquired.

"Why yes, and I believe you must be Barbara Myers," said Anna, extending a hand. "I'm Anna Feathers and I'm pleased to meet you. Would you like to come in?"

Barbara Myers appraised her coolly and stepped into the condo.

Lars was already in the tiny foyer. "Barbara, so nice to see you." He watched her eyes appraising the small space. And then he noticed. "Are you...?"

"I'm sorry to barge in on you," she ignored the implied question. "I've interrupted a celebration. I'd like to see Toby."

"Yes, of course."

"Mom!" Toby was there in a flash. His joy at seeing her was mixed with some hurt and he quickly pulled away from her hug. Her swollen stomach had fleetingly pressed against him.

"My, you've grown so tall, Toby," she said.

Neither of them acknowledged the baby bump. With a touch of shame, Toby realized that he had not said a word about it to his father.

Lars stared for an instant at her tastefully draped stomach, appearing shaken. He regained his composure and said,

"Barbara, you remember Heather? And these are Toby's friends, Chester, his mother Marion, and Alyssa."

Barbara Myers took two steps toward the dining room and smiled at them graciously, her eyes lingering slightly longer on Alyssa.

"You're here to celebrate Toby's birthday," she stated simply with a slight catch in her voice. She turned to Toby. "I have a little something for you. Might I see you for a minute?" she asked, silently appealing to him with her eyes and then added, "I don't want to disturb the party."

They headed to the hallway where his mother handed him a small, exquisitely wrapped parcel. "Toby, I have been trying to get a hold of you. I decided to try the apartment since your father gave me the address. A kindly man let me in."

She hesitated. "I saw that you were involved in that protest... I was worried about you—wasn't it dreadfully dangerous?"

"A bit, but it's okay, Mom. We saved Westwind! Did you see me on the news?"

"Yes, you were wonderful," she smiled. "I'm so relieved that you're okay. I needed to come over to see for myself."

"And are you okay, Mom?" Now Toby looked conspicuously at her stomach.

She put her hand over the bump, cleverly concealed by the elegant drape of the dress she wore. "All's well, Toby. Your little brother isn't due for another two months."

Toby's eyes widened. I didn't ask for a brother, he thought. But still... It might be cool.

"Look, I want us to spend more time together. That is, if you'd like to. I'm pretty settled into my... my current life now. And Toby, if you'd like," she added quickly, "I'd love you to move in with us. It's okay with Richard."

Toby's jaw dropped. "Mom, I—I'm really happy with my life here," he finally managed. She looked horrified.

He thought, but didn't say, *If you had asked me four months ago, I would have been out of here in a flash.* Instead he said, "I've got great friends, there's so much to do here. I like my new school and I get to visit Truewind Island."

His beautiful mother now looked somewhat forlorn. She said, "I understand. Is Alyssa your girlfriend, Toby?" He nodded slowly. "She's lovely." Then she reached out and tousled his hair. "But any girl would be lucky to have you as a boyfriend."

How he missed that gesture. "Mom, I'll call and go visit you some weekend. Or… you're welcome to come here." He almost added *and slum with us,* but caught himself in time.

His mother looked so pleased that Toby gave her a warm hug, baby and all. It still hurt that she hadn't made more of an effort to see him but he realized she was just a very different person than himself.

When Toby went back inside, there was a lively conversation about the occupation since Marion Oldwin still hadn't heard all the details. Chester had his phone out, showing her pictures of the carved sign.

"She wanted to give me a birthday present," Toby blurted out, holding up the package. "She wants me to go live with her."

Silence descended like a curtain.

Toby looked around the table. "But I couldn't leave my dad and the wonderful friends I have here."

His father let out his breath and smiled at him.

Anna said, "Your mother is very beautiful… She seems nice too."

"Yeah, we are going to get together soon," said Toby.

Anna went to get the cake. It was scattered with small birds made of icing sugar. Everyone sang Happy Birthday and Toby blew out all fifteen candles at once. Then he opened his gifts. There was a spider plant in a homemade pot from Marion Oldwin. "Good for air quality," she declared. His father handed him a package, obviously a book. Toby tore it open—it was Lawrence Tanaka's latest book, signed by the scientist himself: *To Toby, an incredible eco-warrior. Thank-you for your hard work on behalf of the birds.*

Alyssa's present was a small first aid kit, which elicited a round of chuckles, especially from Toby. Then he opened his mother's gift—an ornate silver picture frame that held a picture of him and his mother taken a few years previous. As he lifted it out of the velvet-lined box, there was a cheque, signed over to him, which made him gasp.

Chester handed him a box, unwrapped, with a sheepish grin. Nestled inside was a great blue heron carved out of a piece of yellow cedar. Toby picked it up reverently.

"The wood is from your old mansion. When we went there that time, I noticed lots of small pieces littering the ground. I shoved a couple of them into my backpack."

"Wow. It's spectacular, Chester. Thanks. So much."

Then Heather handed him an envelope. "This is a plane ticket for you and Grams to visit Toronto in late September. It's from me, your dad and Anna. I'm going to take you and Mom… er Grams, to Point Pelee, the southernmost point in Canada. Grams' birthday coincides with the autumn migration. It's breathtaking when the birds come through! And easier to communicate with them than during the spring migration—they get crazy then."

"This is the best birthday ever!" said Toby with a gulp. "Thanks everyone." He hugged them all in turn.

It was a lovely warm, summer evening and the group went out to the balcony where there was a slight breeze. Sami flew up for a quick hello. Lars and Marion bemoaned the fact that communicating with birds just wasn't in their repertoire, while the others translated for them.

Alyssa went to get her two little dogs to take them for a walk and they all decided to join her. It was just the sort of evening that Toby remembered from his first evening at Cypress Gardens. It seemed like everyone was out—families, couples and singles—walking, bicycling, running or just kicking a ball around.

They strolled past the tennis courts, and Chi Li called out to Toby, "Where have you been? We need to get together for a match soon."

"Sure thing," Toby waved.

"Here, take one of the dogs," Alyssa said and their hands touched as she handed over Bibbi's leash.

Chester gave him a nudge and he turned to see a limousine driving slowly by. They peered in the driver's window but didn't recognize the man.

"It's not Whenge," said Lars, noticing their gazes. "I'd recognize his limo anywhere. Just some other rich folk driving by to see what they're missing out on."

They all chuckled. It's true, thought Toby.

As they approached the skateboard bowl they saw JB. There was no wheelchair in sight. He looked steady as he went through some basic skateboard maneuvers.

"Looking good, man," Chester called when he was done. Freddie was there too, and whizzed through some amazing moves. She did some big air in their direction, landing at the top of the bowl nearest them. She and JB skated over.

"JB is going to speak at high schools this fall about skateboard safety," Freddie told them proudly.

JB grinned, "Mainly reminding skaters to wear helmets."

Just then, a robin flitted over and perched on the back of a bench. They watched in amazement while he had a quick conversation. "Yeah, well Flame here used to come visit me in the hospital. She saw the accident back in April…"

"That's so great, JB!" Alyssa congratulated him. "I'm only starting to get the hang of bird communication."

JB grinned. "Maybe I'll finally get to see what you Odd S-ers do. Mr. McFru told me I'll be taking some courses with you next year."

"That's cool, man," said Chester but Toby wasn't so sure.

As they headed toward the community center, Lester Oldwin approached. "Sorry to miss the party, but many happy returns, Toby. I'm on my way to the skate-bowl—I like to see how the young fellow is doing."

"He visited JB in the hospital and then at the Rehab Centre," Marion murmured quietly.

"I'll be home later tonight," Lester told her. "It's pretty slow at the homeless shelter. Always a good thing," he added.

The group turned homeward across the large expanse of green. People with shovels were digging in one corner. To their surprise Marion announced, "A group of us got permission from the city to turn a section of this green space into a community garden. You've all been so busy, but Meagan Tanaka helped our group to get the project going. She wants the students from Willow Heights to mentor elementary classes. Her friend, Mr. Getty, will bring a class over from St. Zallo's whenever he can."

"Maybe there's still hope for Milton Turf," Toby joked, but saw that Chester was nodding his head earnestly. *Really, it was only a joke.*

With dusk approaching the streetlights turned on, but there were still lots of people out and about. Toby wondered if it were possible to be happier, even if the fuming face of Suchno Whenge occasionally impinged on his mind.

But then, his final birthday present arrived.

People in the vicinity began shouting and pointing up.

As Toby and his friends looked up, a giant bird swished slowly toward them. It made a wide, slow circle and to the delight of the onlookers, descended onto the grassy field. Children cried out with glee as the giant heron (is Beogall on a growth spurt? Toby wondered) alit.

Toby walked toward the bird, smiling. Boy and bird looked at each other.

Sometimes in a friendship, nothing needs to be said.

Acknowledgements

First and foremost, thanks to Ron Neilson, both for his ideas about the book in progress and for his support during the writing.

For helping to get the book ready for print, many thanks to my editor Jan DeGrass, unfailingly cheerful and professional. If there are mistakes, they are mine alone.

I owe a great deal to Xwu'p'a'lich, Barb Higgins, a Shishalth elder and writer, who gave me permission to use her song to Grandmother Eagle, exactly as written in chapter 8. The Grandmother Eagle character was inspired by a walk I went on with her. She also gave me valuable feedback about some of my First Nations characters. The Part 2 quotation is from her grandmother, Mary Ellen Paull.

I would also like to acknowledge Sheila Weaver who has offered many valuable suggestions. As well as being a writer herself, Sheila is a photographer and gave me the picture of Beogall found at the beginning of Part 1. Several other fellow writers have provided feedback and no one could have asked for a better sounding board. Thank you Colleen Friesen, Theresa Huntly, Stephen Sell and Joan Wilcox.

Penny Hall gave me permission to use several of her bird photos; the one of the Steller's jay and the barred owl for Part 3 and 4 and the two beautiful images for the front and back cover. Her gorgeous photos can be seen at: www.flickr.com/photos/pennyhallphotography/

Artist and photographer Tella Sametz, kindly allowed me to use the one of a bald eagle in Part 2. See her pics at: www.tellaphoto.com/

Finally, thank you to the friends and family who have been supportive throughout this endeavour – your kind words have meant a lot to me.

For the legal beagles among my readers, Toby's court case borrows elements from both criminal and civil law and great liberty has been taken with both.